''Tell me what happened
that night,'' the killer said.
''Tell me in your own words.''

THE VIOLET HOUR

"Sensational . . . The suspense is high, the writing is
compelling . . . and the ending is a great surprise."
Detroit Free Press

"Montanari keeps the reader deliciously off-balance
throughout, letting the novel accrue horrors and deft
misdirections right until its gory end."
Publishers Weekly

"A thrilling *Halloween* for grown-ups."
Kirkus Reviews

"A strong dose of suspense, murder, and revenge . . .
Montanari has a talent for razor-sharp writing with
interesting characters and fast moving plots."
Abilene Reporter-News

"Surprising . . . thoroughly enjoyable . . .
a chill a minute thriller."
Midwest Book Review

"Once again, Montanari has created an erotically
charged thriller . . . *The Violet Hour*
is top notch suspense at the hands
of a new and promising master."
The Book Report on AmericaOnline

RICHARD MONTANARI

THE VIOLET HOUR

A NOVEL OF SUSPENSE

AVON BOOKS ◆ NEW YORK

This is a work of fiction. Names, characters, places, and incidents either are products of the author's imagination or are used fictitiously. Any resemblance to actual events, locales, organizations, or persons, living or dead, is entirely coincidental and beyond the intent of either the author or the publisher.

Excerpt from "The Waste Land" in COLLECTED POEMS: 1909–1962 by T.S. Eliot, copyright 1936 by Harcourt Brace & Company, copyright © 1964, 1963 by T.S. Eliot, reprinted by permission of the publisher.

AVON BOOKS, INC.
1350 Avenue of the Americas
New York, New York 10019

Copyright © 1998 by Richard Montanari
Inside cover author photo by Rocco Tamm
Library of Congress Catalog Card Number: 97-32290
ISBN: 0-380-79532-9
www.avonbooks.com

First Avon Books Paperback Printing: September 1999
First Avon Books Hardcover Printing: June 1998

AVON TRADEMARK REG. U.S. PAT. OFF. AND IN OTHER COUNTRIES, MARCA REGISTRADA, HECHO EN U.S.A.

Printed in the U.S.A.

WCD   10 9 8 7 6 5 4 3 2 1

For the infinitely gentle things

Once again, for being my magnetic north, thanks to Elizabeth Ziemska at Nicholas Ellison, Inc.; and to Christina Hacar, for fighting my wars in faraway lands; thanks also to my sister for reading those cryptic early drafts and swearing it all made sense, and to my father for finally letting me pick up the occasional check; thanks to Lou Aronica, Jennifer Hershey, Jennifer Sawyer Fisher and everyone at Avon Books; a transoceanic *ta, mate!* to Luigi Bonomi; thanks especially to T.S. Eliot for staying just beyond my ragged, scuttling claws all these years, and to the City of Cleveland, burg of my birth, for letting me create suburbs and move things around again.

Lastly, for the window, thanks to the master: Shane Stevens.

I kneel a thousand feet below you.

At the violet hour, when the eyes and back
Turn upward from the desk, when the human
   engine waits
Like a taxi throbbing waiting . . .

T.S. Eliot

one

Jaguar and Marmoset

1 The air in the closet was damp and oppressive, fat with female smells, smells that seemed to invade his skin, silently, deftly mingling with his own sharp odors, his own cloying musk of fear and excitement. Some of the dresses stank of cigarettes. Nighttime clothes, he thought, party-girl clothes. Others offered a thick mélange of deodorant, Dentyne, drugstore perfume. Good-girl clothes, these: school, work, church.

But there was another fragrance beneath this wash of career-girl respectability, one that whispered of fornication, of animal secretions in the dead of night. The casually deployed blood-red teddy, he imagined, hanging by an eight-penny nail in the blackness. The maddening sachet of female sex on expensive silk.

He singled out the aroma and breathed deeply.

It stirred him.

But even though it urged him in a way he knew was not unnatural, the feeling still unnerved him a little, still prodded a primal churning at the base of his belly that no amount of rational thought nor moral reckoning seemed to be able to soothe. He knew that he had to stay focused, though, and that the path that had brought him to this place, this moment, this *act*—the long road that had led him to this woman's closet, a gram of pure heroin in one hand, a scalpel in the other—had to be followed, had to continue forward, onward; a sleek ball of mercury inexorably seeking its final level.

For twenty years he had thought about these nights to come, enacting them over and over in his mind, his *How-do-you-dos* and *Let-me-help-you-with-thats* meticulously rehearsed, his

3

workaday world a dull, perfunctory prelude to his nights; nights that had found him on their fire escapes and tree limbs and driveways and patios, observing them all from afar, waiting. He watched the suburbanites barbecue their steaks, mow their lawns, clean their gutters. Completely unaware. And the urban-dwellers, usually all *too* aware, had nonetheless done the most amazing things with the shades up. He had seen them eat and read and fuck and bathe and masturbate and cry, and he had even seen one of them kick a dog beneath its chin so hard that its yellowed teeth flew forth into the afternoon sunlight like wood chips from the blade of a circular saw. It was the cruelest thing he had ever seen in his life, the kicking of an old dog. Far more cruel, he believed, than anything he was about to undertake.

In twenty years he had witnessed a thousand misdemeanors, heard a million lies. He knew where all of their skeletons dangled. And thus he knew which effluence, in the end, would compel them.

Five friends, twenty years. How quickly the time had passed, he thought. How agonizingly slow the erosion of his grief . . .

He regarded their adult lives not with envy, nor hatred, but rather with an overwhelming sense of sadness. Pity, at times. One of them had a pretty wife, a cute-as-a-button daughter. One, a retarded sister to whom none of this would mean a thing. So much to lose. They did not know it, but he had already integrated himself into their lives, had already staked a place on the outer rim of their daily routine. He might have been the man in the business suit, the man in the overalls, the man in the uniform. Who knew? He might even have been the man who stood at the altar, resplendent in white satin, holding the Holy Eucharist on high.

The young woman whose salt now toyed with his senses had probably been no more than a toddler on that Halloween night twenty years ago, off to bed at eight, her aromas then so sweet and innocent. Now she was a woman. Now she covered her odors with roll-ons, lotions, perfumes, hygiene sprays.

Now she fucked men for great sums of money, and the job demanded that she smell like a harlot.

And from where he stood, she did.

The young woman's name was Kathleen Holt, but her professional name, her *nom de boudoir,* was Kiki. He had met her at the bar at Piccolo Mondo about a year earlier, and considering her profession, she had been easy enough to approach, if not extremely expensive to entertain. That night he played the slightly rumpled Ivy League academic, right down to the Bass Weejuns, Harris tweed blazer, and boyish cascade of hastily trimmed hair over his forehead. During their twenty minutes together at the bar he had used words like *egregious;* phrases like *mise-en-scène.* She had nodded, baffled, yet seemingly comfortable in her bafflement. In this setting, Kathleen Holt looked to be just another young professional in her conservative navy blue dress and matching pumps.

But he already knew who she was, what she was. What she *cost.*

And to that end, without too much tango, they got down to business.

The first time she seduced Johnny Angel for him, it took more than a month, and cost nearly a thousand dollars. Women who looked like Kiki didn't come cheap, regardless of the relationship, and men in Johnny Angel's line of work had long-entrenched defenses against them. But, eventually, the animal in the man surfaced, poking its wet nose through all the sediment of Roman Catholic guilt, through all those richly colored vestments in which Johnny had been so tightly swaddled in the prime of his sexual life.

Because, no matter what the constraints of this life, nor the perceived fires of the life hereafter, all men, all *people,* could be made to act like animals.

He was counting on it.

Kiki had followed up with a phone call, as per their agreement, and told him that Johnny Angel had fucked her and wept that night, fucked her and wept. A pathetic act of contrition, he had thought upon hearing this, the puny wail of a man who once thought himself divine, at least to some degree, only to find himself so sadly out of uniform, debauched with middle age, the stain of roadhouse whiskey on his breath, the briny scent of a common whore on his cock.

Yet that night, six months ago, had simply lit the lamps for this night, this gloriously luminous night. It had finally come after seven thousand dark others, a night during which Johnny Angel would meet both his God and his Devil, and discover, after so many years of unflagging self-denial, they were one and the same.

From the closet, he watched Kiki sort through the small stack of CDs on the dresser; pale, gently freckled breasts just inches away from his hands. She selected a CD, summoned forth the rack, and within a few seconds, sashayed back to the bed to the sounds of "Miss You" by the Rolling Stones.

The music was very loud. That was good.

He watched her hips move exaggeratedly from east to west, the half-moons of her breasts appearing briefly on either side of her torso as she danced to the music. Hypnotic, he thought, the female form in motion. He felt himself harden, then directed his attention to the bed, for it wasn't Kathleen Holt he was there to see. Not right away, anyway. It was an old college friend with whom he had unfinished business.

Johnny Angel.

Johnny looked softer, older—as they all would beneath their clothes—but still seemed to have about him the innate grace of a dancer. Johnny Angel had always been the theatrical one. The irony of that nickname was not lost on anyone, though, considering what Johnny Angel did for a living now, considering the party animal he had been in college.

But college was a long, long time ago. . . .

He straightened his hair, eased open the closet door, and stepped into the room.

"Yesssss . . ." said John Angelino, his mind, incredibly, on something other than the beautiful woman in front of him. Or, more accurately, on *top* of him.

And how could this be?

As the new associate pastor of St. Francis of Assisi Church on Highland Road, one of the largest Catholic parishes on the east side of Cleveland, his list of distractions ran nearly as deep and wide as his dark chasms of guilt. Because, God forgive him, this was the second time he had shattered his vow of celibacy. Twice now. Could *once* be forgiven? He doubted even that. But twice meant that it would happen a third time, and then a fourth. It meant that once again he would leave his collar and cassock folded neatly in his closet at the rectory and visit this woman's bed, only to suffer the yoke of penitence for months to come. He had resisted for so long, so very long. He had known so many other priests driven mad by the shackles of celibacy.

But when Kiki's car had broken down in the church's parking lot that day, more than six months ago now, everything changed. The scent of her perfume, the curve of her breasts as she leaned under the hood of her car. Yet even in the face of her beauty, her Salome charms, the seduction had taken a while. Crosses planted deeply fall hard. But eventually he realized he could not rid her from his mind, not even with prayer, and he had given in to his temptations.

And now it was happening again.

God forgive him.

Father John Angelino closed his eyes tightly, trying not to bear witness to his own fornication, and, in the instant before his world went dark, thought he saw a shadow dart across the wall, a quick, raptorlike slash of gray.

Or did he?

Maybe it was just a cat. Did Kiki have one?

Or maybe, John Angelino thought, the acid of his crimes eating at his stomach, it is just the Holy Spirit, finally come for him, its invisible sword keened to perfection, its target, the engorged genitals of a once obedient servant.

He stole to the foot of the bed, his presence masked by the blaring music, by the frenzied movements of the two bodies snarled on the sheets.

John Angelino was lying on his back, naked and hairless;

his legs spread wide, his toes darting outward with every labored thrust. His eyes were closed. The girl straddled him, preparing to take him into her body, looking slender and pale and perfect in the soft light cast by the solitary votive candle on the nightstand.

He crept onto the bed.

Hands, then feet.

He knelt behind Kathleen Holt, carefully rocking to her rhythms, to the rhythms of the music, naked now himself, his own full erection straining just inches away from the smooth, sweat-slicked planes of her back. He watched, for a moment, transfixed by the contractions of her back muscles, by the steady rotation of her hips, and *felt the blood course through his veins heard the creet-creet-creet of the rusted joints of the bed smelled the raw redolence of sex saw the room fully illuminated by the carbon blue light of the stereo system*. . . .

"Julia," he whispered. The woman sat upright.

And he attacked.

He wrapped his arm tightly around her neck and entered her at the same moment, the sensation at Kathleen Holt's throat and the much harder, much larger presence in her vagina seeming to compete for her terror. He took the opportunity to avail himself of a few strong parries, before turning his attention to Johnny Angel.

Then the woman's hands came to her neck, the instinct to preserve her life more important at that moment than the one to protect her womanhood. A thin shriek escaped her lips, and it was a sound he knew well, a plaintive cry that had stalked the maze of his memory for two decades: the squeal of the maiden, taken.

The last tendrils of Mick Jagger's voice crawled to silence as a three-inch hypodermic needle entered a vein in John Angelino's right arm, releasing a fatal dose of heroin into his system. The GemPac—the four-by-four-inch folded square of glossy paper some drug dealers rely upon to market their wares—would be found on the nightstand, laden with the dead man's fingerprints.

One side of the GemPac would bear the rubber-stamped likeness of a red jaguar.

The other, a blue marmoset.

As the drug hurtled through his veins, and the lightless veil of death descended slowly upon him, Father John Angelino heard his murderer's request, over and over and over, a monotone mantra recalling a hundred nightmares, a thousand sleepless nights. Julia. Julia Raines. And what the five of them did to her that Halloween night so many years ago.

"Tell me what happened that night," the killer said. "Tell me in your own words."

But for Johnny Angel, there would be no more words. No benedictions, no sermons, no homilies. Only the sea air in his face now, the sound of his mother's voice. Only the silence of the seminary and the smooth flight of the white swan beneath him.

He injected Kathleen Holt with a proper dose of heroin, a street fix, just enough to allow her some pleasure from the last sexual encounter of her short life, just enough to experience none of the unpleasantness of what was to happen afterwards. He then propped her on the windowsill, her back against the glass, and took her as long and as hard as he could. When he was finished, he held the base of the condom with his left hand, lest she take it with her and spoil everything, and in his right hand he took her face, gently, almost paternally, and kissed her softly on the eyes, the lips, the forehead.

Then he leaned backward for leverage and pushed her head-first through the glass.

He stood for a moment, watching her body falling to the night-blackened earth a hundred feet below him, her skin a soft white blush in the darkness, her life ending with a hollow slap of firm young flesh on cold asphalt.

A few minutes later, when he passed the body on the way to his van, he didn't look at it. There was nothing there for him now. But there *was* a message in that mound of spilled woman, he thought, and the message was this:

It is reunion year, class of 1978, a time of remembrance. A time of celebration. A time of reckoning.

And the party, old friends, has just begun.

two

This Slow-Gathering Storm

2•Right in front of him. They were copulating *right in front of him.*

It wasn't the hour that bothered Nicholas Stella so much—although he had never been much of a morning lover, and 7:45 A.M. seemed either excessively early or excessively late. It wasn't even the fact that they were doing it on the ledge outside his window. What bothered Nicky most was that a four-and-a-half-ounce sparrow was getting some and he was not.

Jesus Christ, Nicky thought.

Birds.

He opened the window, the phone loosely at his ear, and banged on the windowsill with a rolled-up issue of *Gregg's Cleveland Business.* In doing so, he found that, although he contributed four or five freelance articles per year to the publication, using it to roust fornicating birds was probably the full measure of its worth. He hated the magazine's style. He marveled at the way they took a piece of art, sucked out every ounce of creativity, then rushed it into production. Still, if it weren't for magazines like *Gregg's Cleveland Business,* he wouldn't be able to keep himself in a two-room efficiency apartment, and behind the duct-taped wheel of a fourteen-year-old Oldsmobile.

And they say you need a degree to make it in journalism.

But at least he had a laptop. A good one, too.

Nicky banged the paper against the windowsill again, as the line rang. The birds immediately took raucous flight, cursing him in Sparrow. Nicky immediately felt like an asshole. Then the woman's voice on the phone. "St. Francis, how may I help you?"

"Hi . . . may I speak to Father LaCazio, please?"

"Just a moment. I'll see if he's up."

Up? Nicky thought. As long as he could remember, Joseph LaCazio—technically Father Giuseppe Danilo LaCazio of St. Francis of Assisi parish on Highland Road, Nicky's first cousin and the only white sheep of the family—had risen at five o'clock to either attend or say mass. Yet, in spite of the hundreds of marriages, masses, baptisms, and eulogies he had performed, in spite of the collar he seemed to wear 99 percent of the time, the notion of cousin Joey being a priest was *still* an elusive concept for Nicky. Because Joseph LaCazio was the quick-fisted kid who used to kick Irish and Puerto Rican ass up and down Clark Avenue when they were kids. It was Joseph LaCazio who handed Nicky his first, dizzying Lucky Strike, standing on the roof of Lujak's Dairy on Fulton, tending to Joseph's pigeons. Joseph knew his birds, loved birds in general. Right down to that very unpriestlike tattoo he had gotten in the navy.

Gil Strauss, the rectory handyman at St. Francis, had called and left a message the night before, reminding Nicky of the upcoming food drive. Nicky hadn't talked to his cousin Joseph in a while, and figured to kill two birds here.

Click. "This is Father LaCazio," the voice said weakly. Nicky put the gym sock over the phone and lowered his voice, wondering if this was the right time for a practical joke. He doubted it, but he plunged ahead anyway. "Yes, Father LaCazio, I was wondering if you could tell me how to make holy water."

"I beg your pardon?"

"I want to make my own holy water. Can you tell me how to do it?"

Pause. "You want to make your own holy water," Joseph said, a fathomless well of patience when it came to his flock. "At home."

"Yeah," Nicky said. "I saw the recipe once. It said, 'Put

the water in a pan, put the pan on the stove, and boil the hell out of it.' ''

There was a brief silence, then: ''I'm going to kill you, Nicky.''

''Boil the hell out of it. C'mon. It was funny. Admit it.''

''Not that funny,'' Joseph said, laughing anyway. Then, after the appropriate pause, ''How's your father?''

The question reminded Nicky that they were all getting to be an age when a long-delayed phone call usually meant a death, a sickness, something bad. This time, everyone was okay. ''He's good, Joseph. The same. You know. Still chasing the waitresses around Fort Myers.''

''God bless 'im,'' Joseph said. ''He's a good-looking man, your father.''

''Gets it from me.''

''You wish,'' Joseph said. ''And how's your sister?''

''She's fine. Everybody's fine.''

''So what's up? You gonna make it to the food drive, help out on the dock?''

''I'll be there.''

''Donating some canned goods too, right?''

''Of course.''

''Good, good . . .'' Joseph said, drifting off.

The two men fell silent for a few moments. Nicky sensed a weariness in his cousin, who was usually the one to cheer *him* up, clerical duty and all. He asked. ''What's the matter, cuz? You don't sound too good. And what's with you rolling out of bed at eight o'clock in the morning?''

''Long story, Nicky. We've had kind of a tragedy around here over the last few days. I didn't get to bed until four o'clock this morning.'' There was a slight pause; Nicky heard his cousin draw a troubled breath, release it slowly. ''Johnny Angelino is dead.''

''*What?*'' Nicky said. John Angelino was one of his cousin's oldest friends. Joseph had been elated to learn recently that Father John was finally transferring to St. Francis after fifteen or so years at other parishes in the diocese. And now this. ''What happened?''

"It's not a pretty thing, Nicky. They say he overdosed on heroin. There's an article in the paper this morning."

"Hol—" Nicky began, then bit back his *holy shit*, considering the circumstances. He had met John Angelino once and remembered being impressed with the man's striking looks and calm, affable manner. Father John could have been a recruitment poster for the priesthood.

"They say he was with a prostitute. They say she fell from a window," Joseph said, the anger in his voice now outpacing the grief. "Needless to say, it's been pretty rough around here."

"Did you know he was ... uh ... you know ..."

"Not a clue," Joseph said, lowering his voice. "And that's what pisses me off more than anything. I walk around thinking I have some sort of divine insight into the human condition."

"Don't beat yourself up," Nicky said. "It can't possibly be your fault."

"I don't know. ..." A few moments of silence, then, "Listen, Gil just walked in, and I gotta go. You guys work out a time. I'll call you in the next few days, we'll talk."

"Okay, cuz."

"God bless you," Joseph said.

"Thanks," Nicky replied. He always said "thanks" when Joseph blessed him. And he always felt better for at least a day.

"Hi, Nick," Gil said, getting on the phone. "How ya doin'?"

"I'm just fine," Nicky replied. Gil Strauss was the jack-of-all-trades at St. Francis; the kind of guy who probably wanted to be a priest at one time, but couldn't hack the rigors of the seminary. Nicky wasn't sure if he lived at the rectory or not, but he always seemed to be there, fixing something, painting something, bringing a long-dead appliance back to life. Nicky had noticed immediately that the sun was now missing from Gil Strauss's voice. "What's your schedule?"

"Busy as heck," Gil said. "We're looking to collect a lot more food than last year. When can I come by?"

"Any day this week after six is okay with me."

Nicky heard some scribbling, the rustle of paper. "Looks like tomorrow or the day after is good for me."

"No problem," Nicky said. And at that moment, for no discernible reason—or none that he would be able to determine later—he decided to write the story. "Terrible thing about Father Angelino, eh?"

There was a pause of a few seconds. Nicky had only met Gil Strauss a few times, but knew him to be an emotional man. Gil was the guy who had to make funeral arrangements for the elderly nuns and priests at St. Francis. Joseph once told him that Gil took their passings rather hard. "Yes. Priests shouldn't die like that," he replied.

"Did you know him well, Gil?"

"Not really. Met him years ago. But Father LaCazio was so fond of him. So *proud* of him. I just don't understand. . . ."

Nicky decided not to press the issue for the time being. Gil Strauss was probably not going to be the gateway to the story anyway. He exchanged a few more pleasantries and signed off, then wrote "John Angelino" at the top of a fresh page of his notebook.

Hector's was a fifty-year-old diner on Murray Hill, near Mayfield, in Little Italy; a small, brick building with parking for ten or twelve cars, depending on what the winters did to the asphalt. Inside were a dozen tables draped with red gingham oilcloth, a fifteen-stool counter. On the walls, the perennials: Caruso, Di Maggio, Sinatra, De Niro. It was a place where Nicky found it easy to relax, to slip into his Italian-American rhythms. Especially with Paulina Catalano: the fastest, tallest, sexiest, leggiest waitress to ever serve a meal where Lou Groza once split the Lord's blue sky with a tumbling pigskin.

"When you gonna marry me, Paulina?" Nicky asked, loosening his tie. Whenever he was working, whether he had an appointment or not, he always wore a suit. His grandmother had taught him that. Today it was an off-the-rack glen plaid.

"*Sheee-it,*" Paulina said, meaning the entire word. She was standing at the stainless steel pass-through to the kitchen, waiting for an order, stealing a few hits on a cigarette. She wore a very tight black rayon uniform, white ruffled blouse. "Maybe when you get a respectable job, Nicky. Like a normal Italian."

"A respectable job. Like *what*?"

"Like something in the trades. Cement. Carpentry. Something like that."

"Look at my hands, Paulina."

Paulina leaned against the counter, obliging him, feigning boredom, snapping her gum.

"Mozart had hands like these," Nicky said. "El Greco had hands like these. You can't put hands like these at risk."

"Risk? What are you talking about? You write articles about Amish dairy farmers."

Nicky grabbed his chest. "My God, that's what you think I do? No wonder you never go out with me. I craft *stories* with these hands, Paulina. Parables of life."

"I don't go out with you for a number of reasons, Nicky," Paulina said, filling her tray with the order and swinging toward the dining room. "That's just one of them."

Nicky knew that all of this was harmless sparring. If, somehow, Paulina *did* call his bluff and arrange to meet him at a motel some afternoon, Nicky had the feeling he would probably faint with anticipation. It had been that long. "Would another reason be that you happen to be married to a very large, ugly Homo sapien named Mario?"

"That too," Paulina said, stepping through the door. "And he's not ugly."

Nicky looked down the counter, searching for corroboration. He found it in Flavio Bucci, a fixture at Hector's since the Eisenhower administration. "Is he ugly?" Nicky asked.

"He's ugly," Flavio said through a mouthful of *baccalà*.

"All *right*," Nicky answered as he smoothed his hair, creased his pant legs, shot his monogrammed cuffs like a Jersey mobster, and stepped through the swinging doors into the dining room.

He scanned the newspaper while he ate breakfast. He found the article tucked away in the Metro section of the *Plain*

Dealer. That was good. It meant that most of the other free-lancers in town had probably missed it.

Jesus, Nicky thought, reading the piece. Pure heroin. A Catholic priest.

Nicholas Anthony Stella—having survived thirty-five years of living with both the curse and the blessing of his mother's fine Abruzzese features, her smooth olive skin, her dark wavy hair—had grown up in a world where priests were either the kindly Spencer Tracy types, always ruffling your hair and spouting Catholic witticisms, or the younger Sal Mineo types, street-wise guys who provided a real dilemma for Nicky. If they were cool *and* priests, there had to be something about the God business after all.

The death didn't jibe with the world of his grandparents' house on West Forty-seventh Street, a place embraced by the aromas of sweet basil and Roma tomatoes in the backyard, Louis Stella's beloved, commemorative-stamp-sized parcel of urban green; the sounds of sentences begun in halting English, only to be finished in machine-gun Italian. A time when kids carried squirt guns, and priests all lived to be ninety, died in their sleep, and took the express train to heaven.

Nicky tried to imagine a priest sitting on the edge of a bed, tying off his arm, mainlining heroin. He immediately banished the image from his mind, as if the act of thinking about it might tack on a few more years to his already epochal sentence in purgatory.

The article also stated that the heroin packet found on the scene bore the mark of a red tigerlike animal on one side and the mark of a blue monkey on the other.

But . . . *was* it an accident? Nicky wondered, sipping his coffee. His father had been a Cleveland cop for twenty-eight years, and Nicky had inherited the instincts, the innate skepticism. How does a Catholic priest—graduate of Case Western Reserve, graduate of Chicago University School of Divinity—get sucked down the heroin rabbit hole?

Then came the next logical thought, as morbid as it might have been.

Cover story in the *Cleveland Chronicle*. Eight hundred bucks.

He did the math in his head. If he could get the paper to cough up a five-hundred-dollar advance, he could pay rent, buy food for the week, and make a payment to the gypsy.

He dropped a ten on the register, winked at Paulina. Paulina smiled back.

And it was that piece of sunshine that Nicky Stella took with him as he stepped through the door, out into the October rain, five days before Halloween.

3 Madeleine Catherine Saintsbury stood by herself, as usual, dwarfed by her name, dwarfed beneath the monolithic bell tower that had called every generation of Montgomery School girls to class since 1936. She was small, even for seven, but her face made up for it with huge inquisitive green eyes, framed by an electric shrubbery of pumpkin red hair. Sometimes, in her bicycle helmet and glasses, Maddie Saintsbury looked not unlike Marvin, the little Martian that used to zap Daffy Duck with his ray gun.

Amelia smiled as she turned off Fairmount Boulevard and swung the Toyota around the U-shaped driveway of the school, noticing that her daughter was once again standing in the rain, with her hand out *into* the rain.

Her little alien.

When Amelia had attended Sunview Elementary, a public school on Cleveland's east side, she, like her friends, had generally looked upon private school girls with a combination of public disdain and private envy. Laurel girls, Hathaway Brown girls—they all seemed to have an attitude, as if to say they were just that little bit better than everyone else, even though everyone knew that it just meant that their fathers had better jobs.

And now, Amelia thought, nearly three decades later, her daughter was a Montgomery girl.

Where *had* she gone wrong?

"Hi, Mob," Maddie said, climbing into the car, hopelessly stuffed up again. "What's for subber?" The brim of her oversized floral rain hat tipped, depositing a splash of water onto the car seat.

Amelia reached over and straightened it. "Seat belt," she said.

"Seat belt," Maddie echoed on cue, pulling on her belt, clicking it home.

"I have no idea about supper, sweetie," Amelia said, blotting the water on the seat with the unread Life section of *USA Today*. "It's still sitting at the grocery store, waiting for us."

"Can we have Stouffer's Pizza?"

The head cold turned "pizza" into "beetsa." Amelia felt her daughter's forehead, found nothing out of the ordinary, and said, "We'll see."

The streets of Collier Falls were black and slicked with a full day's drizzle; the traffic, such as it was on the half-mile strip of shops that bordered the Falls, was light. But then again, it was a weekday, and most of the people in greater Cleveland didn't fall victim to the town's quaintness until the weekends.

A tidy bedroom community, Collier Falls, twenty miles southeast of Cleveland, was surrounded by enough greenery to feel rural, yet still plugged into the arteries leading to town and beyond. A couple of twists of the MetroPark system were all that separated the town's five thousand or so residents from the freeways, and within fifty minutes, on a good day, you could be standing on Public Square. There was a first-run duplex theater and two or three chi-chi eateries, a video store with a fairly extensive foreign film rack. Collier Falls, Ohio, was a snoozing upper-middle-class hamlet, mostly hidden from view and quietly delirious about that fact.

But it was grocery-shopping day, and that meant it wasn't toward the Saintsbury home on Wyckamore Lane, a quiet cul-de-sac at the northern end of town, that Amelia pointed the Toyota. Instead she headed west, first to CompUSA, and then to the Food Fair on Bellingham Road, which was certain to be a zoo.

"How is Molson?" Maddie asked.

"He's fine."

"Did you get his poop?" She looked at Amelia, her nose wrinkled into a small pink fig.

"Not yet, honey. Mommy will."

Molson was their ten-month-old retriever (full name, Molson Golden Retriever, courtesy of Maddie, Roger, and ESPN), which had recently been phone-diagnosed as potentially having worms. The assignment that Amelia was dreading with every olfactory synapse in her body was the task of collecting a fresh stool specimen to shuttle down to Dr. Weiss's office so that he could look for the alleged offending worms.

"Don't forget to check for the truck, too," Maddie added. "We don't want to forget about the truck."

"I won't," Amelia said, lying through her teeth.

The prevailing theory was that one of the miniature yellow dump trucks that belonged in Maddie's Tiny Town set had somehow catapulted itself out of Maddie's bedroom window and into Molson's outside water dish. And considering the very limited cranial capacity of even the brightest golden retriever, an elite subspecies into which Molson was clearly not born, it was not surprising that the dog had immediately lapped it up. That was the last anyone had seen of it. Amelia had already decided that if Dr. Weiss was going to be looking for worms anyway, he could just as easily look for a dump truck.

It was bright yellow, for God's sake, Amelia thought as she pulled into a parking space at CompUSA and cut the engine.

How hard could it be to spot?

"What sort of word-processing software are you interested in?" the salesman asked.

He was twenty-five, and far too short to be her main character, Gaspar. He had the skewed, oversized features of a Slavic fisherman and wore too much cologne for daytime, but he had a pleasant smile, he dressed well, and he sported no pinkie rings.

One of Gaspar's cousins perhaps, Amelia thought, hoping she would remember his face and manner long enough to get to the car and her journal. She simply *had* to get one of those microcassette recorders. "I'm writing a novel," she said.

"Isn't that interesting?" he lied, gesturing her over to the three-hundred-dollar-software-for-the-Ohio-housewife-who-thinks-she-can-write department.

"Well . . . we'll *see*," Amelia answered, hoping he wouldn't ask her any specifics.

He did not.

If buying a computer had been the most exasperating experience since she and Roger had bought a new car two years earlier, buying computer software beat them both. At least with cars and computers you only had to think in terms of cylinders and megahertzes and RAMs. Add a couple of megabytes here. Subtract a few mpg's there. But software meant you had to finally do something. Something creative. Something important. Something meaningful.

Something.

And the names made it worse. WordPerfect. FoxPro. LapLink. Sidekick. Paradox. No one could understand it all. But she was very pissed off at Roger these days, and seeing as it was his company's Visa, she decided that three hundred dollars for software sounded about right.

Would she be doing any spreadsheets? the salesman asked.

Only on laundry day, Amelia thought. Maybe. She didn't know. Probably.

How about modem communications? A mouse? A trackball? Did she want integrated software or dedicated software? IBM or Mac?

In the end she bought an integrated software package called LilyWorks. It had "everything for the PC novice." Amelia was sold when she found out she could choose from three dozen color combinations for the type and background of her screen.

On the way to the Food Fair, she and Maddie decided that her novel should be written in magenta on black.

They ambled into the grocery store, rain-soaked in their matching green slickers, and fell into their happy, familiar routine. Maddie bounded over to the rack where the current coupon books were displayed; Amelia tried to round up a cart with four functioning wheels. Then, as the custom went, they would get something from the soft drink machine that was strategically placed by the deli counter. Today it was a Grape Crush.

"Do we need dog food?" Maddie asked, a thin purple mustache above her upper lip.

"It's on the list," Amelia said. "Maybe we can get him one of those rawhide bones, too. Keep him from chewing up the Ethan Allens. Remember that when we get to the doggie section."

"Okay," Maddie replied, handing Amelia the bottle of soda, then heading off toward the produce section, which was always their first stop.

Twenty minutes later they stood at one end of the fluorescent tundra of frozen food that ran the entire depth of the store. The rule was, nobody cooked on grocery shopping day, and that meant that Maddie always got her choice of microwave dinners.

In the end, they both selected something called Shrimp Maria—a "light and piquantly satisfying" entrée with only 290 calories—from the concerned folks at Healthy Meal.

As Amelia and Maddie Saintsbury moved through the checkout line, neither of them noticed the man in the dark overcoat standing behind them, three aisles away. He wore a tweed cap, brown leather gloves, and tinted glasses, all purchased from a mail-order company in Boston, all delivered to a post office box in South Euclid, Ohio.

It was grocery day and that meant Amelia and the little sprite went shopping together. Suburban clockwork. Usually they came to this Food Fair, but sometimes, right before a dinner party, they went to the Russo's at the top of Cedar Hill.

From the shelter of his gradient lenses, he watched Amelia remove items from her cart, her faded denim skirt sliding up her smooth, pretty legs. He glanced down at his singular purchase, a national brand of cotton balls. He always bought national brands because, in the unlikely event that he would

leave something behind, it would be far more difficult to trace
than a house brand.

He looked back at Amelia's soft skin, the inch or so that
appeared enticingly between the waistband of her skirt and the
bottom of her sweater as she leaned over the counter. He
closed his eyes for a moment and imagined swabbing a small
spot of that skin with a cotton ball, then slipping a hypodermic
needle through the translucent surface, into a deep blue vein.
He thought of the scarlet nimbus of blood swirling into the
glass syringe, and knew in his heart that, for two decades, it
had never been *just* about the blood. Not for him, not after
what they did to Julia, and how they did it.

There would always be the semen, too. The red and the
white, mingling forever; thick pink liquid stuck to the mil-
dewed pages of a yellowing yearbook.

The AdVerse Society had taken Julia from him in 1978, and
now the interest had grown to the point where the lives of the
members alone would not be sufficient payment. He would
take their *worlds*, if he felt like it. And everyone in them.
Wives, daughters, mothers. Little girls and bigger girls.

Julia, all.

It would be a few more days until he lived his dream fully,
but in the black wake of twenty years, a few more days just
meant a few more stains on his pillow. No more. No less.

Still, he thought about how easy it would be to take her
now, in the parking lot, to hold her by the throat, to push her
tight skirt up around her waist.

"Two sixty-nine," the cashier said to him.

To dispatch the sprite and fuck her mother in the backseat
of the family Toyota, to mist the windows with the humid
smells of sex, of blood.

"Two sixty-nine it is," he said, handing her a five-dollar
bill. Another glance at Amelia. She was almost out the door.

"Thanks for shopping Food Fair," the cashier added.

"My pleasure."

He took his change and, with the cool swagger of a man

full of secret knowledge, headed to the parking lot, awash in the wisdom that, in addition to buying national brands, he always paid cash for everything.

Always.

4. The Police Athletic League gym on St. Clair Avenue was a peeling, patchworked building near East 140th Street, a converted banquet hall built in the 1930s. At one end of the huge rectangular main room was the gym's solitary boxing ring. At the other, a tableau of greasy full-length mirrors, a trio of taped-up heavy bags.

Nicky had spent most of the day at the Cleveland Heights main library on Lee Road, doing cursory research, cruising the InfoTrac, trying to find some background on John Angelino. A pair of *Plain Dealer* articles reported on the father's charity works. A *Sun Press* article showed him leading a pack of three- and four-year-olds on a nature walk through the North Chagrin Reservation. But there was nothing that tied him to the seamier side of this life, no inner-city drug-outreach stuff that might have put him in daily contact with dealers and users.

Okay . . . I'll just have to scratch a little harder, Nicky thought as he opened the door to the gym, momentarily drenching the room with sunlight, drawing every head toward him in the collective hope, at least among the twenty or thirty young men scattered about the room, that a shot, any kind of shot, was walking into their lives.

The one thing all boxing gyms in the world have in common is a Resident Superstar, that one kid on the fast track up. This PAL, on the day that Nicky Stella first learned of John Angelino's death, had Terry Jackson. Black Lightning, he called himself. Nineteen, a body cut from stone. Nicky had seen a lot of fights, had retired as an amateur welterweight with a record of twelve and five, and had never seen anyone as fast as Terry Jackson.

Nicky changed into his sweats, warmed up a bit, then worked the heavy bag for a full three minutes, feeling every cigarette, every Hot Sauce Williams short-rib dinner, every ounce of whiskey he had ever ingested in his thirty-five years. But he did the full three, working hard from buzzer to buzzer—that shrill, omnipresent timepiece that keeps all boxing gyms on their rigorous three-minute-one-minute-three-minute schedules. Nicky felt he was in fairly good shape for a guy his age, no more than ten pounds overweight, but the truth of the matter was that he didn't want to be *anything* for a guy his age. He just wanted to be *it*, whatever *it* was, no qualifiers. He was going to fight this middle-age thing as hard as he could.

Because, for as long as he could remember, he had celebrated each new birthday in terms of the fast-living icons he had outlived. He made it past Buddy Holly at twenty-one. He had survived twenty-seven, the age that had claimed the big three: Jimi Hendrix, Janis Joplin, and Jim Morrison. He had bypassed John Belushi at thirty-three. The next one was John Lennon at forty. Then the Kahuna: Elvis. Forty-two. He'd hit the bag a little harder, he thought, recalling Elvis's Orca in Sequins tour, his last. The big gut, the jet black hair.

The buzzer buzzed.

Out of the corner of his eye, Nicky watched a Hispanic kid to his left work the heavy bag—sixteen, tall and rangy, Tommy Hearns kind of build. Smooth. Bap-bap-bap. The kid was hardly breathing. But something happened when he began to pick up the pace, as it often does when heavy bags are lined up in a row, as they often are. Two fighters falling into the same rhythm. The kid started shooting quick combinations, and for some reason, Nicky was able to keep up. Jab, jab, jab, straight right hand, left hook to the body. Repeat. Nicky no longer felt the impact in his hands and wrists and arms. It was as if he were in someone else's body, a world champion's body. He continued to punch, faster and faster, each impact resonating loudly through the gym—bob, weave, duck, slip, counter. *Bam!*

Awesome.

Then, at the exact moment he realized he could go on forever, at the precise moment he seriously considered being the oldest guy in history to try out for the Cleveland Golden Gloves competition, the buzzer sounded. He'd done the full three. And then some.

Nicky staggered back, triumphant and spent, heavily lathered, absolutely certain that the entire gym had seen and heard his violent demolition of the heavy bag. No longer would he be just the lone, crazy white boy who dared walk into this building.

He was Rocky Fucking Marciano.

As it turned out, someone *had* noticed. As Nicky tried to catch his breath—his muscles shrieking their discontent, his lungs a pair of raging lava floes—he felt a gloved hand land on his shoulder. He spun around. It was Terry Jackson.

"You pretty good, man," Terry said. He handed Nicky some headgear. "Let's get it on."

"Erique. Wassup?" Nicky tried to sound hip-hop and it immediately made him wince. The gym always had that effect on him. He was standing at a phone booth on St. Clair, across the pitted parking lot in front of the PAL gym, having given Black Lightning Jackson a very tentative rain check on the sparring session, a chit the lithe and dangerous Mr. Jackson actually seemed to think Nicky would one day cash in.

Right, Nicky thought. Only if you spot me a grenade launcher.

"Hello, Nicholas," Erique said. Erique Mars was Jamaican, early thirties, the managing editor of the *Cleveland Chronicle*, the city's big alternative weekly newspaper. "How are things?"

"Got a hot one," Nicky said. "Definite cover story."

"Hit me."

"Well, to begin with, there's some pure heroin making the rounds."

"Drugs?" Erique said, his boredom sucking a measure of energy out of the idea. "Been there. Brought home a lunch box."

"Yeah? How about a face-to-face interview with a midlevel dealer?" Nicky began, not having the slightest idea as to how he would pull *that* one off. "How about pure Chinese heroin making the rounds with the Catholic clergy?"

"Clergy?" Erique asked, suddenly a little more interested.

"Yeah. Dead clergy." Nicky flashed on John Angelino's ready smile and suddenly felt like a pimp. "I mean . . . you know . . . *deceased* clergy."

Erique was silent for a moment, the headline evidently forming in his mind. "We have dead folks?" he asked.

Got 'im, Nicky thought. "Yes. A priest and a young woman. Found him in an apartment on Cedar, found her splattered on the sidewalk."

"Yeah . . . okay . . . heard something about it."

"They also found a heroin packet stamped with a red tiger and a blue monkey. It *has* to be Chinese dope with marks like that, right?"

"Probably . . ."

"Plus, the priest was in my cousin Joseph's parish. I can get *way* inside this." When Erique had been silent for a full twenty seconds, Nicky continued. "Think of it as a community service piece."

Erique Mars burst into high-pitched laughter. "Oh . . . you want to do a public service announcement? Suddenly you're the ad council?"

"C'mon, Erique."

"All right . . . get me something on paper by tomorrow at noon. I'll see if I can fit you in as a City Streets item."

City Streets was midbook, a quarter-page feature. No more than three hundred words. No more than two hundred dollars, either. "City Streets?" Nicky said. "Man, why you insult me, bruh?"

"*Bruh?*" Erique asked.

"Yeah . . . you know . . . *bruh.*"

"I went to Cornell, Nicky. I don't say *bruh.* I've never said *bruh* in my life. I played *hockey*, for God's sake."

Nicky thought about it, and decided he knew Erique well enough to ask. "Yeah? Well, if you're so far from the hood, why do you have a name like Erique?"

"Because I didn't *name* my own ass," Erique said, sinking effortlessly into urban street patois. "Y'unnerstan 'm' sayin? I had *parents* for dat."

"Okay, okay," Nicky said. "Touché."

"Tooshay? That's mah sistuh. Wutchoo want mah sistuh Tooshay fo?"

"All *right*, already. Jesus. You wanna quit with that?"

"Whatever you say, soul man," Erique said, laughing.

Nicky pulled his heaviest weapon. "Remember that crack piece I did for *Sunday* mag?"

"Who can forget? Don't you bring it up every time you pitch me a cover?"

"Well, I'm still tight with the two cops I worked with on that one. I knock, I'm in. Simple as that. I can get under this like nobody you know."

"Tell you what. You put seventy-five words together as a cautionary blurb about this red-tiger dope and I'll stick it in the Murmurs section up front. If you can get anywhere near the investigation into the deaths, I'll give you a cover."

Yes. "I want to French-kiss you, Erique," Nicky said. "You know that, don't you?"

"Don't go *Jungle Fever* on me, Nicholas," Erique said. "Tomorrow noon on the front of the book piece, right?"

"Noon," Nicky said, thinking that he would hit Erique for the advance when he turned in the Murmurs piece. Which he knew he would begin writing around eleven forty-five the next day. "Not a minute later."

5. When they opened the side door and edged into the small foyer, they could already see some of the mess in the living room. When they stepped into the kitchen, they saw the extent: an overturned planter, a dumped magazine rack, and a very penitent-looking Molson lying under the dinette table, trying to get small. His tail was on hold for the moment, straining to wag because his family had just returned home, but at the same time, clearly indicating culpability in the living-room caper. He was still too young to know whether the destruction he had wreaked made him a *baddog* or a *reallybaddog*.

Amelia put the groceries on the countertop, exchanged an expectant glance with her daughter, and followed Maddie into the living room. The initial damage report had been accurate. The TV was still intact, as were all the lamps and end tables and Hummels and eight-by-ten pictures. No Buick-sized holes in the drywall, thank God. Amelia looked at Molson and swore that the dog had put on another ten pounds in just the past week.

"I'll get the DustBuster," Maddie said, already assuming some of the blame for this. It was officially *her* dog, so it was officially *her* mess, she supposed.

Later they ate their Healthy Meal Shrimp Marias in front of the TV, deciding, by consensus, that Maria could cook for her own family in the future. Maddie offered the rather astute observation that Shrimp Maria tasted like a combination of tuna fish and candy apple.

Roger was supposed to make a pit stop today, a brief appearance with his family between flights. Amelia glanced at

the day's mail on the hall table and surmised that Roger hadn't
yet been home. There was a time, and not too long ago, that
her husband would leave her love notes and tea roses on his
stops, but there wasn't a whole lotta love to make note *of*
around Casa de Saintsbury these days, Amelia thought sadly.

Was there something wrong with *her*? There had to be. Why
else, after nine years of marriage, does a man stray?

After dinner, Maddie changed clothes and asked if she could
run over to Caitlin MacGregor's for what she promised would
be no more than a half hour. Although the Saintsbury house
stood alone at the end of Wyckamore Lane, the MacGregor
house was a mere two hundred or so feet away, toward Falls
Road, and Maddie had no major highways to cross to get
there.

"Wear a jacket," Amelia yelled as Maddie walked toward
the front door.

"Okay, Mob," Maddie answered.

A few moments later, the front door closed, and the house
was silenced.

Amelia dialed Paige's number.

"Well, I've done it," Paige said. "For the first time in my
adult life I've actually gone twenty-four hours without food.
The very first time. Does this make me, like, anorexic or something?"

Amelia said, "I don't think that it—"

"Am I bulimic now? Is this what happened to Karen Car-
penter? Jesus *Christ*, I'm nervous."

As a thirty-three-year-old working woman, Paige didn't get
to see too much Oprah or Sally, so her catalog of women's
afflictions was a bit backlisted. Still, it didn't prevent her from
coming down with every single one of them—sometimes three
or four at a time.

Paige was taller than Amelia by an inch or so at five six.
Where Amelia's shoulder-length hair was a woefully lifeless
auburn, Paige had thick, wheat-colored hair that argued its way
to the middle of her back, and conversation-halting aquama-
rine eyes. She was a little bustier than Amelia (then again,

Amelia thought, who wasn't?), but she foolishly considered herself plagued by that little bit of tummy that simply refused to go away.

Yet, when you cleaned her up and put her in a little black sheath and heels, Paige was a knockout. Amelia had caught an inebriated Roger Saintsbury gawking at Paige at many a friend's wedding. "It doesn't make you bulimic," Amelia said. "And—no offense, I say this because I love you dearly—it's not like you're up for the Feed the Children poster-girl spot. Maybe it'll be good for you. Cleanse the system."

"But what if I pass out tomorrow? What if I'm talking to someone and I just faint, or fall into a book display? What if I *swoon*?"

At that moment Molson decided to break his self-imposed exile under the dinette table. He clicked across the kitchen and parked himself at Amelia's feet, then raised a paw, à la the closing credits on *Lassie*. Amelia shook it, wondering exactly what sort of cryptic canine message was being relayed here. Perhaps it was a peace offering for dumping over the ficus plant.

"You're going to be there tomorrow, right?" Paige asked.

"Of course," Amelia said. "Will you relax already?"

"Relax. Right. I need a drink. I need to get laid."

"Eloquent as always. Can't *imagine* why they're not kicking your door down."

"I'm serious," Paige said. "I seem to remember having sex a lot in my twenties. What the hell is going on here?"

"You were married for most of your twenties."

"Okay, then maybe it was my teens. I just know that I had a lot of sex during one of these decades, and it sure as hell isn't my thirties."

"Yeah, well, things will pick up. Don't worry."

"Speaking of picking up," Paige began, and Amelia immediately sensed that the conversation was shifting to the Saintsbury soap opera. And that meant they would shift to their much-practiced verbal shorthand. "Is Roger—"

"I don't think so. Of course, I'm the one who was completely clueless the first time he cheated on me. Big, stupid lap dog. Who's to say?''

''Have you guys—''

''Nope.''

''Wow. How long has it—''

''Too long,'' Amelia said. ''Long enough for me to think about it every time I pick up a gourmet cucumber at Food Fair.''

''Hmmm. A *gourmet* cucumber.''

''Hey,'' Amelia replied, trying to make light of a feeling that had churned the acid in her stomach for the past two weeks, constantly, an emotion blender set on low. ''That's my cheating husband you're speculating about.''

Paige laughed. ''You know, if you need any—''

''I know. Thanks,'' Amelia replied, recalling Paige's appropriately hued pink vinyl gym bag full of adult sex toys. Roger Saintsbury, one of the three lovers in Amelia Randolph's entire sexual repertory company, had been the one to open her up sexually, the one who had first brought her to orgasm, the one with whom she dared to be free. They had even done a few kinky things over the nine years, had even braved a few public places with their amorous adventures. It was just one of the thousand reasons she was so saddened and outraged at Roger's indiscretion.

How *could* he?

Paige, having made the offer, returned to her own woes. ''Be there for me, Sparky,'' she said.

Sparky. It was a goofy term of endearment they had foisted upon each other ever since they had met at junior college fifteen years earlier. Pre-Roger. Pre-Maddie. Pre-Suburbia. Pre-Roger's-Midlife-Crisis-Affair-with-the-Blond-Paralegal.

Pre-Everything.

''Just try and keep me away,'' Amelia said, transferring over to the cordless phone, knowing Paige's moods about as well as she knew her own.

This was going to be a long one, she thought.

Might as well get some dishes done.

*   *   *

It was nearly an hour later when Amelia got her LilyWorks software loaded. Maddie, having dutifully held her nose and swallowed a dose of children's cough syrup, was watching TV. Amelia could hear the standard rhythms of a sitcom drifting down the hall.

So, as she stood in front of her small desk in the downstairs bedroom, with her steaming mug of Celestial Seasonings Lemon Zinger tea at her side, Amelia took a deep breath, closed her eyes for a moment, opened them, sat down, arranged her weight on the navy blue swivel office chair, and typed:

This Slow-Gathering Storm
by Amelia Randolph Saintsbury

She looked up and placed her hand over her mouth, as if she had violated some ancient literary law, titling something before it was written. But it was a start.

Now she could begin.

With Andress already dead and the others looking for her, Vesta knew she had no choice. She cocked the pistol and waited for Gaspar to mount the stairs; the sound of his big boots, once so enticing, once a sound that kept pace with her accelerating pulse, would now be the knell that brought him death.

Her breathing became more labored with each moment that passed, the voice of Gaspar Sencio's child within her, begging her, imploring her not to pull the trigger, not to take the life of his father, not to—

"How's it going?"

Roger Saintsbury was a man of just over forty years, just over six feet, trim and athletic, collegiately handsome. A perfect salesman specimen, Amelia had thought when they met at a party at Case Western Reserve University so many years ago. But if Roger Saintsbury had anything, he had grace. A track star in high school, Roger Saintsbury could sneak up on a mongoose.

"Let's see . . ." Amelia began, "except for needing my Huggies changed, I'm okay."

"Did I scare you?" he asked, for the three thousandth time since they were married.

She had caught him in The Big Lie two weeks earlier, a lie that had led to a wine-soaked confessional, a tearful gusher of a Saturday night that had Roger ultimately owning up to a brief, dispassionate, midlife-crisis affair with Michelle Roth, the Fashion Bug bimbo from his office who represented everything Amelia hoped her daughter would not become—loud, garish, always playing stupid and helpless for the boys. Shelley Roth was a pox on womanhood, a viper in cheap shoes.

But Shelley Roth had fucked her husband, and for that she wanted to gut the little bitch with a rusty Ginsu knife.

Her initial reaction had been to grab the first bag boy who smiled at her at the Food Fair, taking him back to his parents' house and banging his brains out for revenge. It was her second and third reaction, too, although she hadn't acted upon the impulse. Neither had she ruled out the possibility of her own adult indiscretion. Why not? It would be a freebie.

No guilt!

As a contract lawyer for TRW, Roger traveled a great deal for his job, but since his disclosure, he had been spending even more time on the road. And when he was home, he seemed to linger endlessly in the garage, suddenly interested in organizing the Saintsbury supply of nails, screws, nuts, bolts, and washers.

Amelia had not yet decided whether she would forgive him.

When she didn't answer, Roger leaned over and kissed her on the cheek. "Whatcha got?" He jockied for position to get a better look at the computer screen. Amelia leaned back and let him see her nonbook.

She had not gotten past the title. The screen was still blank. For some reason, the thoughts and scenes and words and actions and plots all came to her head so easily, as did the descriptions of the characters and settings, right down to the smallest details, but nothing seemed to come out her fingers. She saw it all. Heard it all. *Felt* it, at times. So how come she couldn't write it?

Because you're not a real writer, Sparky. See . . . you're a thirty-four-year-old housewife with two years of college, a couple of adult-ed courses, a cheating husband, and a subscription to Writer's Digest *magazine, as opposed to an actual—*

". . . writer in the house," Roger said. "I think it's kind of cool. Kind of sexy, too." He stood behind her and cautiously ran his right hand gently under her right breast. Although the desired effect was the actual effect—they had not had sex now in more than a month—Amelia couldn't let him know that. She shrugged her shoulder to let her husband know that Tits were off-limits.

"I'm gonna grab a few shirts and head back to the airport," Roger said, awkwardly, his plan derailed. He looked at his watch, clearly unaware of the emotional eddy he had just narrowly averted. "It looks pretty good in Chicago. Should go smoothly. I might even get back in a few days. Only four stops." He kissed Amelia on top of her head. "Love you."

As Amelia watched him move gracefully toward the stairs— the crystal sconces in the hallway highlighting the chestnut in his hair, the silhouette of his broad shoulders stirring a deep need within her—she had no way of knowing how much would happen to her little family by the time she saw her husband again on Halloween night.

Nor did she know that by that time, everything that made him recognizable to her, everything that made him Roger Alan Saintsbury, would already be gone.

6. The Villa Corelli Nursing Home was a four-story, stoic brick bear on East 152nd Street near St. Clair. It had seen better days when it was known as the Erie Arms hotel, back in the thirties and forties, but for the most part, its sixty rooms were clean and safe and well run. The home was all male, all Italian. Nicky's grandfather Louis Stella, now ninety-one, lived in a room on the fourth floor. As Nicky passed through the small lobby and signed in, he was immediately accosted by the standard nursing-home scents. Disinfectant, long-boiled meats, flatulence. Geezer smells.

When he turned the corner in to his grandfather's room, Nicky had a bag of candy in his hand, a plastic sandwich bag containing a few green jellied spearmint leaves, his grandfather's favorite. The bag was a lot smaller than the bags they sold at the stores because Nicky made it himself, putting four or five of the spearmint leaves in a Glad bag, then stapling the paper label to the top. He had used the same label for two years, managing to sneak it out of the room every time he visited Villa Corelli. Left to his own devices, Louie Stella would eat five pounds of the shockingly sweet green candies if they were left in front of him, as he once had.

"Hi, Grampa," Nicky said. He leaned over and kissed the old man on his stubbled cheek, and immediately winced. Someone had given his grandfather a bottle of Brut cologne, and it appeared that he was wearing the whole thing.

His grandfather looked up, squinted. "Vincent?"

"No, Grampa. It's Nicky." Nothing. Not a glimmer of recognition in the old man's eyes. Nicky spoke a little louder. "*Nicky*, Grampa. Vincent's *son*. Nicky."

"Vinny?"

"Nicky."

Louis Stella gave his grandson the once-over. Slowly. Like he was sizing him up for a spanking. "Vincent?"

Nicky looked to the other side of the room. "Hank . . . you want to give this a shot?"

Hank Piunno was his grandfather's roommate of ten months, an emaciated, birdlike man in his eighties, a classic anal retentive who always had the items on his nightstand arranged with euclidean precision. "It's Nicky, Louis," Hank said. "Your grandson. Nicky. Not Vincent. Nicky."

Louie Stella smiled, oblivious. He looked at Nicky. "Howsa you fam'ly?"

"I don't have a family, Grampa," Nicky said. As always, the stating of that fact chipped away another tiny piece of his heart. Meg. *God*, how he still missed her. He started talking before his emotions could seize his words. "You're my family."

Louie Stella appeared not to have heard. But Nicky knew that he just as likely might have been back in Italy somewhere, adrift in time, a cocky, muscular kid walking his donkey through the crags and cairns of Bari. He looked up. "You catchada baggize?"

Nicky rolled his eyes. "That's Vincent, Grampa. That's my father. Your son. He's the cop."

Nicky stood up, took out his Walkman CD player, put the headphones over Louie's head. Like all the rituals in his life, Louie expected this, looked forward to this. Every visit, Nicky would play something from Mascagni's *Cavalleria Rusticana* for his grandfather. Like all Italian men, Louie Stella misted up and began to drift with the opening strains of the inter-mezzo.

Nicky studied the old man for a few moments, seeing his father sitting there in a few years, himself. Three generations of emotionally brittle men. Louie Stella had been a bullworker his whole life, a man who offered the world the intellect of his hands, the strong, unyielding muscles of his back. But now his hands were gnarled into something hardly recognizable as human. It was difficult for Nicky to believe that they were the same hands that used to magically find half-dollars in his ears, the same hands that used to go under the hood on those numbingly cold Cleveland winter mornings, fumble around with a few wires, and miraculously start the ocean blue Buick Le Sabre, the only car that Louie Stella had ever purchased new. Now his hands were idle, useless.

"Look at this, Grampa." Nicky placed a copy of the *Edition* on his grandfather's lap, an issue that was already ten years old. He had shown his grandfather the article a number of times, and he had had a lot of things published since, but neither of those points mattered. What mattered was that his byline was set in twenty-four-point type.

After a few moments, Louie's eyes drifted down to the page, and recognition settled over him like a sunset. *"Look,"* he said, pointing to the page, animated by the notion of seeing his own last name unexpectedly. "Look, Nicky."

Bingo. "Yeah, Grampa. That's me. I wrote that."

His grandfather smiled broadly. "You?"

"Yeah."

He held the magazine up to Hank Piunno's face. "My grandson," he said.

"I know, Louie. I know," Hank said, not looking up from his paper. "You showed me last time."

Undaunted by the chilly response, Louie Stella looked back at the magazine, marveling at it again for the very first time. Nicky smiled, opened the bag of candy, and put the label into his back pocket.

"I hate to bring this up, of course. And we usually handle matters like this through the mail. But it's already over a thousand dollars. I'm afraid his pharmaceutical costs keep going up," said Jimmy Corelli. Jimmy—in his early fifties, rotund and prissy, manicured—had cornered Nicky in the lobby and asked him to step into the office. Nicky knew this meeting was coming, he was just hoping it wouldn't come for a few more weeks. "I'm afraid that if it's not paid, and paid soon, we'll have to move your grandfather to Villa Paese on One Hundred Eighty-fifth. It's not so bad, really."

But it was. The two months that his grandfather was there, before a room was available at Villa Corelli, Louie Stella had cried every day. And while that was not at all unusual for Italian men, who, as they got older, cried at the drop of a hat, Nicky knew it was because Villa Paese was one step away from a welfare hotel. Forget the fact that, as Jimmy Corelli was giving him this speech, Nicky could see the back parking lot through the window, a lot that was dotted with late-model luxury cars bearing vanity plates like BCORELLI, JCORELLI, MCORELLI. Business was business.

"Let me talk to my family, okay?" Nicky said, knowing that his father was tapped out, and that his uncle Chuck in San Diego had recently learned that he had lung cancer, and therefore would not be contributing any longer. "Can you give me a week?"

Jimmy looked at his clipboard, as if the answer might be there. He looked back up. "One week, Mr. Stella. And then I'm afraid my hands will be tied."

Nicky got into his car, started it, flipped on the heater, waited. He tried to push the image of his grandfather warehoused at that scuzzy place on 185th Street out of his mind. The Corellis owned four homes, and of them, Villa Corelli was the best. It was where they put their own aging relatives.

But where was he going to get a grand? He was already into the gypsy for four thousand dollars.

When the Olds was as warm as it was going to get, Nicky pulled out onto East 152nd Street, deciding to drive through the Euclid Creek end of the park, hoping there was still some fall color left in the trees, hoping there was still enough light to see them.

As he turned in to the park, he thought about the fact that John Angelino—Johnny Angel, his cousin Joseph used to call him—was only a few years older than he. A young man, really, and *his* final autumn had already come and gone.

7.Macavity was his favorite name, although it was not the only name he used. God, no. Over the past twenty years he had been so many people. Still, he liked to keep his aliases in the realm of T.S. Eliot's poetry, if he could. He liked Mr. Mistoffelees, but it wasn't very practical, as aliases go. He liked Bustopher Jones a lot. Now, *that* was a kick-the-door-down name, there. *Bustopher*. You needn't pack a second day's worth of charm if you had a name like Bustopher. But it was getting harder to use them, primarily due to that heretical, two-hundred-dollar venus's-flytrap set for every midwestern rube who dared set foot in midtown Manhattan on a weekend theater package. That desecration of T.S. Eliot's *Old Possum's Book of Practical Cats*.

Julia would have hated *Cats* with a passion.

Of that, he was certain.

On those occasions when he needed a formal first name, he used Tom. That was Eliot's first name. Thomas Stearns Eliot. Julia had told him that Tom was what they called T.S. Eliot in his younger years.

For the most part, though, for him, it was simply Mac. Macavity was the Mystery Cat, see. The Hidden Paw. "Hey, Mac," the Cleveland street people would say to him, the only people who saw this keen edge of his life. It was easy for them to remember. "Morning, Mac, how are ya?" they would say. And that suited him fine.

He got up from the MetroPark bench, stood, stretched, prepared to run. He had changed his clothes. He now wore navy blue sweats, a dark knit watch cap.

Mac-avity, Mac-avity, there's no one like Mac-avity, Julia had so often recited, reading from her dog-eared Eliot primer, her constant sidearm. *He's broken every human law, he breaks the law of gravity.* . . .

He imagined Julia, barefoot, standing in the lagoon by the art museum . . . Julia cooking spaghetti on her dorm-room hot plate . . . Julia crying over Shel Silverstein's *The Giving Tree*. He breathed deeply the unsullied air of the MetroPark, eyes closed now, filling his lungs with the scents of the suburban forest. Another phrase from Eliot descended—*flesh, fur, faeces.* . . .

He opened his eyes, saw a jogger, a young woman of nineteen or twenty. Julia's age. She leaned over to sip water at the fountain, the outline of her ass high and firm and inviting. She stood up straight, unzipped her windbreaker, struck a pose. A chill cut across the park, and even from thirty feet away, he could see her nipples fighting the spandex for room. Her hair was a raw honey color, soft, ponytailed, perfect. She scanned the park, the nearby pavilion, looking around slowly, slowly, finally in his direction, then rather quickly away. It was a look that women gave to men when they found them attractive but, with their highly attuned female whiskers, sensed they were dangerous as hell.

You . . . cannot . . . *have* . . . me, the swing of her ponytail said as she turned her derriere to him and trotted, fawnlike, up the asphalt path and into the greenery.

But he *could* have her if he wanted her. He knew that. While the other runners navigated the paved asphalt trails of the park, he usually attacked the cliffs that bordered the Chagrin River: shale, limestone, granite. City-hard surfaces that made him strong.

He took off his cap for a moment, fingered his hair. His features were sharply drawn, nearly aristocratic in their symmetry. As often as he had been described as handsome throughout his life, he had been described as plain; as often over six feet as under.

When he had to, though, he could be small, very small. Add a three-day beard, an unkempt shock of hair, a khaki jacket, and he could blend into any crowd, float unseen through any city. A gray ghost among gray buildings.

He walked to the river's edge, found an area near a copse of sycamores. Perfect, he thought. Julia would like this place. He found a hole, dropped in the extra daffodil bulbs, covered them with the rich earth.

Flesh, fur, faeces . . .

He put his cap on, scanned the immediate area, saw no one, then turned on his heels and began to trot along the all-purpose trail, a hundred or so yards behind the pretty blond jogger.

Not much of a head start, he thought a few moments later as he entered the canopy of trees, just about hitting his full, smooth stride.

Not much at all.

8 The idea of a used bookstore had not flourished in Collier Falls at any time in the previous fifty years, nor had an enterprise of any sort managed to prosper for more than three or four years in a row at 3223 Marble Lane, just off Falls Road, the village's main commercial thoroughfare.

But still, Paige Wellington had had her sights set on owning a bookstore since she was a little girl, and nothing—not a rotten marriage, nor lousy credit, nor a less-than-supportive family—would deter her from her dream. She'd raised the thirty thousand dollars she'd needed by putting together a consortium of literary types in the area, as well as other contacts she had from her previous employment as a fund-raiser for the Cleveland Orchestra.

And while it was true that she had unofficially gone back to her maiden name, Paige Wellington, she *had* married Pete Turner for better or worse. So, as she threw open the doors on that warm autumn day, her stomach could feel no worse than it did, nor could she think of any better name than the corny neon masterpiece that graced the window of 3223 Marble Lane in Collier Falls, Ohio.

PAIGE TURNER BOOKS was open for business.

The handful of patrons who had lined up at the door at nine o'clock proved in short order that they were there mostly for the free refreshments. By the time Amelia showed up at a little after ten, the register had registered the grand total of $6.52, the gross receipts for a used copy of *The Thought Gang*, by

47

Tibor Fischer, and a pair of Erma Bombeck paperbacks that smelled a little bit like used kitty litter.

The doughnuts, a good measure of Paige's confidence in this enterprise, were gone by ten-thirty.

The coffee held out until two.

Business picked up before dinnertime; mostly magazine sales, mostly college kids. For a while, Amelia and Paige were hard-pressed to keep up. The small, trilevel space was abuzz with lively chatter and the dulcet sounds of a ringing cash register. For that half hour or so, Paige Turner Books had all the trappings of a bona fide enterprise.

By six o'clock, closing time—at least until the marketplace dictated otherwise—the day's take was out of the register and laid across the counter. Paige counted it and, after a few clicks of her calculator, she had the good news.

She'd made $160. On her very first day in business. Ever.

She turned to Amelia with a look that Amelia knew very well. A look that screamed two words.

Party time.

Before going out that night, Amelia called the Swissotel Chicago on East Wacker. She was told that yes Mr. Saintsbury had checked in, but no, he was not in his room. Would she like his voice mail? the desk man had asked. "No, thanks," Amelia said, not really knowing why she was calling him. Habit, she supposed. Making sure he got to where he was going. "I'll try later."

She hung up the phone and sat down at the computer. She had decided to keep the computer switched on twenty-four hours a day (one of the manuals said it was okay), and whenever she had a book idea, she would just run in and type it up on her Windows Notepad program.

She took the mouse in hand and clicked over to the Program Manager, but before she could click on Notepad, she noticed an icon she had not seen before. A small graphic of a laptop computer with a picture of the earth on the screen.

World Online, the letters beneath the icon read.

It sounded vaguely familiar to Amelia, as if it were software that had come already loaded on her computer, but she couldn't remember ever having explored the software's features. She seemed to recall that World Online was one of those internet services like Compuserve or Prodigy. Something you sent e-mail over. Maybe Roger had loaded it, she thought. She decided to check into it later, then realized, as she returned to Notepad, that she'd forgotten her book idea.

New rule, she decided. Sit down at the desk and *immediately* write down that brilliant, Pulitzer-worthy, industry-shaking idea that brought you over to the IBM in the first place.

She walked into the kitchen just as the soup she was heating for Maddie's dinner boiled over.

"Can I go to Aunt Paige's?" Maddie asked, already at the counter with spoon in hand.

"I'm going *out* with Aunt Paige, honey," Amelia said, grabbing an oven mitt and removing the pot from the stove. She ladled the too hot soup into Maddie's favorite blue bowl and placed it on the counter to cool. Then she poured herself some coffee, knowing full well that she should eat something if she was going to drink, but eschewing dinner in favor of finding an outfit that was going to fit. Before drinks, she had her writing class at seven, so whatever she wore couldn't be too wild, although she felt like dressing up for some reason.

"Oh," Maddie said. "Is Becky coming over?"

"Yes."

" 'Kay, Mom," Maddie said. She looked at the ceiling, doing some sort of math in her head. "Will Daddy be back for Halloween?"

"Yes," Amelia answered. "Sure he will. He'll take you out."

"Yay," Maddie said brightly. "Can we go trick-or-treating at Gramma's?"

"Sure, honey," Amelia replied.

After shoveling the dinner dishes in the sink, Amelia showered and slipped into her black Guess jeans and an oatmeal

Pringle sweater. She ran a brush through her hair, clipped on a pair of pewter earrings, and then, for no reason at all—or none that was apparent to her at that moment—spritzed herself with her most expensive perfume.

Twice.

9. He had rented the warehouse at the corner of Euclid Avenue and East Fifty-first Street, a hugely dilapidated yet structurally sound parcel that had been vacant for five years, gathering dust and spiders and pigeons and rats, everything but tenants. He had paid two years rent in advance, meeting the building's owner only once, a chain-smoking Armenian who insisted on meeting at night.

But the top floor, the tenth floor, *his* floor, was clean. Spotless. Once a month he sprayed for bugs; the rodent traps were constantly set. He had spent a month reglazing all of the windows. Electricity and phone lines had been no problem, but running a gas line up was. So he relied mostly on electricity. When needed, he would fire up the electric space heaters, and in fall and winter, they did just fine.

Inside, on the first floor, accessible from the alley that cut behind the building, through a corrugated steel door, was space for his car and his van, exceedingly ordinary vehicles that were both as benign and invisible as the man in black who sat in the window of a filthy stone building at which no one ever looked.

In the northwest corner of the top floor, his space, there sat a card table and chair, a cot, a set of free weights, a portable shower. The only luxury—indeed, at times, the only light in his cavernous home—was his laptop computer.

The other two corners of the top floor, the ones facing northeast and southwest, were also blocked off by ten-by-ten-foot sheets of thick canvas, creating small, square rooms at either end, rooms no other living person had ever seen.

*   *   *

Early evening. He looked at the screen of his laptop computer, at the familiar handwriting, at the four familiar lines of poetry. It was one of those remembrances that still sent a crippling torrent of sadness and loss through him.

Julia had copied the verse of the poem on a white legal pad and passed it to him during an English composition class in 1978. It had begun to yellow years ago, so he had bought a digital scanner and turned it into a computer file, so that it might live forever.

He had sent out a copy of the poem to all of them by e-mail—most of them were on World Online—then instantly regretted it. Childish. It meant an extra, dangerous step. It meant he would have to get to all of their computers and erase the file, if he wanted to be on the safe side. And he wanted to be on the safe side. For after he had pushed aside those initial thoughts of suicide so many years ago, he discovered that life was still worth living. Although he had run right past her, without even a glance, the honey blonde from the park was all the testimony he would ever need on that point.

Those who had the right software would read the poem, in Julia's own handwriting, and perhaps they would remember.

Those who didn't would never see him coming.

He knew that the face he would present to them would not be recognized (he had dealt with that small bit of business years ago, a series of painful surgeries he had explained away with a dozen intricate lies), but he also felt that they had all probably forgotten what happened in that loud, smoky dorm room when Carter was still in the White House and the Bee Gees owned the charts. And that bothered him most of all.

Because for him, it was a night before which the world had existed on a different plane. He had breathed different air before that night, drank different wine, made different love.

He looked back at the screen. The passage was from T.S. Eliot's "Preludes," one of Julia's favorites:

I am moved by fancies that are curled
Around these images, and cling;

The notion of some infinitely gentle
Infinitely suffering thing.

He clicked over to Lotus Organizer, his calendar and address book software. He checked their schedules for the evening.

Geoffrey had nothing. Not surprising.

Jennifer's palsied sister Greta had a physical therapy session.

Dr. Crane was probably going to watch his wife disrobe from the comfort of his backyard lounge chair. Again.

Amelia had her writing class.

Whose compulsion would he feed this night? he wondered. Who among them would sniff the air, finding his scent?

He showered and shaved, then slipped on a pair of faded denim jeans. He sat down at the card table, donned a pair of thin rubber gloves, and began to fold more GemPacs, the sage geometry of it second nature to him now.

Jaguar and marmoset, he thought.

Suffer no more.

10• Amelia had signed up for a four-week-long writing class that met twice a week for ninety minutes, taught by a local newspaper editor who had once gotten something into the *Los Angeles Times*; a graying teddy bear in his fifties named Lawrence Price.

At seven-forty, just as Mr. Price was handing out the night's agenda, a man walked into the room where they met, at Mildred Burroughs Middle School, and took a seat directly in front of Amelia. He hadn't been there the first week, and he drew Amelia's attention immediately. Youngish, nice-looking, slender, he wore jeans that hugged his narrow hips, a black pullover sweater, black cowboy boots. His hair was dark, lustrous.

At first Amelia thought: Paige could definitely be interested in a guy like this. Cute and literate. The rarest of breeds.

Then she thought: I could too. If I was that kind of woman.

She booted that thought out and tried to zero in on what Mr. Price was talking about. Something about dialect, and the wisdom of using it sparingly.

The class moved along briskly; Amelia took copious notes. More than once, though, she found her eyes wandering to the man sitting in front of her, to his dark curls, the soft ringlets that fell across the ribbed collar of his sweater.

At eight-twenty, just as Mr. Price began to explain about how one must never write dialogue just to hear characters talk, Amelia cruised the man's left hand and saw that he was not

54

married. She then cruised her own left hand and discovered that, of course, she *was*.

She felt guilty for a few moments, but that soon passed. She reminded herself that she had officially entered the realm of the cheated-upon, the cuckolded, that select group of a billion or so women whose husbands have decided to seek comfort in the fold of another woman's bosom.

Amelia made a conscious decision to never feel guilty again.

At least, not about her harmless fantasies.

At nine o'clock Mr. Price adjourned the class, and while Amelia was gathering her purse and other belongings, the man who had been sitting in front of her managed to slip out of the classroom; unseen, unheard, unmet.

Of the handful of vehicles in the parking lot, Amelia's car—a ten-year-old maroon Toyota—was the only one producing a gray cloud of vaporous exhaust.

Amelia looked at all of the cars, including her own, and saw that they were empty. But her car was *running*. It took a few moments to register, to seep into that part of her brain reserved for the monumentally stupid things that she managed to do with frightening regularity, but eventually it sank in: She had gotten out of the car, left the keys in it, left it *running*, locked the doors, and casually sauntered off to class. Not a care or a clue. Edith Bunker on Prozac.

Kinda distracted these days, lady?

"I can see it now. *The Mystery of the Idling Car*. It'll be a best-seller."

The voice came from behind her. Just a few feet away. She spun around, startled.

It was Dark Curls.

"Oh, uh, yeah, I, uh, um, well . . ." Amelia said, doing a passable impression of Annie Hall. "I guess I, uh, decided to keep the car warm while I was in, uh, class." How had he managed to walk up to her so quietly?

"And you don't have a spare key. . . ."

Amelia buried her head in her hands, her face beginning its tour of the red palette. "No," she said. "That would make life *far* too easy."

Dark Curls laughed. "Hey. Don't be embarrassed," he said, circling the car, looking in the windows. "I was late for a class once. Parked my car quickly, locked it, ran off to class, even though the engine was doing that preignition thing it was so fond of—*popata-popata-popata-popata . . .*"

"You mean, like, where it won't shut off for a while?" Amelia asked. "Then it does a big wheeze when it's finished?"

"Yeah, that's it. Forty-five minutes later I came back and the car was still at it—coughing and sputtering and belching exhaust. The parking lot attendant, who sat there the whole time, told me it sounded like a forty-five-minute Keith Moon drum solo. So you're not the only one that stuff like this happens to."

Amelia laughed, thinking: He remembers Keith Moon. He can't be *that* young. "Okay. I guess I'm not so embarrassed now. I think." She began to rummage through her purse. "But I also guess that it's time to call Triple A." I also guess? Amelia thought. Who the hell says *I also guess*?

"Hang on a sec." He walked around to the far side of Amelia's car. In addition to his jeans and cowboy boots, he wore an Indiana Jones–type brown leather flight jacket; scuffed, of course, in all the right places. "Don't waste the call. You've got the window down a little here. Let me go back inside the school and get a coat hanger. I'll get you inside in no time."

"You can do that?" Amelia asked.

"Just anudder vestige of me misspent yoot," he said with a rakish smile, then turned and trotted back to the school.

Amelia glanced into the window of her car, at her fun-house reflection. She poked at her hair, smoothed her cheeks, thought about freshening her lipstick, but she didn't think she would have enough time or light to do a proper job.

Wow, she thought. Am I *flirting*? Is this how it all started with Roger and Shelley Roth? Did Roger do something really

gallant for Shelley Roth in a parking lot one night and then
they talked for a while and then they laughed for a while and
then they had a drink and then One Thing led to the proverbial
Other? Is this how people who are allegedly happily married—

"Nice sweater," Dark Curls said from behind her, nearly
making her jump. Again.

"Oh, uh . . . thanks," Amelia said, wondering: Did he see
me primping? *Shit*.

He walked to the passenger side of her car and, within seconds, said: "Got it!" He opened the passenger door, unlocked
the driver door, got out. "Score one for the criminal mind."

"Wow," Amelia said. "I'm impressed."

"I draw the line at safes, though," he said, folding the coat
hanger and dropping it into a nearby trash can. "Well, *big*
safes, that is."

"Damn," Amelia said, playing along. "There goes the Re-
public Savings job I was going to invite you on." Jesus. She
was flirting.

Dark Curls laughed and walked around the back of the car.
"There'll be other burglaries," he said. "Just keep me in
mind."

"I will," Amelia said, sliding into the driver's seat. She
had left the heat on and it felt like slipping into a toaster oven.
Her glasses instantly fogged over and she whipped them off
and dropped them on the passenger seat. "I guess I'll see you
at the next class then."

"Sure thing," he said. "Have a nice evening."

"You too," Amelia replied. As she reached for the door
handle she looked up. The streetlamp behind him created a
halo of light around his head.

He smiled.

A single butterfly loosed itself in her stomach.

Amelia slammed the door on her seat belt and drove off.

The weeknight crowd at Celine's on Falls Road had been more
local in flavor than it was on the weekends. Paige made up
for it by dancing with every breathing male between the ages
of twenty-two and sixty. Amelia nursed a single glass of wine

for two hours, her mind returning over and over again to her rescuer.

She dropped a very giggly Paige Turner off at midnight and drove home.

After a quick look around the house, searching for signs of whether Becky's boyfriend had paid a conjugal visit to the Hotel Saintsbury, and finding none, Amelia paid her and drove her home.

It wasn't until one o'clock that Amelia's head hit the pillow. Sleep came within minutes.

And, in its wake, a very erotic dream about a man in a soft leather jacket.

Seventy-five feet away, at the mouth of the driveway, a blue van cut its engine and rolled, silently, to a stop. For a brief moment the brake lights shone brightly; red knives slitting the darkness.

Then the night regained control, and the Saintsbury house, the lone structure at the end of Wyckamore Lane, was once again clothed in black.

three

Crack Alley Blues

11 From the windows of his office at Clark Hall, a suite of dark-paneled rooms he had occupied for twenty-three years as head of the English Department at Case Western Reserve University, Sebastian Keller looked out at the rich fall colors that blanketed University Circle: Severance Hall, the Cleveland Museum of Art, the lagoon.

Sixty-one, he thought. Young, really. But it would be his final year of life.

He turned back to his desk and looked again at the newspaper. John Angelino. The theatrical one. Mr. Angelino, he recalled as if it were just yesterday, was the one who never missed an opportunity to burst into show tunes. Nice-looking, serious about his faith. A natural for the priesthood.

They had called themselves the AdVerse Society, he remembered. Their main purpose in life—aside from the sampling of any alcoholic concoction that had ever dampened the cocktail napkins of Dorothy Parker and the Algonquin Round Table—had been the trashing of the allegedly overrated, the deconstruction of the so-called greats in modern poetry: Emily Dickinson, Walt Whitman, Ezra Pound.

John Angelino, dead at forty-two. The newspaper confirmed it.

But it was the next day's newspaper that Sebastian Keller dreaded, and then the one that would come the day after that. Because one day, and soon, a *Plain Dealer* would show up on his desk and let him know that another one had died. Another member of the AdVerse Society had died in the prime of life.

Heroin *indeed.*

He glanced at his watch, at the second hand, and moved slowly, painfully, toward his chair. The myriad pills he took every day barely assuaged the pain that racked his lungs, his lower back, his hips, his genitals. The cancer had drawn a deep red outline of his manhood and now it had begun to flame.

He sat down, closed his eyes, conjured up the young woman's body, the way it had moved beneath her simple cotton dresses; the unthinking, unspoiled way she would cross her legs beneath her desk, her paper white thighs a beacon at the back of the classroom.

And then he recalled the way she had looked on that Halloween night, her perfect young breasts in the candlelight, the streetwalker's makeup.

He downed his pills, sipped his water.

He would watch the newspapers, he thought. He wasn't sure whether he would have enough time or strength to do anything if it happened again, but he would watch the papers.

Watch, and wait.

12. The article that Nicky Stella firmly believed was his best work, the one he figured he would eventually resell to *GQ* as his ticket to the big time, was entitled "Crack Alley Blues," a diary-style journal of three days inside the Cleveland Police Department's Narcotics Unit. He had sold it to *Sunday*, the *Plain Dealer*'s magazine. "Sensitive and riveting," one reader had written in a gushing encomium.

Nicky had spent three nights with two undercover narcotics cops; cops who, to this day, Nicky knew only by their street names, Birdman and Willie T. The detectives always rode around in disguise: wigs, hats, tinted shades. Willie T was black, short, and powerfully built, given to tank tops and left hooks; Birdman was a lean, wise-cracking Anglo who seemed to have a thin veneer of procedure covering long-simmering sadism.

They would pick Nicky up at the Burger King at East Eighty-fifth Street and Euclid Avenue every night about eleven, then head straight into the Third District, straight into hell. During the entire time Nicky was on the assignment, including a number of follow-up interviews, the two police officers never divulged their identities, never dropped the disguises. All Nicky knew was a phone number.

Five days before the article was published, Nicky met Willie T at a cop bar on Payne Avenue. He gave him an advance copy. Willie T took it into a booth, along with a tumbler of Jack Daniel's, and read it. Twice. Forty minutes later he had come out and marched the length of the bar with what Nicky would swear under oath was a tear gathering at the corner of his eye. Willie T hugged him.

Later that night the two police officers took him into the supply room at the back of the bar, reached into their respective pockets, and pulled out a stack of bills. In unison they each peeled off a single hundred-dollar-bill, then ripped the bill in half. They each handed a piece to Nicky, tokens of their appreciation. Birdman spoke first. "Your next two misdemeanors are on us, as long as you fuck up inside city limits. Cross the line, make it even a felony three, we don't know you."

"Uh-huh," Nicky replied, only marginally understanding what was going on.

"Or maybe you'll need a source," Birdman continued. "Either way, you ever meet with us in the future, you bring your half. Understand?"

"Yeah," Nicky said. "I get it."

"But don't you go walkin' around cocky. Like you got license to do some shit," Willie T said. "This ticket will take you about as far as my mood on the day you fuck up. Capeesh?"

Nicky understood, and for a long time the half bills had burned a hole in his end-table drawer, as did the image of Willie T's misty eyes into his mind.

He dialed the number, got the machine, as always. *"This is Willie T . . . Leave a message at the beep."*

"One-one-six," he said, as per instructions, and then hung up.

He sat on the couch, found the remote, flipped on the television: CNN was in Bosnia, Bob Barker was giving away a trip to Puerto Vallarta, Larry Hagman was looking awfully vexed at something Barbara Eden had done. Round and around the cable wheel he went.

It used to drive Meg crazy.

Nicky glanced at the calendar. Could it really be five years?

He had met Margaret Connelly one steamy August night at the Holiday Inn Rockside, a night that found him in the right suit, the right cologne, and, somehow, in possession of the right words to say to the girl who would be the love of his life. Bouncing to the music, feigning disinterest, he walked by her table no fewer than five times that night, five separate passes before he was able to roust the courage to ask her to dance, and when she accepted, he prayed a quick novena for the wisdom to avoid saying anything stupid. Unfortunately, that par*ticular* prayer went unheard, but during their second slow dance, when he leaned back and looked at Meg closely— emerald eyes, the sexy crooked smile, the way she reddened, head to toe, a full Irish body blush, when he told her she was beautiful—he knew that this was the woman he was going to marry.

Within three months he proposed to her. Meg Connelly said no. So Nicky Stella asked her again and again and again— fifty days in a row. Didn't miss one. He'd show up at her desk at work, he'd leave balloons in her car, he'd send her telegrams. He even tried the corny old mariachi-trio-under-the-window routine. Cost him two hundred sixty bucks to rent Luis, Chatto, and Little Diego for that hour, but still she resisted.

On the fifty-first day he gave up, got plastered. And it was just before midnight that night that Margaret Connelly appeared at his front door and said yes.

They had been in love, they had married at city hall, and then one perfect spring day Meg went to the doctor's office and never fully returned. She was twenty-five when they found the cancer, twenty-six when Nicky sat next to her bed, holding her frail hands as she slept, hands that once smoothed his hair when they kissed, hands that once electrified him with the slightest touch, hands that now lay still and empty. Dry, seasoned twigs stacked by a dying fire. She was one day shy of twenty-seven when they all stood in the cold rain at Holy Cross cemetery: steel gray silhouettes against a dirty scrape of winter sky.

He kept her clothes for the longest time, along with a hundred slightly out-of-focus pictures. He wore her powder blue hospital bracelet for a year.

The bill for losing Meg had been $77,300, and Nicky paid every last cent, taking every job he could manage to fit into a twenty-hour day, reserving the final four hours of each day for his booze, his ventless corner of sorrow. He had not been out of the city in five years, had not purchased a new suit in six.

Now, though, he had a solitary snapshot left. Meg, smiling, her face forever young; her eyes, evergreen. He had long since donated her clothes to Catholic charity. Everything, of course, but her beret. The raspberry-colored beret still hung on the rack by the front door, as if it had all been a cruel hoax, as if the strong young woman who could all but wrestle him into submission hadn't become a ghost in front of his eyes, as if one day he would open the door and find the beret gone. And that would mean that Meg was at the store, that Meg was coming back.

Every day, though, the raspberry beret remained where it was. A warm whisper of Margaret Jane Connelly at the bottom of the stairs.

And in spite of a half dozen one-nighters—faceless bodies in his bed, always gone by morning—there had been no woman since Meg who had turned his head, his heart. Yet he knew it was time to move on.

He was ready.

The day after he had paid the last of the medical bills, the day after he had gotten deliriously drunk at the accomplishment, his ancient 286 computer decided to commit the digital equivalent of suicide.

On that day Nicky knew he had to act fast, for without a computer, he had no way to earn a living. He also knew that there wasn't a bank or a finance company this side of Indonesia that would lend him a dime. So he did the next dumbest thing. He let his cousin Paulie talk him into seeing a "friend" of his, a loan shark named Frank Corso, a six-three, three-hundred-pound blond gypsy miscreant who, as a "favor" to cousin Paulie, gave Nicky a good rate and monthly payments.

Paulie set up the meet, Nicky got his four thousand dollars and bought the best laptop computer he could get.

For the past ten months Nicky managed to make the payments, never touching the principal. Except this month he was late. And so Frank Corso had shown up at Nicky's door six days ago and informed him that he would return in one week and, at that time, would leave the premises with either the four large, or Nick Stella's testicles in his hand. What Frank had failed to tell Nicky at their first meeting was that, if you miss a payment by more than two weeks, you suddenly owed the whole principal.

It was a good thing he was Paulie's friend.

On the other hand, it was the first time in Nicky Stella's life he found four thousand dollars to be a bargain for *any*-thing.

The phone rang during *General Hospital.*

"This is Nicholas Stella."

"What d'fuck's up, *homes*?" the voice said brightly, immediately recognizable as Willie T. He sounded playful, content. It probably meant he had recently chewed some gang-banger a new asshole or dropped a midlevel crack dealer with the fourteen-shot nine-millimeter pistol he carried under his arm. It was a perfect time to ask for a favor.

"*Yo*, Willie *T*," Nicky exclaimed, trying to sound as street as possible. "*Mah* man."

"Where y'at?"

Willie T sometimes drifted into a New Orleans kind of drawl, and Nicky wasn't sure, at those times, if he was offering a *how ya doin'* greeting by way of his *where y'at,* the way they did in Louisiana, or actually asking him where he was. Seeing as Willie T had just dialed his number, he chose the former.

"I'm good, Willie. Takin' care a business."

"Ain't seen your name in the papers lately."

Tell me about it, Nicky thought. "Yeah, well, trying, you know? It's one of the reasons I'm calling. I'm working on a cover story for the *Chronicle*. But I have bigger plans for it."

"Yeah?" Willie T said, sounding genuinely impressed. "So what can I do for you?"

"Well, were you by any chance in on this case about the priest who overdosed?"

"Heard somethin' about it."

"He was my cousin. . . ." Nicky lied. "John Angelino was his name."

"Sorry, man."

"The paper said the junk had a red tiger and a blue monkey on it."

"Yeah, right. I didn't catch the case, though. If there isn't anybody buying or selling it, I don't get the call. You know what I mean?"

"Have you run across the tiger and monkey marks before?"

"No," Willie T said. "Don't ring a bell. But these dealers change these marks all the time."

"Sounds Chinese though, right?"

"Yeah. I would say. They're really into that animal shit."

The first push. "Got any connections on the local Chinese chain?"

"Yeah," Willie T said, a little skeptically, recognizing the pressure. "A few. Why?"

Nicky decided to just say it out loud. He closed his eyes, spoke clearly. "I want to talk to the dealer, Willie. Some mid-level guy. You know what I mean? No holds barred, completely anonymous interview. We'll get some really arty shots of him in shadow. I'll quote him in dialect, even. Real street-theater piece. He'll be a fuckin' star. He'll be the new Monster Kody. It'll get him laid for years."

Willie T laughed, a little more patronizingly than Nicky would have liked. *"What?"*

"I'm serious."

"Number one, drug dealers need absolutely no help gettin' pussy. You know what I'm sayin'? None. Drug dealers got pussy like you and me got *gas*. Like *all* the motherfuckin' time. Okay? And two, this is some dangerous shit you talkin' about, man. I mean, do you know who these people are?"

"Hey . . . did I not ride around with you and see firsthand?"

"You think that's who you talkin' about? Man . . ."

Up came the Italian. "I *know* what I'm talking about. I

know *who* I'm talking about. You think I discovered drugs when I met you? Gimme some fuckin' credit, Willie.''

"A'right . . . a'right . . .''

Nicky continued. "Look . . . I want to know if he has any more conscience about selling killer shit than he does about the other shit. I mean, I'm not on some crazy crusade because this guy was my cousin,'' he lied. "I just want to know. It'll be a great story.''

"You got brass, Nicky. I will give you that.''

Second push. "All I need you to do is find out who's dealing it. Get me an intro. I'll do the rest,'' Nicky said.

"Where you gonna be?'' Willie T asked.

"Around,'' Nicky said. "You tell me where and when.''

Nicky heard Willie T cover the phone with his hand. After a few seconds, Willie T said, "I'll call you back.''

Later, while Nicky was at a David Cronenberg double feature at the Cinematheque, hoping to avoid Frank Corso at the door to his apartment—*Videodrome* and *Scanners*, as if his life wasn't bizarre enough—Willie T left a message. Willie T said that there was only one man to see about the red-tiger heroin.

The good news? The good news was that Willie T told him where he could find the guy, and how to get on the drug dealer's good side.

The bad news?

The man's name was Rat Boy Choi.

13. Dr. Bennett Marc Crane, one of the most highly respected plastic surgeons in all of western Pennsylvania, graduate of Case Western Reserve University and Harvard Medical School, sat on a lounge chair, in the shadows behind his house, the beginnings of a fairly strong erection thickening between his legs. He was twenty feet from the sliding glass doors that led to his dining room, and the expensive track lighting that looked, from Dr. Crane's somewhat inebriated and aroused perspective, like black cocks dangling over his wife's head, spewing thin streams of sperm-light.

Elizabeth Crane walked out of the room, down the hallway, toward their bedroom. Bennett Crane hoped she was off slipping into a new outfit. He was ready for a new outfit.

Behind him, the trees shimmered in a late October breeze. Above him the clouds lashed a thin veil of purple over a bone-colored moon. Midnight. Next to him, on a wrought-iron end table, sat a large pitcher of vodka martinis, now half-empty. Next to that, a compact video camera, top of the line.

Dr. Crane—forty-three and slightly balding, tanned year-round, always in Milano high fashion—wore a powder blue scrub set from the hospital, no shoes. He had had so much lightning-quick sex in hospital settings over the years that he almost needed the feel of the soft cotton against his skin to get a hard-on these days. The Beefeater's helped sometimes. It helped soften the edges of his fantasy, helped to putty in the imperfections that had begun to erode his wife.

But Elizabeth always knew what to do, knew all the moves. And in the proper light, in the proper mood, she still looked

70

very good. The teak-colored hair, long and thick and luminescent. The eggshell skin.

He poured himself another martini as Coltrane's "Wise One" came thundering forth from the house. The sliding glass door was closed, but the music was loud. This fed his fantasy, of course, and Elizabeth knew it. It meant she trusted him completely tonight. He wondered what she would be wearing when she came around the corner, into the dining room, and was instantly gratified when she stepped into sight wearing a very short red cocktail dress, red elbow-length gloves.

The phone game.

She answered the phone that wasn't ringing, spoke animatedly into it, a game they often played: she the fiery Italian film actress; he, the debauched producer, watching her talk dirty to an ex-lover.

Dr. Crane observed her from his cove of darkness, his eyes running slowly up her legs, over her hips. In this light, at this distance, she was Rita Hayworth at her fuck-me prime. He was a very lucky man at the moment.

He was just about to untie the top of his scrubs and begin to deal with his now furious erection when a shadow crossed the patio stones in front of him.

Someone was there.

Someone was *right there*.

"Jesus Christ!" Bennett Crane jumped from his chair, his hand clutched to his chest.

A broad-shouldered man about his size stepped from the shadows, stopped. There was something in each of the man's hands. "Hi, Doc," the man said, softly.

Inside, Elizabeth Crane sat on a dining room chair, drew the hem of her dress up to her thigh, continued to talk into the phone. She reached into her bag, produced a long cigarette, lit it, drew deeply.

Outside, her husband looked around for a weapon. There was nothing. He froze.

"I've always liked her in that dress," the man said. "Very sexy."

Bennett Crane tried to gather his senses. He looked carefully at the man and recognition soon dawned. *"You."*

"Yes," the man said, stepping closer. "It seems so."

"What the hell do you want? I-I thought we were through. Years ago. I thought we were even." Bennett Crane tried to see what the man carried. The left hand held something boxy, black. The other hand was turned away, hidden from view.

"Even? Are you serious?"

"That was fifty thousand dollars worth of work I did. For free."

"That was a long time ago," the man said. "And nothing's free."

"But you said—"

"What I said was, your secret was safe with me." The man stepped closer, two full steps. "I said I'd never go to the police and tell them about your role that night. I haven't."

Elizabeth Crane unzipped her dress, stepped out of it. She wore a short black slip. She sat back down on a dining room chair, facing the window, and began to run her hands over her thighs, her stomach.

Coltrane bucked and roared.

"So tell me what happened that night, Dr. Crane. Tell me in your own words."

Bennett Crane glanced at the window, back. "You were there. Why do you—"

"Who was the pirate?"

"I-I'm not sure," Bennett Crane said. "After all these years, I always assumed—"

"Don't lie to me, Doc," the man said. He was inches away now. Then, from his right hand, came a flash of silver. Bennett Crane glanced down, recognized the scalpel as his own. The man who stood in front of him now had demanded it as a souvenir so many years ago, a badge of his courage. He looked back at the man's face, his own handiwork now more visible in the moonlight. Crazily, Bennett Crane thought he had done a hell of a job.

"Johnny Angel's dead," the man said, an expression of mock sadness on his face. "Just like you."

Bennett Marc Crane turned to run, but the man slammed a

Taser unit into the side of his neck and instead he slumped to
the ground, his limbs flung spastically out to the sides, his
brain now a vicious tangle of unfettered impulses. The man
fell instantly on top of him, pinning his shoulders to the damp
earth. He held a shock of Bennett Crane's hair in his left hand,
the scalpel in his right.

The woman in the window unsnapped her bra and let it fall
from her shoulders. She moved suggestively to the music for
a while before she sat back down, faced away from the window, spread her legs, and began to fondle her breasts.

A few moments later, as the blade of the scalpel was drawn
across his face for the first time, Dr. Crane remembered, in
agony, a question he'd pondered for years, a question about
how it *felt*.

The blade returned, again and again.

Blood steamed the night air.

And Bennett Crane had his answer.

14• At the age of sixty-nine, there were three things that Dag Randolph still welcomed over his threshold. One, of course, was his Social Security check. As a retired postal worker, he knew the importance of the godsend check's timely delivery, and George Sitz, his current mail carrier of five years, did a mighty fine job. Except in the rain. Sometimes George let the magazines get wet.

Two, the nice young lady from Domino's Pizza, the one who always flirted with him.

And three, the one person for whom he would trade the first two in a heartbeat. The one precious person he would trade anything and everything for.

His granddaughter Madeleine.

Amelia angled into the driveway at her parents' house at 1728 Edgefield Road, unbuckled Maddie's seat belt. Maddie got out of the car and ran up the stone steps to the front door, where Dag Randolph stood: the furious shock of thick white hair, the now de rigueur red flannel shirt, the ever trim figure of a man who spent his life walking. Five days a week Dag Randolph still walked his old route.

Dag grabbed Maddie's hand and led her into the living room. Amelia followed, a close but undeniable second. "Uh, hi, Dad," Amelia said, removing her jacket.

"Hi, honey." He planted a cursory kiss on Amelia's cheek, then sat down on his threadbare La-Z-Boy recliner, the one Amelia and her mother were plotting to replace that Christmas. The aroma of baking banana-walnut bread filled the house. A college football game was on the TV in the corner, the sound turned down. Dag Randolph was in his milieu.

Maddie was visiting.

Amelia wandered into the kitchen, kissed her mother hello, and poured herself a cup of coffee.

"Guess what," Maddie asked.

"What?" Dag replied.

"Mom said I could trick-or-treat *here*!"

"Well, you *better*," Dag said, tapping his hand on his knees. "I was counting on it. I've got it all mapped out for us."

"What do you mean?" Maddie said, climbing up onto her grandfather's lap.

"Got it right here." Dag reached to the end table, flipped on the lamp, and retrieved a yellow legal pad that had a rather detailed map of a five-block radius drawn on it. "We're shooting for name-brand candy only this year," he said, slipping on his bifocals, plotting a course like Hannibal surveying the Alps.

"Right," Maddie said. "Like Twizzlers."

"Twizzlers are good."

"And Peppermint Patties."

"You bet. No point messing with the cheap stuff."

"No point," Maddie echoed.

"I figure we'll start on Sunview, work our way toward Huron Road, catch the Singers and the Callahans early that way. You got a full-size Snickers last year at the Singers' . . . and a popcorn ball at the Callahans'." Dag, of course, had all of this cataloged. He had delivered mail to these people for nearly three decades. He knew who the cheapskates were.

"Yum. I like popcorn balls," Maddie added.

"I do too," Dag said. "Too bad they pull my damn teeth out every time I eat one."

"Daggett!" from the kitchen.

Dag shrugged.

Maddie giggled.

*   *   *

Amelia lowered her voice. "Is everything okay with Dad?"

"Oh yes. He's just a little tired," Martha Randolph said. She was a slight woman, five three in heels, the original owner of Maddie and Amelia's bright green eyes. She had worked in some sort of retail establishment her entire adult life, the longest stint being the ten years she had put in at Connor's Ice Cream, but lately Amelia had noticed that what once was a single spry step across this very kitchen was now three, what once called itself vigor now answered to lethargy. Her mother's movements were slower, more deliberate of late. *Older,* Amelia conceded. "He stayed up late the last couple of weeks watching the Indians in the World Series. It messes him up for a month if he doesn't go to bed at ten-thirty. Besides the fact that he gets so damned involved in the game. Shouting, even."

"Well . . . okay," Amelia said. "If you say it's—"

"Then there's this business with your brother."

Whenever Amelia's only sibling was in trouble with his parents, he was referred to as *your brother*. In happier times, which was most of the time, he was Garth. The current business with Garth Randolph, who, at thirty-nine, had already made and blown two fortunes, centered around his refusal to take a handout from his parents.

And his habit of dropping out of sight for long periods of time.

Garth's business cycle was currently at low ebb; everyone knew it, just as everyone knew he would rebound and probably make another million dollars someday. Because Garth Randolph was brilliant, a renaissance man, even though he had never finished college. He had started off like gangbusters at CWRU—his first year he carried a 4.0 average—but eventually his substance-friendly extracurricular activities became his curricular activities. The last straw came after a five-day binge when, as editor of the yearbook, he mixed up the names of sixty-four students. The yearbook made it to press in that condition. It was an all-time university record.

Yet Amelia *did* get something out of her brother's brief college career at Case Western Reserve University. Her own

400-level course in tolerance. It was Garth Randolph who had
introduced her to her Roger.

That's okay, big brother, Amelia thought with an inner
smile. I forgive you.

"Have you talked to him, Mom?" Amelia asked.

"Just yesterday, in fact," Martha said.

"You're kidding."

"Just called out of the blue."

"Really?"

"Funniest thing . . . I haven't talked to him since maybe
Easter," Martha said. "So I ask him where he's been—as in,
what has he been doing with himself?—and you know what
he says?"

"What?"

"He says: church."

"What?"

Martha laughed, acknowledging her son's lifelong resistance to organized religion. Garth was always the sulking,
dark-eyed teenager in the Rolling Stones T-shirt, slouching in
the St. Clare vestibule, thoroughly miserable and bored. By
the time he was fourteen, he just said no to his parents, and
that was that. To Amelia's knowledge, he had since set foot
in a Catholic church only once, and that was to attend her
wedding. "That's what he said," Martha said. "But I think
he meant he just *came* from church."

"Still . . ."

"I know. Garth near holy water. It's a miracle."

"Where is he living?" Amelia asked, more than a little
surprised by the news, wondering why Garth hadn't called her.
His pattern, after being out of touch for a long time, was always to call Martha first, then Amelia. Then he'd show up.

But *church*?

Her *brother*?

"Didn't say," Martha answered. "But you know
Garth. . . ."

I used to, Amelia thought as she poured more coffee into
her mother's cup.

I used to . . .

Keep this *tiger out of your tank.*

Murmurs hears that there is an awfully nasty batch of heroin on the streets of Cleveland these days. It has the distinctive markings of a red tiger on one side and a blue monkey on the other, both rubber-stamped onto a white GemPac. Creative stuff? Well, unfortunately, there's also some creative alchemy at work here, too. This red-tiger smack is far too pure and it has already proven itself deadly. If you've ever visited the offices at the *Chronicle*, you already know that no one here is in a position to tell you not to indulge in illegal substances. We're merely suggesting you don't indulge in this one. After all, we need the readers.

—Nicholas Stella

15. She worked at the opium house on East Thirtieth Street by night and probably went to some vocational school by day, he thought. He had seen her there when he had scored from Rat Boy, but she had never seen *him*.

He was small when he bought his drugs.

The girl was walking up Fourth Street between Euclid and Prospect, dallying, appointment-free, peering into store windows, fluffing her hair, looking slight and waiflike as the business crowd muscled its noontime way around her.

He knew the minute he saw her in the sunlight that he would own her.

He stepped out of the doorway, directly into the young woman's path. She was nineteen, street-savvy, smart enough to know that she was being hustled for something. Hand on purse, pivot toward the curb, eyes down. Urban survival maneuvers.

"Hi," he said, blocking her way.

"Hi," she answered, the small-town Pennsylvania girl rushing to the surface, betraying the makeup. There was a tiny tattoo of a butterfly near the outside corner of her right eye.

"What's your name?" he asked.

She wore tight black jeans and a blue leather motorcycle jacket. Knee-high black suede boots. Her hair was a cantata of blondes and browns and rusts, falling just past her shoulders, soft bangs in her eyes. She tried to step around him, but at the moment he was big. He filled her path, her near future.

She seemed to resign herself to his presence. "Um, Taffy," she said. "What's yours?"

"Mac."

"Oh . . . okay . . ."

"Mind if I walk with you, Taffy?" he asked.

She looked him up and down. "Free country, I guess."

They walked in silence for a few storefronts. The smell of diesel fumes mingled with the scent of tomato sauce and garlic coming from the pizza parlor on the corner, then slipped beneath the girl's perfume, a perfume that was probably too expensive for her, a fragrance she'd probably gotten out of a magazine, he thought, or as the result of a quick run through a department store. Rap music raged out of the wig store. She spoke first. "So . . . what are you up to today, Mac?"

"Oh, Taffy," he said. "Important things."

"Is that right? And I suppose that means that you're an important man?"

"Yes," he replied. "I'm an important man, and I do important things."

She smiled, and it made her look younger. Seventeen, maybe. A high schooler. Younger than Julia. "Oh yeah? Important things like what?"

She had a slight gap between her front teeth and he liked that. "Taking care of unfinished business, you might say. I'm the kind of man who doesn't like loose ends in his life."

"*Tell* me about it," Taffy said, opening up to him a little. "I'm exactly the same way."

"Really? How so?" He offered her a cigarette. She took it, stopped walking, allowed him to light it for her.

"Well, for one thing . . . *guys,*" she said. They turned the corner, leisurely, heading east on Prospect. "I cannot start with a new guy until the old relationship is over. Over, over. You know? And I don't mean the stage when you're still sending cards, or calling in the middle of the night just to hear the other person's voice. I mean over-over-over. Believe it or not, some of my girlfriends can't leave a relationship until they have the next guy hooked. Not me. Can't do it. Nope."

"Do you have a lot of boyfriends, Taffy?"

"Hah!" she exclaimed. "Not these days."

"Really? A pretty girl like you?"

Taffy gave up a half smile. Sexy gap. "Oh . . . I betcha say that to all the girls."

"Just the pretty ones."

Taffy giggled. "Betcha say *that,* too."

They stopped at the corner of Fourteenth and Prospect, waiting for the light.

"Hungry?" Mac asked.

Taffy smiled, flicked her cigarette to the curb. She looked at her watch, coy, demure. "I could eat."

The northeast corner of the huge, drafty room was blocked off by two sheets of white canvas, suspended from the high ceiling; creating, in effect, a ten-by-ten-foot square room that looked down onto Euclid Avenue from one window, and a side street from the other. Thank God there were space heaters, Taffy thought.

Ten stories below them, the rush hour was just starting to flag.

Although she had never officially attended college, Taffy Ann Kilbane, late of East McKeesport, Pennsylvania, had been to many a frat party since she had come to Cleveland on a Continental Trailways bus when she was sixteen. So at the moment she stepped through the canvas, she recognized the layout, the setup. It seemed a little freaky to her at first, a little out of sync with what she expected to see when she pulled back the corner of the canvas, but there it was.

A dorm room. A *girl's* dorm.

It appeared as if her new friend Mac had built a replica of a college dorm room in the corner of the top floor of an empty warehouse. Single bed, student desk, wardrobe, tiny fridge, hot plate, portable TV.

Above the bed, and on the wall next to it, were posters. But neither seemed to be about anything or anyone current. One was that old poster of Robert Redford, the one from *Butch Cassidy and the Sundance Kid;* the other, a baby-faced Al Pacino in *The Godfather.*

Taffy walked over to the desk, which was L-shaped and
made out of that blond wood that was so popular in the fifties
and sixties. It reminded her of her grandmother's house in
Meadville. The desk butted up against the wall in the corner,
below the two windows. On one end was a tarnished silver
tray with some makeup items. A brush, liquid foundation, a
powder compact, a collection of eye shadow, tweezers, a half
bottle of Ambush *eau de toilette*. She'd never heard of Ambush *eau de toilette*. It looked old, just like all the rest of the
makeup. The cut crystal of the cologne bottle had a filmy,
greasy feel to it, as if it had been in a plastic makeup bag for
years, stuck in somebody's damp basement. On the right side
of the desk was an old Magnavox turntable/eight-track combo.
Next to that, a few dozen albums. Taffy began to flip through
them. They were all squaresville, too. Unbelievably ancient.
Allman Brothers. Carpenters. *Frampton Comes Alive*. Well, it
looked as if there was *one* good one. *Saturday Night Fever*.
Taffy's mom had played the *Saturday Night Fever* soundtrack
all the time when she was small. She took the album out of
the jacket, placed it on the turntable, and started the record
player. Within moments, Barry Gibb was scratchily explaining
about his Night Fever. It made her feel good, protected.

She had taken the clothes he had given her and stepped
inside the canvas-room, wondering if this guy was a peep-
show freak or what. Not that it mattered much. The hundred-
dollar bill he had given her in the rickety freight elevator on
the way up had pretty much insured that he could have whatever he wanted over the course of the next few hours, short
of any rough stuff. Besides, he wasn't all that hard to take for
an older guy.

So if he got off on watching girls change clothes, there were
certainly enough places he could be hiding. Nonetheless, she
still rushed through the part where her breasts were exposed.

On the other hand, she discovered that she liked the clothes.
A lot. She really dug the seventies-retro look, and this outfit
was dead-on. Faded denim bell-bottoms, a white cotton wraparound halter, a pair of white boots. The jeans were a little
tight on her, but she didn't think Mac was the kind of guy

who would object. Mac struck her as a tight-jeans kind of guy.

She walked over to the full-length cheval mirror; this piece, a *real* antique. The mirror was losing some of its silver, but she got a pretty good look at herself. And she looked *hot*. The bottom of the halter top caught her just beneath her breasts, pushing them up and together. She even had a hint of cleavage.

She got her own brush out of her purse and ran it through her hair just as Mac peeled back the canvas and stepped into the room carrying a bottle of wine and two glasses.

Mac had not changed his clothes; he still wore a pair of dark blue corduroys, Timberland loafers, a white shirt with the sleeves rolled up. Strong forearms, Taffy noticed, even though a small table lamp and a blue lava lamp were the only lights in the room. There were no blinds or curtains over the windows, and every so often the brake lights from the street below would spray-paint a spooky, ethereal orange glow onto the buildings across the street.

Mac sat next to her on the bed, handed her a glass of wine. They clinked glasses, drank, sensed each other's sexual presence, drank some more. Taffy could feel the wine warming her. She wished she had a joint.

Eventually she decided it was time to make conversation, and this very strange place, this very strange world, was about all she could think of to talk about. "You live here?"

"Not all the time," Mac said. "I have another place."

She nodded, sipped her wine, pointed to the wine bottle on the desk. "Spanada?"

"Yes," he answered, as if he had been waiting for her to ask.

"Spanada?"

"Yes, why? You don't like it?"

"Cheese *Louise*. Where do you find this stuff?"

"At the beverage store, of course."

She looked at him skeptically, sipped her wine. "I don't *know*. . . ." She picked up the bottle, perused the faded label. "I've bought a lot of cheap wine in my time, okay? I've had a fake ID since I was, like, thirteen. *Lots* of fortified crap. Night Train, MD Twenty/Twenty, wine coolers. Never seen this on a shelf. Ever.''

"You're just not going to the right stores.''

"But I'll tell you where I *have* seen it,'' Taffy continued. "In old pictures of my mother's house when she was having parties. Spanada bottles on the dining room table, Allman Brothers records on the turntable. Just like here.''

"Well, let's just say that I'm a nostalgic kind of guy, Taffy,'' he said, moving closer to her, taking the bottle in hand. He poured them some more wine. "This was a very good time in my life.'' He recapped the bottle. "What's wrong with that? What's wrong with reliving the good times?''

"Hey . . .'' Taffy began, holding up her right hand, as if she were being sworn in. "Whatever grabs your rabbit, right?''

"Pre*cise*ly.'' They clinked glasses.

Taffy continued. "But answer me one thing, okay, Mac?''

"Sure.''

"We're not drinking twenty-year-old jug wine, are we?''

He laughed. "Of course not.''

"I mean, I'd hate to think about what kind of weird friggin' protozoa might be growing inside a twenty-year-old bottle of drugstore wine,'' Taffy said, offering unrequested proof of her education. She'd actually gotten a B in ninth-grade biology.

"No. It's just a funky old bottle I like to keep around. I assure you, the cheap wine we're drinking is fresh.'' He lifted his glass to his lips, took another deep swallow.

Taffy looked at her watch, pointed to the television. "Um, can we watch the news?'' she asked. "I kinda like to stay informed, you know.''

"Sure,'' he answered. "Whatever channel you want. Go ahead. The on/off knob is on the side.''

She got up from the bed and crossed over to the desk. She turned off the Bee Gees and flipped on the television, a thirteen-inch Philco black-and-white model. Another antique. Beige plastic, bent rabbit ears, a couple of knobs missing. After a few moments, it warmed up. The reception was remarkably clear.

"What's this? Where's Dan Rather?" Taffy asked, sipping her wine.

"This is Walter Cronkite. He does the news."

Taffy looked at him. "Uh, excuse me. Dan *Rather* does the six-thirty news on this channel. I'm not *ignorant*."

"Well, Walter's filling in for Dan tonight."

"I also happen to know who Walter Cronkite is too, dear. And he's a *lot* older than this. Look at his glasses. Nobody wears glasses like that anymore. In fact, I'm not sure he's still *alive*. This must be some kind of cable show."

She flipped the channel, over to channel five, just as Frank Reynolds was going to a commercial. "*. . . back with more news, in a moment.*"

Then came a station promo.

"*. . . tonight on channel five, at eight o'clock,* Eight is Enough, *followed by* Charlie's Angels *at nine, and at ten, Robert Blake is* Baretta *. . . and then stay tuned for all the day's news, sports, and weather at eleven on Channel Five.*"

Flip, flip. Channel Three. John Chancellor.

"Where's the rest of the channels? Don't you have cable?" Taffy asked.

"Not yet," he replied.

She left it on Channel Three, sat back down on the bed.

John Chancellor said: "*. . . and in a surprise move by the White House today, President Carter signed into law a bill that most Washington insiders believed he would veto. . . .*"

Taffy emptied her glass, poured them both more wine. She reached for the TV again. Back to Cronkite, who signed off by saying: "*And that's the way it is, October twenty-eighth, 1978.*"

Taffy looked at him, her clear blue eyes a twist of confusion. "You're a *very* weird guy, Mac," she said.

Taffy stood, crossed the room, turned off the TV. She found the Peter Frampton album, put it on the turntable, clicked it to life. She swayed to the music, moving around the room. She played with the bow at the front of her halter top. "Got any pot, Mac?"

Mac flipped his hand out to his side, like a magician. And,

magically, a joint was there. He smiled, lit the joint, passed it to her.

She took a few deep hits, passed it back, continued to dance. She twirled, her hands moving expressively about her face, her body. Taffy had danced at a club on West Twenty-fifth called the Iron Gate. It was only for three nights, but she was a quick study. She knew the moves. "Hey, sailor," she said, pushing his knees apart as he sat on the bed, stepping in between. "You lookin' for a date?"

She stepped back, untied the bow, let the halter top slide down over her shoulders, over the tops of her arms, and onto the floor. Her breasts were small, adolescently firm. And she was proud of them. Ever since she was fourteen, Taffy Kilbane had worn her T-shirts extra tight. The boys had always looked. The men, too.

Mac removed his shirt, reached for her as she moved to the music. She danced away, then back. "Wow," she said. "Nice tattoo."

Instead of answering, he reached out and took hold of her. Taffy didn't struggle. As she stood in front of him, she could feel his hot breath on her stomach. He pulled her closer and dipped his tongue inside the waistband of her jeans, ran it along her smooth skin to the curve of her left hip.

Taffy Kilbane gasped with pleasure. "You're a naughty boy, Mr. Mac."

He unbuckled her belt, then slowly pulled down her zipper.

"I know what *you* want," she said.

He pulled open her jeans, ran his tongue gently around her navel, then lower, lower. Then Mac lifted her high into the air and eased her down to the bed, his erection beginning to gather, to evidence itself to the world in spite of his baggy trousers. Taffy noticed, reached for it, fondling it through his pants, her hand gaining purchase from the ribbed corduroy, squeezing him hard.

"Julia," he said, softly, his eyes floating shut.

She looked at him, at the cant of his features, and immediately understood. All of it. The dorm room, the clothes, the wine, the music. He wanted her to be someone else, someone very specific. She had met them before, men who never got over someone, men who were still pining for a long lost love. It had never been anywhere near this elaborate, but she'd seen it. She had been Peggy, once. Rosemary, too. Why not Julia?

She unzipped his zipper, unbuckled his belt. By the time she removed his pants he was very hard. And she noticed right away that Mac was way above average in size. She straddled him, lowered herself down. "Mac . . ."

He would tell her that he loved her, but it wouldn't be for an hour, an hour later when Taffy reached her orgasm, sitting on the windowsill, naked, her hot skin pressed against the chilled glass of the October night, the sound of her sighs rising and falling, entangling the city sounds that rose, like steam, to meet her.

Fifteen feet above their heads, mounted to the ceiling, a closed-circuit camera watched—silent, digital, dispassionate, as vigilant as the Hidden Paw himself.

Taffy Kilbane left in a cab at ten-thirty. A second hundred-dollar bill in her hand, a clear message burned into her memory. She would call if anybody came for Ronnie Choi. Ronnie Choi was unaware of the jaguar and marmoset marks, but he could easily pick Mac out of a lineup. If it ever came to that.

And it could never, ever, come to that.

He decided not to go home just yet. At home he was nobody special these days. A cold marble rattling around a dark, loveless drawer.

In his corner, though, high above the city, cocooned amid his sensitive and far-reaching equipment—his computer, modem, scanner—he was *some*body. He sat in front of his laptop, the active matrix screen now the only light in his room. He accessed the photographs, the black-and-white smiling faces he had scanned from the yearbook; coifed and sprayed and toothy and smugly perverse in their youth, their promise.

The remaining members of the AdVerse Society of 1978. *Macavity, Macavity, there's no one like Macavity. . . .*

He looked at the credit card receipts he had taken from

Geoffrey Coldicott's trash. Three were from the Shenanigans nightclub near the airport. All late at night. He decided to scan the receipts, study them more closely on his computer screen. Besides, they were beginning to smell a little. Geoffrey favored smoked fish, but always bought too much.

He placed the receipts facedown on his flatbed scanner, fired it up, just as another computer jolted to life twenty miles southeast of him, no distance at all in cyberspatial terms, its data bits flying through the circuitry like milk blue lightning slashing across the Cuyahoga River.

16. Amelia sat at the computer and clicked on the icon called: *World Online.* Immediately the hard drive whirred to life and, within a few seconds, she heard the modem dialing out. Then, that very strange noise a computer makes when it hooks up with another computer.

"You have new mail," the computer said. Out loud.

Amelia jumped a foot.

"What the *hell's* the matter with you?" she said, her hand to her breast. She had never heard any sound come out of the computer other than the occasional *ding* noise it made when something was finished. This was an actual woman's voice.

After she regained her composure, she was able to intuitively click around the software, and, after a few more turns of the hard drive, she had her e-mail message.

It was five full pages of gibberish. Numbers and symbols and strange-looking characters.

At first, it appeared as if some of it may have been Russian. But, Amelia thought, even Russian didn't have characters as strange as this. Did it? Maybe it was Arabic. Or Hebrew. Or Greek. She'd never seen anything quite like it.

There were no paragraph breaks, no indentations, no recognizable words, let alone sentences. One of the characters looked like an upside down Q.

This isn't Russian, Amelia thought as she hit the Print button, starting her HP DeskJet in motion, making a copy of the message.

This is *Martian.*

four

Subterranea

17• Six-twenty A.M. Nicky stood in the doorway to Volk's Jewelers on Prospect Avenue and attended the street as it slowly came alive. He sipped his coffee, yawned. This was the worst part of his job. He was always waiting for somebody, something.

But, as always, it was the thrill of the hunt that energized him, the thought that he might actually pull it off. This time, a story from the dealer's point of view.

He closed his eyes, leaned against the window, imagined his byline in *Esquire*, *GQ*, *Playboy*, *The New Yorker*. . . .

Six twenty-five. Gil Strauss entered the back door of the rectory at St. Francis, as he had every autumn and winter weekday for many years, and prepared to heat the sacristy for the priest offering seven-o'clock mass. The sky was leaden, promising snow, and Gil brought with him a chill that seemed to follow him down the long, dark hallway that led to the church.

Dark, as always, except . . .

Except this morning there was a wedge of light from one of the vacant rooms, a room that was going to be Father Angelino's when he arrived. Gil walked around the corner, pushed open the door, and saw a figure standing near the window.

"Good morning, Gil," the figure said, without turning around.

"Good morning, Father LaCazio. How come you're—"

"A priest doesn't leave this earth with much, Gil."

"Excuse me, Father?"

Joseph turned toward him, slowly, a cigarette in hand. He gestured toward the two large cardboard boxes on the bed. They were unsealed, either just arrived and opened or ready to be taped and shipped.

Gil asked: "Are those Father Angelino's belongings?"

"Yes. They came from St. Michael's yesterday."

"Is that everything?"

"Yes," Joseph said. "Two boxes. That's what he accrued in this life. He lived forty-two years, helped thousands of people, and he got two boxes of junk for it."

"But a priest isn't supposed to—"

"Two boxes. You could fit his whole life into the trunk of a car." Joseph opened the window slightly. A frigid breeze stole across the room. "It all goes to his sister, Carmen."

"Do you want me to take them to UPS?" Gil asked.

Joseph was silent for a few moments. He flicked his cigarette out the window, closed it. "Perhaps," he said. "Or maybe I'll go. Maybe I'll take a drive after mass. I'll let you know."

"You should let me do it, Father," Gil said. "Your bad back and all. You shouldn't be—"

Gil made a move toward the boxes, but Joseph froze him with a glance. "I'll let you know, Gil," he said softly. "After mass."

"Okay, Father," Gil said, stopping in his tracks. He tapped his watch. "Speaking of mass."

Joseph waved, absently, in Gil's direction. "I'll be right up."

Gil hesitated, then left the room. The last thing he heard as he ascended the steps to the sacristy was the low-volume hum of a spiritual, "Just a Closer Walk with Thee," one of Father LaCazio's favorites.

At six-thirty Nicky looked up from his *Plain Dealer* and saw Beverly attempting to cross the street, lithely sidestepping traffic, almost balletic in her movements, waiting, now, for a bus to pass. Beverly was tall and arrogantly statuesque, and this morning wore a mauve satin bolero jacket, short white skirt, seamed stockings, and perilously high heels. Her thick black hair was swept dramatically back from her face and secured by a pair of huge African-ivory barrettes. Her makeup was gaudy and theatrical; her legs, perfect.

Beverly Ahn was black/Asian, a stunning transvestite in her early thirties, one of the thousands of exotic Vietnam war hyphenates populating the large cities of the eastern United States. She had just come off duty as a hostess in a club called Shangri La on West Twenty-fifth Street, a mostly transvestite bar that served the city's fairly active cross-dressing population, but also one that drew a large tourist clientele—gay, straight, and everything in between. Nicky had once done a series of City Streets pieces on alternative bars, and Beverly had been his unofficial guide to subterannea. They'd been friends ever since, running into each other at concerts, film festivals, and the like.

Nicky watched Beverly click across Prospect, a sleek, polished illusion of womanly grace and confidence. For any number of reasons, not the least of which was simple respect, Nicky always thought of, and referred to, Beverly Ahn in the feminine.

"Hi, gorgeous," Beverly said. "Sorry I'm late." She stepped onto the sidewalk, towering over Nicky by three or four inches.

Nicky felt himself color slightly at the compliment. He bullied it back. He was never quite sure how to react to compliments from men. Especially men who wore lace camisoles. "Good morning, *bella aura*," Nicky replied. He always countered Beverly in faux Italian because she loved things like that. And this morning Nicky needed all the flattery he could muster. It was a point that Beverly Ahn lost no time in acknowledging.

"You don't know what I'm going to have to go through to talk him into this," Beverly said, stepping into the doorway. "The man's a *beast*."

"Well," Nicky began, trying to think of some charming way to placate her, "they don't call me the Beastmaster of Euclid Avenue for nothing, you know."

Beverly just glared at him. "And why am I doing this again?"

"Because you like me. Because I'm the coolest white boy you know. And because I'll take you to dinner anywhere you want. But not for a week or two."

"Anywhere?"

"Yep."

"You'd walk into Sammy's with me dressed like this?"

The funny thing was, Nicky would. Wouldn't even think twice about it. Ever since his early rock-band days—Nicky Starr and the Constellation—it seemed as if he was born to shock. "Beverly. It would be my pleasure."

Beverly laughed. "You do go on, Nicholas." She reached into her bag and retrieved a compact. She opened it, did some maintenance on her face, then added, "Just keep an eye on this fucking creep for me, okay, hon?"

The creep in question was a Chinese hood named Ronnie "Rat Boy" Choi. Willie T had pointed him out to Nicky one night at Lancers on Carnegie, and the first thing Nicky had noticed was that the man looked every bit of his name. Willie had also told him about Choi's thing for cross-dressers. Nicky figured that Choi probably liked his transvestites a lot younger than Beverly, but Nicky also figured that Beverly had something pretty special going for her. Something she had long ago stopped offering to Nicky. "You don't have anything to worry about," Nicky said.

"No?" Beverly replied, raising a solitary, sculpted eyebrow. She grabbed Nicky's coffee cup and sipped.

"Of course not," Nicky said. "I'll be right there. All you have to do is talk him into an anonymous interview with me. One hour, anywhere he wants. No cops. No tape."

Beverly pouted for a moment, letting Nicky know that she was fully aware of the fact that nobody could protect her from a butcher like Rat Boy Choi. In one drug-crazed moment he could, and would, slit her throat for no reason at all. Because he didn't like her perfume, perhaps. Because he decided that he just didn't feel like having a half-black boy-whore today.

She tossed the cold coffee into the street, grimacing at the bitter taste. "Okay. Let's go."

Nicky produced his most charming smile, looked skyward, put his hand through a crook in Beverly's arm, and hailed a cab.

Elegant Linda's was an opium house that operated out of the basement of a warehouse on East Thirtieth Street, near Superior Avenue. After passing muster with a pair of gargantuan Anglo thugs at the unremarkable front door, and paying in advance, Nicky and Beverly descended a long narrow staircase, passed through two more doors, then entered a dimly lit womb of damp red carpeting—floor, walls, and ceiling. The lounge at the back of the room, where one could sip tea or cocktails while waiting, was a haphazard jumble of mismatched red vinyl furniture, maroon draperies, and filigreed gold fixtures. Two men sat at the back, one black, one white. They wore matching motorcycle jackets, mirrored sunglasses, leather chaps.

In contrast, the two hostesses were garbed in virginal white *cheongsams,* slit provocatively up to the thigh. They were white, around twenty, and made up like extras in a David Lynch version of the Peking Opera—high black hair, pasty white faces, red bows. They seemed to be in constant motion, designating the opium girls to customers, dispatching the twosomes to their private rooms with even, quiet authority. Above them, from cheap speakers buried somewhere in the thickness of the carpeting, a pan flute played.

Beverly talked to the prettier of the two hostesses, the one with a small butterfly tattoo by her right eye, and found out rather easily which den was occupied by Rat Boy. Nicky hoped there would not be any repercussions. Within moments, he and Beverly found themselves being led through the elaborate web of rooms, rooms closed off from the narrow paneled hallways by thick velvet drapes. The girl who led them was Chinese, about twelve years old, dressed in the traditional *samfoo,* the black pajamalike clothing of north China. She took them nearly a full city block into the basement, carrying with her a long bamboo pipe and a small leather pouch. Along the way, Nicky could hear the sounds of the trade, the wet and raspy coughing, the incoherent babbling, low and hypnotic. In spite of a half dozen years in rock and roll, in spite of five years in college and an association with some of the more bohemian types in the city throughout his life, this was an extreme end of the drug lifestyle that Nicky knew absolutely nothing about. More than once he had to remind himself that he was in Cleveland, it was the middle of the week, and that it was still twenty minutes until the start of the *Today* show.

When the girl got to Rat Boy's cubicle she stopped and cast her eyes to the ground.

Nicky peeked through the curtains and saw Choi, supine on a jute mat, his huge ocherous belly and thighs mercifully covered by a white towel, a young girl refilling his pipe. Rat Boy's pipe was a showpiece, very ornate, with an ivory mouthpiece and delicate carvings along the shaft. The deep metal bowl was etched with Chinese characters.

Rat Boy's eyes were closed, but in the candlelight Nicky could see that his face bore the vacuous half smile that came from years of indulging in the brown, sticky paste; the stone-set features of the opium habitué. Nicky relaxed a little, realizing Rat Boy's reflexes were probably slowed to the point of rigor mortis.

Beverly stepped inside and spoke softly to Rat Boy's girl, who was also very young and Chinese. The girl finally understood, reluctantly handed Beverly the pipe, and retreated to a corner of the small room, where she sat, cross-legged, on the floor, waiting for something to go wrong. Within moments, Choi slitted his eyes, sensing another presence in the room. He smiled when he saw Beverly standing over him, offering up a thick row of uneven yellow and silver teeth. Rat Boy pulled off his towel. He pointed to his lips, then gently tapped his shriveled penis.

When Beverly straddled Rat Boy, placing the pipe once again to his mouth, touching a long wooden match to the candle's flame, Nicky retreated to an empty room. His opium girl stood in the doorway, pipe in hand, a little nervous about not being able to fulfill her duty, a little confused as to what Nicky wanted her to do. He walked her inside and gestured for her to sit on the edge of the mat. He offered her a cigarette. She refused, blushed, looked at the floor.

Nicky put his ear to the thin paneled wall.

He smoked.

And waited.

Twenty minutes later, Beverly stuck her head into Nicky's den and beckoned him with one long, enameled fingernail, the color of ripe strawberries. Within moments they made their way hurriedly through the narrow corridors, across the lounge, up the stairwell, and out onto East Thirtieth Street.

After the dank claustrophobia of Elegant Linda's den, Nicky welcomed the now-teeming workaday crowd, the diesel fumes, the noise.

As they walked toward Euclid Avenue, Beverly told him the bad news. Ronnie Choi wasn't dealing heroin that bore the marks of either a tiger or a monkey. And neither were the other triads.

The marks, he had told her, were Anglo marks.

"When are you going to settle down, Beverly?"

They were standing at the corner of East Twenty-fourth and Euclid Avenue. "When men like you stop looking at my legs, I guess. You know what I mean? Straight guys?" She flipped her cigarette into the gutter, lifted her short skirt a little higher, drawing the attention of a pack of young schoolboys on a bus stopped at the light. "You look at my legs when you see me, don't you?"

Nicky found no reason to lie. "Sure I do, Beverly. You've got great legs."

She smiled wanly. "For a boy, you mean. Right?"

"No," Nicky said. "I mean, for anybody. Tina *Turner* doesn't have legs like you, Beverly. Honest to God." Nicky pointed at the boys on the bus. "They seem to think so."

Beverly glanced up and shook an accusatory, maternal finger at the boys, who immediately took a collective nosedive

onto their respective seats in a flurry of long-sleeved white
shirts and thin black neckties. She looked back at Nicky.
"You're a doll," she said, noticing a cab, raising her hand.
"But I know you're full of shit, too."

She stepped into the cab, shut the door, smiled again at
Nicky. In the morning light Nicky observed that her makeup
had begun to crack a little; the lines around her eyes and lips
were a lot more visible than they were in the provocative illumination of Elegant Linda's.

But before he could discern any other of the new day's
realities, the cab jerked into the vortex of rush-hour traffic on
Euclid Avenue, preserving, for the moment, the illusion that
was Beverly Ahn, lead hostess at the Shangri La Club on West
Twenty-fifth Street.

Preserving, for the moment, her *bella aura*.

18. Taffy called at noon.

He dropped the man at the door with his Taser unit, a brief blue and yellow shock to the side of the neck that sent an immediate message to the man's extremities that services were no longer required. He heaped the bodyguard at the bottom of the stairs, away from the windows, relieving him of his firearm in the process.

But, as soon as he started up the steps, the man stirred a little, his hand instinctively moving toward his now empty holster, as if to say . . . *one more please, sir, I'm not quite out of the fight . . . you see, I haven't taken quite enough pain for my employer . . . the guy who pays me just enough money to buy my suits at Sears and my whores on Carnegie . . . more, please, sir.*

Mac obliged him. He lifted his right foot parallel to the floor, about waist-high. He held on to the handrail for leverage and brought his boot down with a violent scissor kick, his heel catching the man on the right side of his jaw, splintering the man's teeth onto the dusty hardwood floor in a spout of bone and soft red tissue. The man fell unconscious.

Mac ascended the steps to Ronnie Choi's apartment.

Five minutes later he descended, stepped back into the alley. Ronnie Choi had been sleeping, defenseless until Mac entered the room. He begged for his life.

Mac had said no.

Mac looked both ways, lowered his sunglasses into place,

and turned up the collar on his khaki jacket. Small. Very small. He walked toward Euclid Avenue, toward the lunchtime crowd.

And disappeared.

19. Maddie cleared her throat, stepped to the edge of the stage for her audition, and launched into:

"The sun'll come up tomorrow . . ."

Amelia had Maddie in the exact center of the camcorder's viewfinder, a little flourish of professional videography she had learned from Roger's brother Neal, the family's official historian and gadget high priest. The problem was that she didn't have the greatest seat in the auditorium, and the sound quality would probably be a little bit lacking.

On the other hand, she had the feeling that the only sound she was going to get was Paige's sniffling. Paige loved kids, Paige wanted kids, Paige Turner had the loudest biological clock in Collier Falls. She looked over at Amelia, her bottom lip aquiver, as Maddie turned the corner on the first verse.

"Tomorrow! Tomorrow!"

By the time Maddie had finished the song—a rather atonal rendering, if one were to be even Christian about it—it became clear that she didn't have a chance at playing the feisty, carrot-topped orphan when Collier Falls Community Theater mounted *Annie* for the third time in the past decade.

Afterwards the three had lunch at the Applebee's on Fordham Road, a repast during which Maddie made a project of rearranging peas, and little else.

But by the afternoon Maddie had brightened a little and she and Amelia made an angel food cake with raspberry frosting.

Amelia's imagination needled her all afternoon. What was that very strange e-mail message about? she wondered. Was it a business letter for Roger? A *personal* letter for Roger? Was it a love letter from Shelley Roth?

She tried calling the technical support lines at MicroCenter at Eastgate but found out that if you hadn't bought your computer there, you weren't going to get any specific information out of them. However, the pert young lady at Customer Service said that they have daily computer courses and even a 900 number she could call for—

And that's when Amelia bailed. She wasn't going to shell out $3.95 a minute for, well, *anything*. Andy Garcia, maybe, but not over the phone.

Amelia dialed the second number on her list. It was the direct line to the audiovisual section of the main branch of the Cleveland Public library. The AV department handled the library's considerable computer software collection.

"Audiovisual, Rhonda speaking."

"Hi. I was wondering if you could help me with a little computer problem I'm having," Amelia said.

"Well, I'll do my best," Rhonda replied.

"I received some e-mail from someone, but I think it's in some kind of code and I—"

"Excuse me," Rhonda said, interrupting. "I don't mean to cut you off, but you're kind of beyond me already."

"There's no one down there who knows about this kind of thing?"

"To be honest with you, we've only had one computer expert in this department over the last couple of years, and he's no longer with us. We just sort of shuffle and file software, I'm afraid."

"He doesn't work at the library anymore?" Amelia asked.

"I think he may be at another branch. Hang on a second."

The electronic hiss was soon replaced by Muzak as Amelia

waited. It was a Neil Diamond medley. Finally, mercifully, Rhonda returned with a loud click.

"Yeah, he's at our Stillman branch if you want to call over there. Name's Eddie Pankow. Real whiz kid when it comes to computers."

Amelia wrote "Stillman" and "Pankow" on her notepad.

He could see her on the phone, through the front window, but he couldn't hear a word she was saying. She wasn't using the cordless telephone this time. He wondered how much she knew. He wondered if the e-mail meant anything to her, although he doubted it. After all, she had not even finished junior college.

Yet when they were intimate, he thought, when the electricity leapt between their skin and muscles and hair and bone, he wondered just how much of a challenge she was going to be. Quite formidable, he supposed. Maternal instincts and all.

Yet for some strange reason, although he wasn't quite sure why—nor would he be for a precious few more hours—he almost *wanted* her to fight.

At four o'clock Maddie called from her friend Ellie Applebaum's house. Ellie had invited Maddie for dinner, and after a short bit of whining, Maddie got her way. Amelia spoke to Ellie's mother, Dorothy-call-me-Dot, and was assured that Maddie would be home by around seven.

At six o'clock Amelia sat at her computer, a Healthy Meal microwave meal (Mandarin Chicken with Snow Pea Pods) in front of her, and decided she would call information in Stillman, Ohio. She looked in the phone book, got the area code, and was just about to dial when the cordless phone rang in her hand. "Hello . . ."

"Hey, wife," Roger said.

"Hey . . ."

"Miss you."

Amelia remained silent. Did she miss him? Yes. Would she let him know that? Not on your life. But she decided she was getting tired of the verbal sparring. She decided to be pleasant.

"How's my girls?" Roger continued.

"The big one's tired," Amelia said. "The little one's at a friend's house. Where are you? You sound like you're right around the corner."

"Just the wonders of modern science, I guess. I'm in Elkhart, Indiana."

"Ouch. Sounds like something out of *Twin Peaks*."

"It's not so bad," Roger said. "I'm at the Sheraton. Inside, they're all the same. I could be in Barcelona."

"Yeah. But you can't get those Basque McMuffins you like so much."

Roger laughed. "So catch me up. Seems like I've been gone a week."

Amelia related the salient details of the last few days in suburbia, including the grand opening of Paige Turner Books, as well as Maddie's audition. For some reason, she left out the part about her and Paige nightclubbing. And the part about Dark Curls. They weren't lies, really. Just minor, harmless omissions.

Amelia looked less than longingly at her orange glazed chicken. It had already congealed into an amorphous peach-colored mound. Disposal fodder. She'd have a bowl of Trix.

"Great," Roger said, a little too enthusiastically. "What else is going on?"

Amelia told him about the cryptic e-mail message.

"What do you think it is?" Roger asked.

"Some kind of coded e-mail, I guess," Amelia said. "Can't read it. Looks Egyptian or something."

"Are you sure you're *supposed* to be reading it?"

"What is that supposed to mean?"

"Nothing," Roger said. "I'll take a look at it when I get back."

"No . . . I'm serious, Roger. What did you mean by that?"

"Nothing. Jeez. Ease up on the Midol there, babe."

"Don't patronize me," Amelia replied, a little more harshly than she intended.

Roger was quiet for a moment. "Look, all I meant was—"

"Have you used my computer in the last few days?"

"I think I used it once or twice last week when my laptop went into the shop. You weren't home, so I just did a little on-line work," Roger replied. "But I assure you I didn't send any e-mail to James Bond or anything." Roger laughed, but it was a hollow, humorless sound.

"Yeah, well, maybe you should ask me first from now on," Amelia said, although she had no idea why. She hadn't wanted to pick a fight, but the fight just seemed to happen.

"Okay, boss," Roger said in his conciliatory manner that drove her further up the wall.

Amelia growled in frustration and Roger took it as his cue. He said he'd call tomorrow, mumbled a desultory "love you," and hung up.

Amelia listened to the silence of the house, now grown more still and empty since she'd gotten into a stupid argument with Roger. She considered calling him back to apologize, but she found that she really *was* a little pissed off. She wasn't exactly sure why, though. Maybe it was because she really didn't think Roger believed she could actually write a novel.

Or maybe it was just the infuriating vision of Shelley Roth and Roger slapping thighs in a Budgetel off I-271.

Sorry, sugar babe, she thought, hiking her resolve.

See you at the book signing.

20·William Thaddeus Collins sat in a nondescript brown sedan, a double cheese Whopper in one hand, a *Cleveland Chronicle* in the other. He wore a department-issue dark blue watch cap and his customary wraparound shades, but he was clean-shaven and looked to have bulked up to a ridiculous proportion since Nicky had last seen him. Willie T had to be in his late forties, but his body was that of a much younger man.

It was late morning, so the postbreakfast, prelunchtime trade at the East Eighty-fifth Street Burger King was just a handful of cars. The parking lot was peppered with rusted Pontiacs and brand-new BMWs. Nicky backed into the space next to Willie T. Their driver windows were inches apart.

"Hey, Mr. *T*," Nicky said, cutting his engine.

"What I tell you 'bout that Mr. T shit?" Willie said, with what Nicky hoped was good nature. There were times when Willie T looked meaner than the criminals. "And when are you gonna get a fuckin' haircut?"

"Said the man with no hair."

Luckily, Willie T laughed. "I got hair. I just choose not to wear it. Women love a bald black man."

"Is that right?"

"Look around, man. Shaq, Charles Barkley, Michael Jordan. You see any hair on their heads? You see them lackin' in the pussy department?"

"They're rich," Nicky said with a smile. "You're not rich, Willie."

"Yeah . . . but that ain't it."

"Come on. If Charles Barkley was on welfare, you think he'd ever get laid?"

"Fuck *yeah*, man," Willie T said, a little defensively. Obviously someone had once told him he looked a little like Sir Charles. Which, now that Nicky thought about it, he did. "Charles has got it goin' on, man."

They fell silent for a few moments, Willie T working the mouthful of food around. Finally he swallowed and asked, "So you struck out with the Rat Boy, eh?"

"Yeah," Nicky said. "But how could this heroin not be Chinese? I mean, who else would put marks like that on the bags?"

"The Crips, the mob, the Latinos . . ." Willie T said. "The Chinese don't have no patent on that shit."

"Any idea where I could look next?" Nicky said, getting down to business.

"No," Willie T began, "but I do have some advice for you."

"And what would that be?"

Willie T looked up from his newspaper, undividing his attention. "My advice to you is to back off this thing."

"Come again?"

"I mean find another story, man."

It didn't sound like an order or anything. It still sounded like a suggestion. Nicky plowed ahead. "I got some time into this, you know. I *did* go down to that scuzzy place at six o'clock in the morning, putting my life in danger."

"I'm telling you that you don't know what this is about, man," Willie said. "You think this is about white-boy priests and heroin, but you don't know shit. This ain't *about* that."

"Hey . . . Willie . . . wherever this leads, I'm going with it. You know what I'm saying? This is my ticket out, man. If the shit gets deeper, I'll wear bigger boots. C'mon. He was my cousin."

"No he wasn't. You fuckin' lied to me about that."

Nicky tried to stare him down, but all he got back was the fish-eye reflection of his own face in Willie's wraparound sunglasses. It was useless. "Okay . . . he was *like* a cousin . . . close friend of the family, all right?"

Willie T studied him for what seemed like a full minute. "It's bad, Nicky."

"Bad. Bad *how*? Talk to me." Nicky held up his hands. He noticed that they were beginning to shake a little. "Look . . . no pencil. Eh?" He unbuttoned his shirt. "No wire."

Willie T grabbed a napkin out of the bag and wiped his lips slowly, deliberately. He leaned forward, out the window, the sharp smell of just-eaten onions filling Nicky's world. "I'm gonna tell you something that you're not going to know. You hear me?"

"Yeah. I hear you."

"I ain't fuckin' with you, Nicky. I see a word of this in print before the investigation is over, I'll find you and wax your ass myself. Birdman'll hold you down. You rode with us. You know what I'm talkin' about."

Nicky knew exactly what he was talking about. Every crack dealer in the Third District was scared shitless of Willie T. Nicky made a Boy Scout salute with his fingers. Then crossed his heart.

Willie said: "The priest was fucked up. Big time."

"What do you mean, fucked up? Fucked up how?"

"I mean he didn't just die from the smack. It was no accident. He was cut up. Mutilated."

"What?"

"Ugly motherfuckin' scene, man." Willie held up a color photograph that showed a man's body: naked, shredded flesh, a huge sticky pool of brownish blood. The man was hardly recognizable as John Angelino.

Nicky felt the bile head north. "Wh-what happened to his *eyes*?"

"Pulled out. *Cut* out, I should say. Somethin' really sharp."

Willie T took a bite of his Whopper. The reddish brown meat juice ran down his chin, onto his hand, onto the crime-scene photo. Nicky gagged, looked away, found his wind, continued. "Yeah, b-but there's something . . ."

"Somethin' stuffed into the eye sockets? Man, you could be a fuckin' detective."

Willie T was clearly enjoying this, Nicky thought. There was some kind of street lesson in here somewhere. A *be careful what you ask for* kind of thing. Nicky hitched his courage and looked back at the photo. There was something beige and wrinkled stuffed into the eye cavities. The texture and color reminded him of ginger root.

"You ready for this?" Willie T asked. "They're *daffodil* bulbs."

"What?" The word sounded so incongruous, so grotesque, next to the carnage of the crime scene that Nicky almost laughed. But he remained silent, stunned.

"Daffodil bulbs," Willie T repeated, then let out a snort of humorless laughter. "You gotta love this fuckin' *city,* man."

Nicky composed himself, somewhat. This was way beyond anything he had ever tackled before, but he could do it, right? He *should* do it, right? Nobody deserved to end up like that, especially not a priest. "I don't care, man. This makes it a better story. Ten times better."

"Okay, Nicky," Willie T said, placing the photos on the seat. "But I can't get you any closer to the investigation than this. You're a smart boy. You'll figure out where to go next."

Nicky had no idea where to go next, but he didn't want to tarnish his smart-boy image just yet. "So how come this information wasn't in the paper?"

"*Nicky*. Cops withhold shit from the public all the time. You know that. Your old man's a cop. Separates the real confessions from the professional assholes who call and confess to everything."

Over the next few minutes, Nicky tried to make small talk, hoping to keep Willie T there for a few more minutes, hoping some ideas would spill over. "So . . . how *is* the Birdman these days?"

"The Birdman's cool, Nicky," Willie T said as he started the Ford. "The Birdman just flies. He's Homicide now. That's how I got the photo."

"No shit?"

"None," Wille T said. He crumpled the greasy waxed paper his Whopper had come in. "Me? I still like the dope, man. I still like ropin' these cocaine cowboys."

Nicky decided to ask. "Do I, uh, owe you that half of the C note for this little meeting?"

Willie T put his car in drive, his foot on the brake. "You do."

Nicky reached into his pocket, retrieved the half bill, handed it to Willie T. "And what about the other—"

"That's between you and the Birdman," Willie T said of Nicky's remaining voucher. "But I'd advise you to wait and use it on somethin' else. Because this is some dangerous shit, Nicky. The coroner said this guy used a fuckin' *scalpel*. You wanna get close to that?"

"No," Nicky said, the image of John Angelino's eyeless horror mask seared into his memory. He wondered if his cousin Joseph knew.

"You see the Birdman, you tell him I said hello," Willie T said.

Before Nicky could answer, Willie T swung out of his space and headed for the exit onto Euclid Avenue.

The thick, moist smell of fatty meat lingered behind him, and for the first time in Nicky's life, it didn't make him hungry. For the first time in his life, it smelled like what it was. Dead flesh. The dead, fetid flesh of a formerly ambulatory mammal.

The offices of Morris, Goldberg and Dodge, Court Reporters, were located in the sixth floor of the Leader Building at East Sixth and Superior. A reporter for fourteen years, Nicky's sister Maria was one of the firm's real assets. Hence her office was up front, near the reception area. Hence Nicky found it relatively easy to sneak in there sometimes and search Nexis, the huge database of news stories and company information available to corporate accounts.

He always dropped by at lunch.

Today, as he had hoped, the offices were essentially deserted and he managed to slip into Maria's office unseen. He closed the door, sat down at his sister's computer, and called Nexis. While he waited for the connection, he surveyed what he had.

He was pretty sure that he was the only writer in Cleveland who had the information that the priest was hacked up. But why? Why hadn't that been in the papers? Why hadn't it *leaked* to the papers? Did the families know? He knew he couldn't use that information in print, but if he could find some connection to another crime, and *that* source gave him the information . . .

The initial Nexis search screen appeared. Nicky navigated to the news-story database, and requested all articles that contained the words *red* and *tiger* and *heroin*.

Nothing.

He figured he would start specific, then get general. Inputting a search for the word *heroin* would have given him thousands of references. Nexis was huge.

Next he punched in *tiger* and *heroin* and got fifty-four references, including his own short piece in the *Chronicle*. He scanned them. Most were *Hollywood Reporter* and *Variety* stories on a movie called *White Tiger*. One story was about a member of the Detroit Tigers going through rehab. No murders.

He tried *monkey* and *heroin*.

Nothing.

He rummaged through Maria's top drawer, found a half pack of stale Virginia Slims menthols and a fold-up ashtray. He wheeled over to the window, opened it, broke off the filter, fired up a Slim. It tasted like burning VapoRub.

Next search. He typed *priest* and *heroin*.

Eighty-eight hits. Mostly stories about inner-city rehab centers, DARE programs, and the like. Nothing local. Nothing about anyone overdosing on red tiger brand smack.

He was just about to begin a new search when his eyes landed on the day's *USA Today*, opened to the sports section. The articles were about a variety of teams—the Vikings, the Blackhawks, the Cardinals, the Cavaliers, the Panthers, the Buccaneers, the—

Wait a second. Panthers.

He reached for his shoulder bag, extracted the manila file envelope. He took out the original *Plain Dealer* article, scanned it, found the reference. The article said the heroin packet had been marked with a "tigerlike" animal. Not tiger. Tiger*like*.

Nicky began a new search. Over the next five minutes, he tried *panther, leopard, cougar, ocelot, lynx, bobcat, lion*. At one-thirty he keyed in *jaguar* and *heroin*.

There was one reference. A recent article from the *Erie Times News*, the daily paper in Erie, Pennsylvania, ninety miles away. The proximity sent a shiver through Nicky as he hit Enter, requesting the article.

The shiver became an icy hand around his heart when he saw the headline.

ERIE COUNTY DOCTOR FOUND STABBED TO DEATH; DRUGS INVOLVED.

21. The drive south was exhilarating. Amelia knew that she should have called first, but the sky had cleared completely and it was a perfect day. She had Roger's car today, an apple red Acura. On certain days, in certain moods, on certain streets, it made her feel like Audrey Hepburn in *Two for the Road*. She passed through Bath and Hinckley, through Massilon, Zoar, and New Philadelphia. The trees were aflame with color, the air held a hint of woodsmoke and apples. Fall was in full, glorious burn in northeastern Ohio.

By the time she arrived in Stillman, just west of Sugarcreek, she was hungry. She found a spot on Route 36 called Emma's. The waitress told her the lunch specials were country meat loaf, fried Lake Erie perch, and spaghetti with meat sauce. And that they were out of the perch. Amelia glanced around and saw absolutely none of the customers eating the meat loaf.

"I'll have the spaghetti," she said. "And coffee."

The waitress retreated to the kitchen just as a blue van pulled into the parking lot across the street from the restaurant.

"Well, first of all, this is an Internet message. See all this information at the top?"

Amelia nodded. She had handed the floppy disk to the taller of the two young men she had found huddling over a computer terminal at Cybernauts, Inc., a disheveled storefront computer store on Gulliver Street, next to the one and only barber shop in downtown Stillman, Ohio. The librarian at the Stillman Community Library had told her that Edward Pankow had not worked there in a few months, that he had struck out on his own and started a telecommunications company. Amelia, for some reason, had expected a high-tech office with a dozen employees scurrying about on expensive carpeting. When she stepped through the door and saw that the "cybernauts" were really a couple of grunge rockers in their early twenties, she relaxed. She'd find out what she wanted to know.

"This is the routing information," Eddie continued, clearing his long, dirty-blond hair from his eyes, pointing to his twenty-one-inch monitor. "As in, these are the locations of all the computers this had to go through to get to yours. I can tell you right now, this did not come from someone on World Online. This came through an Internet account."

"*We* can tell you that," Andy Bencek said. He was the shorter one, the dark-haired one, the one standing inches away from Amelia.

"Okay," Amelia said, barely hanging on to the thread. "But is there any way you can tell me what it says? Is there any way to, well, *decode* it?"

"Dr. Bencek here is our resident encryption expert," Eddie said, standing up, gesturing toward Andy, giving up the chair.

"Is that right?" Amelia said with a smile.

Andy sat down, hit a few keys, and brought the encoded message onto the screen in what may have been twenty-four-point type. "Initial analysis, Dr. Pankow?" he asked.

Eddie leaned in, looking over Andy's shoulder. "I'd say it was a jay-peg, Dr. Bencek."

"Sorry, Beavis. Watch and learn." Andy tapped a few keys.

Amelia looked at the screen and saw it slowly reveal, from top to bottom, a photograph of a piece of paper—specifically, the bottom half of a torn sheet of paper from a legal pad. On it was a poem written in a pretty handwriting, a woman's handwriting, that was for sure. For a moment it looked like calligraphy, but Amelia looked more closely and saw that it was just that the woman's writing was nearly perfect—fluid, delicate, yet still confident and forthright. A *young* woman's handwriting, Amelia thought. The poem read:

I am moved by fancies that are curled
Around these images, and cling;

The notion of some infinitely gentle
Infinitely suffering thing.

Amelia did not recognize the poem, but then again, her knowledge of poetry was limited to what she had been made to sit through in high school English. But there was something about the tone of this brief verse, something so sad, it filled her for the moment with a liquid sorrow. She thought of how Maddie dealt with the world, her daughter's quiet, gentle nature.

On the other hand, if this was a love poem from Shelley Roth to her husband . . .

"Mystery solved," Andy said as he turned to his partner and high-fived him.

"The doctor is *in*," Eddie replied, fiving him back.

"Well," Amelia began, "do either of you recognize this poem?"

The two young men looked at each other, then at the screen, then at the floor, then out the windows, as if they had just been cornered by a hostile English teacher. "No."

"Okay," Amelia said. "No problem."

"But we *can* get you the real names of these people before you go. We could run a finger check on everyone who got the mail."

"Can you *do* that?" Amelia replied, batting her lashes. She decided she really didn't want to know what a "finger check" was, so she didn't ask.

The co-owners of Cybernauts, Inc., Edward James Pankow and Andrew Martin Bencek, looked at each other, at the computer screen, then at Amelia.

They nodded solemnly.

The only reason Eddie Pankow noticed the blue van was because he was trying to buy one. Cheap. And this one had potential. It looked around ten years old, clean but not perfect. When it rolled to a stop out front, about five minutes after the lady with the poetic e-mail had left the store, he could see a few fair-sized rust spots, and that meant if the van was for sale, there was bargaining room.

But while the van was cool, the guy who got out of it and stepped in front of the store was another story altogether. Tall, dark coat, tinted glasses. He had his hands in his pockets and stood there looking at the window display for what had to be ten minutes. The only things in the display were some empty, sun-faded boxes of Windows 95 programs and a couple of outdated fax modems laid out on some cheesy red velvet. Yet the man stood there and stared at the stuff for the longest time.

Eddie was just about to go get his partner and get *his* take on the lurker when something totally unexpected happened. Davey and Clete stopped in. Davey and Clete Sutar were twins, both Ohio State Troopers, both standing around six two, both weighing in around two ten of muscle, gristle, and attitude. They were Eddie's first cousins and Eddie loved it when they stopped by. It always gave the place an air of security.

After the usual family small talk, Clete said they needed a couple of patch cords for the computer in their cruiser. Luckily, the X-650s were in stock. "You want the gold ends?" Eddie asked, rhetorically.

Clete gave him his patented *Waddayathink?* look. Eddie smiled, stepped into the back to get their order. When he returned to the front of the store he was greeted with a flash of sunlight, sunlight thrown through the front window, the *unobstructed* front window, which would mean—

Eddie looked.

The man in the overcoat was gone. So was the van.

Shit, Eddie thought. Another potential love chariot gone down the road. He bagged the patch cords and tossed the bag to Davey, the slightly bigger of the two huge police officers.

"On the house, gents," Eddie said. "Stop by anytime."

Amelia sat at her kitchen table and scanned the decoded printouts. They'd saved them on disk for her, but she'd forgotten to take it with her. That was okay. The list was plenty to spark her curiosity. Five names and e-mail addresses. Four of them were complete strangers.

Bennett Marc Crane	bcranemd@wol.com
John Angelino	praise@wol.com
Geoffrey Coldicott	hardman@ttk.net
Jennifer Schumann	jenny5@wol.com
Roger Saintsbury	ras@wol.com

What did Roger have to do with these people? she wondered.

Was this some kind of computer mailing list he was on?

Why was it all so hush-hush secretive?

And who the *hell* was Jennifer Schumann?

22. Bennett Crane's widow was a classic beauty: long-limbed and graceful, a former dancer with the Cleveland Ballet. She wore the standard uniform of the young, grieving rich. A Versace black dress, no jewelry.

The house, an imposing colonial in Wolf Run, near Erie, Pennsylvania, told more of the tale. Dr. Bennett Marc Crane had had a very lucrative career as a plastic surgeon, reconstituting a fair number of the sagging rich and near rich between Cleveland and Buffalo, right up until his untimely death and subsequent mutilation at the age of forty-three.

Nicky knew that he couldn't talk to the reporter who had written the original piece in the *Erie Times News*—a staff reporter named Timothy C. Galvin—without arousing suspicion. A city desk reporter at a fairly large daily newspaper was the kind of person who thought that the gas pump had a hidden agenda when it flashed *Have a Nice Day!* at the end of the transaction. For some reason, Galvin referred to the tigerlike stamp as a jaguar in his article, having gotten, Nicky figured, a look at the actual GemPac. But Galvin, too, referred to the animal on the other side as a plain old monkey. It seemed his zoological expertise ended with the big cats.

Nicky thought about calling the media relations officer at the Erie Police Department but ruled that out too. They didn't know him, he wasn't a local, so any inquiries from Cleveland would tip a hand somewhere, Nicky was sure of it. And he didn't want any other writer anywhere to get even the faintest whiff of this story. So he decided to try to contact the deceased's widow on his own. Surprisingly, she had agreed almost immediately to an interview.

He had only been able to con Erique Mars out of a three-hundred-dollar advance, and that, combined with the fact that his checking account balance was balanced precariously around the one-hundred-dollar mark, led Nicky to decide that breakfast would consist of a pair of yesterday's crullers he'd picked up at Unger's on Taylor before the trip, and a thermos full of homemade coffee, brewed with a double pass of yesterday's grounds.

Elizabeth Crane seemed surprisingly calm for a woman who had lost her husband within the past few days, but Nicky figured that people grieve differently. Italians and blacks went nuts, lots of flailing and wailing, lots of swan-diving onto caskets. Irish got plastered. Jews turned their mirrors to the walls, sat shiva. Protestants, it seemed, got quiet.

She met him at the door, shook hands with her icy bone-china fingers, led him to the living room, poured coffee. White piano, white carpeting, white walls, white cups, saucers. Thank God the coffee was brown, Nicky thought. And dark brown at that. Certainly better than the hobo shit *he* had brewed that morning. The coffee warmed him, but he still got the feeling he had been sent to the waiting room outside George Orwell's Room 101.

They sat on opposing white love seats, Nicky on the edge of his, separated by a white marble coffee table, a table bearing a fan of oversized European magazines and a vase full of huge red gladiolas, the only real color in the room. As Elizabeth Crane talked about her husband, and the brutal way he met his death, Nicky found his eyes returning to the bloodred flowers.

She gave him a brief history of her husband's life, through his undergraduate work at Case Western Reserve University in Cleveland, his graduation from Harvard Medical School, fifth in his class, his residency at the University Hospitals in Cleveland. At thirty-five, Bennett Crane moved back to his hometown of Erie and opened a private practice.

They had no children, she said, by choice. She said his only real diversions were golf, gourmet cooking, and his computer.

But for some reason, she said, he had erased his hard drive the day of his death. She noticed it when she turned on the computer to retrieve some financial information for their probate lawyer and found the hard drive empty. No programs, no directories, no files.

She refilled their coffee cups, pensively, obviously distracted. Nicky remained very still; the white room, for a few moments, stealing all sound, all thought. Eventually she spoke.

She said that she found her husband on the back patio, a packet of heroin and a disposable hypodermic needle at his side. And although it took her a while to get it out, she managed to tell Nicky what the papers meant by "stabbed."

The Erie County coroner said that, although the official cause of death was heroin poisoning, the large amount of blood that was found was due to the fact that Bennett Marc Crane's lips, upper and lower, were removed with a scalpel.

Neither were found at the scene.

23. The poetry section at Paige Turner Books was fairly extensive, at least by comparison to the Science Fiction and How-To sections of the store, each of those covering no more than three shelves.

As Amelia sat behind the counter, minding the store, she skimmed a dozen anthologies, read a score of indices to first lines, taking time out to ring up a few sales while Paige ran some errands. Nothing. No poem that started with "I am moved by fancies . . ."

Along the way she read a poem that made her cry—something called "Love Song: I and Thou," by Alan Dugan—and a few that made her laugh; more than a few that made her think, kindling an adult interest in a subject she had so violently resisted as a schoolgirl.

By noon, Amelia had skimmed her way through all the poetry books, including the Pelican Series Shakespeare. Paige returned at one o'clock, a half dozen huge boxes of used books in tow, none of it poetry.

On to the library.

The Collier Falls Neighborhood library was a three-room, ivy-laced brick building on Ludlow Circle, and it was known, locally, to have a fairly extensive audio book collection and a rather fancy schedule of hours. Amelia found the library open and all but deserted when she walked in at a few minutes after one.

She walked the length of the building, toward the darker end of the large main room, away from the windows, looking for the eight hundred section. She found it, stepped down the row, ran her eyes over the hundreds of titles. It was at moments like these that she realized, with equal amounts of joy and sadness, that it was her limited education, and her almost slavish envy of those more schooled than she, that had driven her to Roger Saintsbury's arms in the first place.

She had been twenty-three when they'd met, her love life consisting of a Saturday night dinner-and-a-movie relationship with Jimmy Barone, Jr., then twenty-six, he of the endless pyramid schemes, he of the spotless 1981 Ford Thunderbird and shag haircut. Life, at that time, was living at home, working downtown, and panting her way through a weekly, passionless hump at Jimmy Barone, Jr.'s, tiny apartment at Marsol Towers.

Then her brother Garth invited her to a party at University Circle and introduced her to an old CWRU classmate named Roger Saintsbury.

The first time she saw Roger he was leaning against a wall, a Rob Roy in hand, talking to a young woman who looked like a cross between Bizet's Carmen and a South Dakota truck-stop hooker. Amelia immediately categorized this handsome stranger with the wavy hair, winning smile, and great shoulders. Here was a thirtyish man hitting on a child. Of course, the child was only a few years younger than Amelia, but Amelia felt so much more dignified and ladylike in her tartan-plaid wraparound skirt and turtleneck sweater. And so much more, well . . . un*scrutinized* was probably the proper, unfortunate word, considering the attention that Miss Way to Go was generating by comparison.

Or perhaps it was because she was so instantly attracted to Roger that she felt that way.

Twenty minutes later, when she accidentally spilled a glass of cabernet sauvignon on his lap, she got the opportunity to find out. Amelia's second image of Roger Saintsbury was of him standing in a roomful of people, a roomful of *women*, with a large round target that had, as its bull's-eye, his crotch.

Maybe that should have told me something, Amelia thought.

Maybe that first night should have been an indication of what was to come. Maybe it—

She sensed someone nearby. A flash of color in between the stacks of books.

Amelia drew a breath, bent her knees, looked over the jagged tops of the books, cocked her head, *there*—the sound of cotton on cotton. Someone kneeling down to peruse the bottom shelves. She looked through the openings again, didn't see anyone, listened some more. Nothing.

But someone *was* near.

She could hear breathing. . . .

She looked out into the aisle, around the main room, but the only other person she saw was Mary Ellen at the front desk, nibbling a brownie, reading a LaVyrle Spencer novel.

Oh well, Amelia thought. Must have been my imagination.

Then the man in the dark coat grabbed her around the waist and pulled her into the shadows.

24. The interview with Elizabeth Crane had been a lot more draining than Nicky had realized. Talking to people who have just lost a loved one was hard work. Especially a loved one who got hacked up in such a horrible fashion. How the hell did cops do it?

Nicky remembered his father coming home many nights, pouring an inch of bourbon into a jelly glass and sitting in front of the television, still in uniform, his thousand-yard stare in place. His dinner would sit on a TV tray most nights as the inch turned into inches and the five-year-old Nicky would cry as his mother would have to help Officer Vincent Stella to bed. Big, tough guinea cop being helped up the stairs by the five-two Nicolette Stella, the frail, iron-willed woman he had married after two dates, the woman he would lose to breast cancer before her fiftieth birthday. His father was not a drinker, far from it, but sometimes the craziness got to him, sometimes he had to numb himself to the madness. Now that his father had retired, though, the stories were coming more frequently, with greater ease. And with far less booze.

But what would Vincent Stella do now? Nicky wondered. Call the police? Did he really want to get involved to that extent? Was this some kind of conspiracy? Did he have some sort of moral obligation here?

He realized that he was not prepared to answer a single one of those questions as he turned off Lee Road onto Chagrin Boulevard, and headed for Normandy. He could barely keep his eyes open.

But as soon as he saw his house, he knew something was

wrong. For some reason, his landlord had installed a giant lawn jockey on the front walk. Then he realized it wasn't a mammoth landscape ornament at all.

It was Frank Corso, sitting on his front steps.

Fuck.

Frank looked even bigger than Nicky remembered. He had cut his hair into a spiky crew, and in the afternoon light, even from a block away, Nicky could see the ridges and valleys of a half dozen scars on his face. He also could see that Frank Corso now had a gym bag with him, sitting at his feet like a small, napping rottweiler. What the hell was in there? Nicky wondered. Did he bring instruments of torture?

Nicky slowed down, looked up the street. There was a black Firebird parked across from his driveway. Nicky suspected that it was Frank Corso's ride. Typical. Penis car.

Four grand, Nicky thought. Four grand or my testicles.

He pulled into a driveway about a half dozen or so houses north of his own, backed out, and headed back toward Chagrin Boulevard, checking his rearview mirror, suddenly wide-awake. He saw Frank lighting a cigarette, oblivious. He hadn't been spotted.

Nicky drove to Avalon Road, turned left. He parked, got out, locked the car, and made his way through the backyards. He stopped when he reached his yard. Frank Corso's Pontiac was still parked on the street.

He selected the right key and dashed across his backyard in a dozen silent steps, leapfrogging a Big Wheel bicycle belonging to his downstairs neighbor's son Aaron in the process. His leather soles on the wet grass left a lot to be desired as prime track and field equipment, but he managed to hold his balance and slip-slide to the door.

He quietly turned the key in the lock, stepped inside, and closed the door behind him in one liquid move. He removed his shoes and padded up the steps, put his ear to the door of his apartment, heard nothing, let himself in, did a quick perusal of his two rooms. Intact. He took one of his folding chairs and tiptoed back to his door. He checked the lock, the dead bolt, then wedged the chair under the knob.

That's it, he thought. That's the best I can do. Fort Knox is sealed. If you want me that bad, you fat fuck, come and get me. Give it your best shot.

Bed.

He removed his socks and crashed on the mattress, just asking for bad dreams. He was asleep within minutes.

And the bad dreams obliged.

When the phone rang two hours later, a lipless, blood-drenched Bennett Crane was chasing him through an opium den, right into the arms of Frank Corso, who was suddenly naked, Chinese, and holding a pair of sparking cattle prods.

And in the center of the room—while the *Cavalleria Rusticana* played on—lay a cold Louie Stella, bright yellow daffodils growing from his eyes.

25 "I should kick your ass," Amelia said.

They were sitting in the Bagel Shoppe across the street from the library. She had yelled at her brother for scaring the shit out of her—both the scaring and the subsequent tantrum a Randolph family tradition. But it had started to rain heavily, so the dressing down of Garth Randolph was relatively brief.

When Amelia was done with her harangue, she hugged her brother, then they slid into a booth, dried themselves with napkins, ordered coffee. She sat and stared at him as he looked at the menu, cataloging her brother's features, marveling once more at how everyone she knew seemed to get older except Garth. It had been almost two years, and he had picked up a few lines near his eyes, but he looked to be in very good physical shape. Garth had been a wrestler in junior high and high school, an all-around athlete until the car accident after college that injured his back, and sent him to the hospital in Pennsylvania to have part of his face rebuilt. Incredibly, Garth had come out better-looking than when he went in.

The last time she had seen him he had a long beard and was living on a dairy farm in Orwell, recovering from nervous exhaustion and the collapse of the advertising agency that had once made him rich. He had called her once or twice during that Return to the Earth phase, swearing he was okay and would reenter the world of cigarettes, newspapers, booze, exhaust fumes, and dental hygiene soon. That was two years ago. Now he was clean-shaven. And wearing a very nice suit.

"So . . ." Garth began, "how's your sexy friend Paige?"

"She's fine," Amelia answered. "She's not seeing anyone, you know."

"Still the yenta, huh?"

Amelia laughed. "She has her own business now. She opened a bookstore on Marble Lane. You should stop in and see her."

"A bookstore?"

"Yep. Nice little place, too."

"Cappuccino and latte alongside the John Grisham and T.S. Eliot?"

"Not yet," Amelia replied, the name jumping out at her. Had she looked up her mystery poem under T.S. Eliot? She didn't think she had. She made a mental note to do so. "But one of these days she wants to do the espresso-and-biscotti thing. On the other hand, Paige would have to hire someone to handle the culinary end. I've seen her in the kitchen. I know whereof I speak."

"And how's my *little* redhead?"

"Maddie's good. She misses you." She retrieved a Polaroid that Paige had taken of Maddie at the *Annie* auditions and handed it to her brother. "But I'll be honest, she brings your name up less and less. I'm afraid that she's going to forget you."

Garth handed the photo back. "Did she get the part?"

Amelia laughed, then felt a little guilty. "Let me put it this way. She gets her singing talents from me."

Her brother made a face, obviously recalling the years of Martha Reeves and Joni Mitchell deconstruction that had taken place at the Randolph home on Edgefield Road. "That bad, huh?"

"Yep," Amelia said.

Garth smiled, finished his coffee. "And how are you and Roger getting along?"

Amelia hesitated for a split second, but that was plenty for Garth. Her brother could read volumes about her in that amount of time. "Great," she said. "You know. Good."

"What's wrong?"

"Nothing." *God* she hated it when he did this.

"Meelie."

She hated that nickname even more. "We're fine, okay? Just marriage shit. That's all. Just the soot that settles every day from people rumbling around the same space. If you'd ever get off your high fucking horse and fall in love again, you might get to experience these profound and wonderful joys." Garth, who had never married, was famous for the one-year relationship. She hadn't seen him in love since his college days.

"You only swear when you're hiding something," Garth said. "You gonna tell me?"

"Roger had an affair." Somehow it just tumbled out.

"I see. . . ." Garth said. "Anyone you, uh, *know*?"

"Unfortunately, yes," Amelia replied. "Unfortunately, I *am* cursed with a highly detailed image of the two of them rutting in the slop like barnyard animals."

Garth tapped the back of his sister's hand. "I told you not to marry him."

This was said in jest, Amelia knew, but it still rang true. Garth had not seemed thrilled when Amelia said she was going to marry Roger Saintsbury. "It's a very strange feeling, brother o' mine," Amelia said, calming herself. "I love him, and I want to push him out a fucking window. Does that make sense to you?"

"Yes, Meelie. It does." They fell silent for a few moments. Then Garth asked, "Do you want me to talk to him?"

Amelia smiled. "Gonna slap him around for me, big brother?"

"I'll t'row him a few if I have ta," Garth replied, doing his pug thing.

"He's out of town, Garth. He'll be back in the next few days. You can punch him then."

"Oh well." He grabbed the check. "I'll try and call you later anyway," he added, although Amelia knew it was just Garth-talk. Yet he did appear to be on the fast track again. Maybe he would stay in touch. He kissed her on the top of the head, started toward the door.

Amelia called after him. "I have my writer's class tonight, but I should be home by nine-thirty."

Garth waved acknowledgment, paid the bill, said something to the counter girl that made her laugh. Amelia watched the young woman and realized how much she missed her brother. He could be charming as hell.

She caught him halfway through the door.

"Hey," Amelia said, kissing him on the cheek. "Welcome back, big brother."

Garth smiled, turned up his collar, and stepped into the rain.

She had taken a half dozen weighty poetry anthologies out of the library and stacked the books on the dining room table. She checked the messages. Nothing. Not even a "miss you" call from her husband.

Ten minutes later, while Maddie played a CD-ROM game, Amelia found herself staring at her closet, wondering what she was going to wear to her writer's class. And she knew why. She hadn't exactly fantasized about the man with the dark curls—she'd insist on learning his name tonight—but she *had* thought about him since her last class, thought about the way he had come to her aid, thought about the cut of his jeans. Yet if it was just harmless flirtation on her mind, why did she feel so guilty?

She decided she was being childish. She selected a denim skirt (knowing full well it climbed halfway up her thigh when she sat down) and a black pullover. She laid them out on the bed and went downstairs, poked her head into the computer room. "Pizza okay?"

"Yep," Maddie said as she changed the color of the curtains in Dolly's Dream Chalet computer bedroom.

Amelia called Domino's, found her purse, put the money and a two-dollar tip next to the front door, and checked her watch. What the hell, she thought. She'd do it. There was enough time. She walked over to the linen closet and took down the two boxes of rinses, and found the jar of facial mask. She put them on the counter in the bathroom and changed into her combat sweats, the ripped and stained fleece she wore for heavy cleaning, the clothes she wouldn't wear into the backyard even under the cover of darkness.

A rinse and a facial.

Right, Meelie.

Just what a gal who had no intention of flirting would do.

Twenty minutes later she looked into the bathroom mirror. It was official. With the light green cast of her facial mask and the shocking hot orange of the combination Golden Sienna and Red Copper hair rinses, she looked like a Kabuki zombie mutant from the planet Vanity.

Then, of course, the doorbell rang.

Domino's.

Amelia turned off the ceiling fan and the faucet. "Sweetie?" she called out.

"What?" Maddie answered.

"Would you get the pizza? The money's by the front door. On the table."

" 'Kay . . ."

Amelia heard her daughter's chair roll back on the hardwood floor, heard her cross the foyer, heard the front door open. She turned the ceiling fan back on, ran the water. Then . . . heard something else. A voice? Was it Maddie? Was Maddie calling her? She shut off the fan, stepped back into the hallway, listened.

Silence.

"Maddie? Did you call me?"

"Mom?" Maddie said, soberly, from the foot of the steps. Her voice sounded tiny, uncertain. It was the voice she used when she was suddenly asked to conduct adult business.

"Yes, honey . . . what is it?"

"Um . . . somebody's here to see you."

Amelia stole a glance in the mirror. One of the extras in *Dawn of the Dead* stared back. Jesus *Christ*. Company. "Who is it, Maddie?" she asked, barely managing to move her lips, now that the mask had hardened fully.

Maddie paused. "It's Shelley Roth."

26• Father John Angelino's sister, Carmen Ricci, was a widow with five children, and Father John, it appeared, had been devoted to her, spending two or three days a month at her house on Tillman Avenue, tending to its constant need for repairs. When Carmen had heard of her brother's death she had fainted dead away. She was still in Mt. Sinai, under heavy sedation.

The phone call that had awakened Nicky from his nightmare was from his cousin Joseph, who said that as long as he didn't take anything, he could look through the two boxes of goods shipped to the Ricci house.

As Nicky approached the house, he had a feeling that the inside was not going to be as surgically clean as the house in Erie. A half dozen riding toys littered the front yard, along with a full orchestra of plastic buckets, shovels, rakes, bats, balls, and trucks.

"More coffee?" the woman asked. Her name was Beth Something Polish and she worked for Catholic Family Services. She was thirty-five, plain and scrubbed, sandy-haired, there to take care of the Ricci brood until Carmen was well enough to return home. There were *Good Housekeeping* and *Christian Family* magazines on *this* coffee table, Nicky noticed. A huge contrast to Elizabeth Crane and her *Mirabella* motif. The furniture was all old, not quite antique. Everywhere he looked was a crystal candy dish of some sort, brimming with Brach's pinwheels.

"No, thanks," Nicky said, rising to his feet.

"The boxes are right through here," Beth said, leading him

down a hallway to a small office, a converted first-floor bedroom cluttered with papers, Christian-product catalogs, dogeared hymnals, boxes of church artifacts. In one corner was an oak laminated computer desk, one of those assemble-it-yourself cheapies that you can get for forty or fifty dollars on sale.

Nicky looked under the table and saw a large cardboard box filled with books and pamphlets. He began to remove items from the box.

At the bottom he found an old Toshiba laptop computer, cleverly disguised as a beat-up world atlas. Nicky figured that Father John had glued an old book cover to the outside to make it less of a target for theft when he rode the RTA. Very clever. Except, the computer probably was a dozen years old and probably not worth much anymore.

Nicky booted it up, checked the root directory. Three programs. A word-processing program, a spreadsheet program, and World Online. He found a diskette in the drawer, popped it into the floppy disk drive, then moved to the word-processing files. There were two files from the day before John Angelino's murder, but nothing for three weeks prior. Nicky copied the files onto the floppy. He knew he couldn't read the spreadsheet stuff, wouldn't know what he had if he could, so he didn't even bother with that. He moved to the World Online directory and saw that there had been three pieces of e-mail and one attached file from the week prior to the murder. He downloaded those, then shut off the laptop.

The letters turned out to be parish business. One was to a cement contractor, requesting estimates to repave the church's parking lot. The other letter was to the Ecumenical Council, requesting funding guidelines for the same project.

Nicky had circled his block three times before parking behind Sol's Delicatessen near the corner of Avalon and Chagrin, then scooted once again through the backyards and up the back steps. There had been no sign of Frank Corso.

He sat at his computer, a Giant Lean Corned Beef with extra pickle spread out before him, and moved on to the e-mail files.

Of the handful of e-mail messages, the first two being correspondence that John Angelino had been carrying on with a Reverend Edmund Phillips of Tacoma, Washington, a spirited debate on the concept of immortality, only the last message held any intrigue. It was a message received two days before John Angelino was murdered.

Nicky clicked on the file, which automatically opened his graphics program. After a few moments he saw that the attached file was a graphic file, a replica of a single stanza of a poem, written on lined paper. Instinctively his eye went first to the sender's address. He recognized the **tse@com.hk** as a bullshit address, a forwarding service, a remailer. There were no clues there. Then his eyes moved to the ''cc'' column of the screen. He saw:

Bennett Marc Crane	bcranemd@wol.com
John Angelino	praise@wol.com
Geoffrey Coldicott	hardman@ttk.net
Jennifer Schumann	jenny5@wol.com
Roger Saintsbury	ras@wol.com

His first reaction reminded him of the time his sister had thrown a surprise party for him to celebrate his first piece in a national magazine. He walked into her apartment and saw all these people from his various walks of life, people he *knew* did not know each other, yet there they were, talking and laughing and drinking and discussing the Nick Stella *they* knew. Considering the voluminous closet space he had already dedicated to the skeletons in his life, the notion of all those worlds colliding filled him with an overwhelming sense of dread.

It was that sense of panic that washed over him when the two names appeared on the screen, just a few pixels apart.

No, leapt *off* the screen.

Bennett Marc Crane. John Angelino.

Two men, in two different cities, ninety miles apart, mutilated and poisoned with pure heroin. One man had his eyes gouged out with a scalpel, the other had his lips removed. Not to mention a working girl named Kathleen Holt, who picked the wrong guy on the wrong night, it seemed. Two men on the same e-mail list, both the recipient of an enigmatic verse of poetry about suffering.

Yet it wasn't the fact that two homicide victims just showed up on the same roster that frightened him the most. What frightened him the most was the devil in that other mathematical detail.

There were three names to go.

27●The first time Amelia ever saw Shelley Roth was at a TRW Christmas party. It was out in the parking lot of the Richmond Road offices, and Shelley Roth was standing there, Madonna in the snow, with half of TRW's male middle management falling drunkenly over themselves trying to be the one to successfully give Ms. Roth's car a jump. Although everyone involved knew that it was a jump in the *sack* that was being vied for here, it didn't stop this Grecian Formula horde of suited, middle-aged men from getting their hands greasy or falling knees-down into freezing slush puddles; nor did it stop Shelley Roth from cooing about it, her platinum hair in shrill chorus with the overhead streetlamps.

"Who's the tart?" Amelia had asked, only to be rewarded with one of Roger's *let's be kind* looks. Amelia read it for what it was, and that was a look that said *there but for the spousal proximity of my wife go I.*

Little did she know.

But now, somehow, Shelley Roth was sitting on her couch, sipping tea that Amelia could not remember making. The only things that Amelia could think about, the only things that swirled behind her eyes in a dark tornado of broken logic, were those four words. Four English words that filled Amelia with a bright red rage and a pale blue calm that, in and of itself, was not all that unpleasant a feeling.

What the four words did to her heart was another matter.

"*What?*" Amelia asked, knowing that Shelley would say those words again, starting the cycle of pain a second time.

Shelley Roth crossed her long, shapely legs, sipped her tea, and said: "I think I'm pregnant."

It wasn't until eight forty-five that Dark Curls wandered into the classroom. He wore the same leather jacket, but this time his jeans were black, pegged. His entrance was so unexpected that when he walked in he caught Amelia in the middle of a huge Cowardly Lion–sized yawn.

Like an idiot, she had downed three huge shots of schnapps after Shelley Roth left, trying to calm herself down, trying to talk herself out of driving to Elkhart and beating the living, screaming shit out of her husband with a nine iron. She had a brief, delicious fantasy of chasing him down the hallways of the Sheraton Elkhart, slamming his prized Greg Norman signature clubs into his head, his ass, his back.

But on the other hand, Shelley Roth had not made a very convincing case about being pregnant. Other than confirming what Amelia already knew to be true—that Roger and Shelley Roth had shacked up a grand total of three times—she hadn't taken a pregnancy test, she was only nine days late, and she said she had the father narrowed down to Roger or a guy named Milton Pettigrew in Accounting. She said she just wanted to make sure that everyone lived up to their responsibility.

After Amelia had gone through the roof about the notion of Roger having unprotected sex with her, Shelley Roth had said, yes, Roger had worn a condom. But, she added, condoms had been shown to not be a hundred percent reliable. That was why she wanted to have this talk, she'd said.

Thank you, Dr. Westheimer, Amelia had replied as she escorted Shelley to the door with the instructions to call her the moment she could verify that she was bona fide, puke-in-the-Cheerios preggers.

Until then, Shelley baby, the operative words were *fuck* and *off*.

Amelia estimated that the damage in dinnerware alone, scattered about the kitchen, was in the three-hundred-dollar range. She had sent Maddie over to the MacGregors before her tantrum, and Caitlin's mother, Karen, had said it would be no problem to watch Maddie for the whole evening, clearly sensing the domestic strife in Amelia's voice. Amelia made a mental note that she owed Karen MacGregor a big one for this. Baby-sitting on New Year's Eve or something.

After the ceramic carnage, she had decided to calm down, do a couple shots of peppermint schnapps, and plot this thing out like the woman God created.

By the time she reached her writer's class, she discovered she had decided a number of things.

"May I say how nice you look this evening?"

"You may," Amelia replied, blushing a bit at the compliment, leaning against the brick wall behind the school. "And you may say it as often as you like. You don't even have to raise your hand."

Dark Curls smiled. "Well, we don't want to give you a swelled head now, do we?"

Amelia, with a little help from the schnapps, thought of something *extremely* naughty and crude to say at that moment. She kept it to herself.

Like a gentleman, he had walked up to her after class and asked if he might escort her to her car. He had made a joke about bringing his own coat hanger this time so he would be prepared. They laughed. He had helped her with her coat.

They stood in the lot for a while, talking, watching as the handful of other students waved good-bye to them, started their cars, and pulled off into the clear, starry evening; heading, Amelia was certain, to their perfectly happy, perfectly nuclear families. After ten minutes or so, the lot was empty, save for their two cars.

"So," Amelia said.

"So," he replied.

After a few seconds, their eyes met and they both burst out laughing, both recognizing the sexual tension in the air. Emboldened by the liquor, Amelia decided to break it. She reached into her purse and retrieved the bottle of schnapps. "Buy you a drink?"

He looked around the parking lot. "Sure. Why not?"

Amelia tipped the bottle back, slightly, took a half sip. She may have been acting wild, she may have been the seductive Jezebel enchantress of the Adult Learning campus, but she had a daughter and a house and a car and a dog and a life to think about too. Even this slight amount of schnapps nearly made her gag. She passed the bottle over. He took it, sipped, looking into her eyes the whole time. Sipped again. *Very* practiced at this. And for some reason, that made him even more attractive.

"By the way, my name—" he began.

Amelia placed a finger to his lips. "Don't care. . . ." She kissed him, softly, gently, only the slightest parting of lips, then pulled back and looked into his eyes. She was a little bit drunk, it was a brisk, exhilarating fall evening, and this wasn't her husband.

Wow.

She let him take the lead then as he opened her coat, ran his hands over her hips, around her waist. Amelia closed her eyes for a moment, felt the strength in his arms, his wrists, his fingers. She kissed him again, this time more aggressively, the tips of their tongues touching now, exploring. Amelia let the moment take over and ran her hand down his leg, then slowly back up, the edge of her thumbnail barely grazing the ridge of material over his zipper.

He spun her around, her back against the school building, and stepped between her legs. He put some of his weight on her, pinning her gently to the bricks.

"You know . . ." he said, "you're my kind of writer."

"Is that so," Amelia said, her breath coming in shorter waves, wondering if this was progressing too fast, too far. The hell with it, she thought. It felt good. She looked at his eyes, then at his lips. He was *so* cute. "And what kind of writer . . . *am* I?"

"Sexy," he said, running a finger along the front of her dress.

After the visit from Shelley Roth, Amelia had decided against the denim-skirt look. She had instead put on a sexy little black dress, cut just above the knee, spiky black heels, no bra. She figured that if anyone asked, she would say she was heading to some sort of reception after the class. The dress was cut rather low in the front, so she had pinned it.

But now she reached up and unpinned what she had so painstakingly pinned and repinned a dozen times before leaving the house. The stranger slid his hand inside, fondling her breasts as she leaned up against the rough bricks. He opened the front of her dress and leaned forward, running his tongue over her breasts, her nipples.

She kissed him again and ran her right leg up and down his, and was just about to drag him inside her car when she realized what she was doing.

She stopped. "Oh my God," she said.

"What?" he asked, but it sounded to Amelia as if he knew. He looked experienced enough to know when a housewife was on the prowl just because her husband had cheated on her or had called her fat or had blown the mortgage payment at the racetrack. In that one word Amelia could tell that he knew, in the end, he was going to be teased.

And he was right. Amelia opened her car door, dove behind the wheel.

"Are you okay to drive?" he asked.

"Absolutely," Amelia said. And she meant it. It was only ten blocks to her house, and the realization that she was just now leaning up against a junior high school building, slightly looped, with her breasts exposed to the world, had sobered her up immensely.

"Okay, then," he said. "Rain check?"

Amelia started her car, put it in reverse, backed out of the space. "Rain check," she said, not knowing if it meant a rain check for another drink sometime or a rain check to finish what they started one October night.

She hit the button marked Play Messages.

"Hi, honey . . . how's my girls? . . . Missing you and Mad-die much. . . . Um . . . not a lot going on here. . . . Just finished some road food . . . deep-fried something with a side of deep-fried something else . . . thimbleful of wilted coleslaw . . . a

warm Dr. Pepper, I think. . . . Yuck . . . not sure why I bought it. . . . I don't like Dr. Pepper, do I? . . . Maddie-bear? . . . Do I? . . ."

Amelia was standing in the kitchen, the only light the twenty-five-watter in the range hood, a glass of 2 percent milk in her hand, the highest-percent anything she would drink for the rest of the evening. She leaned against the refrigerator, listened, thinking, once again, how close Roger sounded.

"And I just wanted to say that when I get home I want to do something . . . you know . . . the three of us . . . maybe go get a couple of pumpkins or something . . . maybe go to a movie . . . okay? . . . Or maybe we could even go down to Tower City, do a little early Christmas shopping . . . what do you think? . . . So, uh, I guess I'll try and call tomorrow sometime . . . let you know exactly when old Roger will be pullin' into Dodge . . . and, uh . . . okay . . . I guess I've babbled enough. . . . Sorry, I missed you. . . . Night, you two . . . love you and see you soon. . . ."

There were a few seconds before the click, a few seconds during which Amelia held her breath for some reason, waiting for Roger to say one more thing before putting the phone down, a few seconds when all the sights and sounds and smells of their kitchen, their life together, invaded her senses, especially the autumnal drawings of Maddie's that were deployed on the fridge (the Kelvinator Gallery of Fine Art, Roger would call it). The best of the one-girl showing was the traditional turkey made from an outline of Maddie's tiny hand, and it was a solitary tear that struck the floor the moment Roger hung up without saying another word, a single glistening drop of salt water that would surely dry by morning.

28• Coldicott and Crowe, Inc., was an antique jewelry emporium in the Old Arcade—the highly ornate, multistory arcade that spanned from Euclid Avenue to Superior Avenue, right around Fourth Street. The store was located on the first level, near the food court.

Nicky sat at one of the miniature tables they put out into the arcade, the Barbie and Ken furniture that had chairs big enough for two thirds of the average ass. From his vantage he could see the entire showroom of Coldicott and Crowe—three women, one man. It was clear just who Geoffrey Coldicott was in that group, Nicky thought. Geoffrey was tall and spidery, about forty, gravedigger-pale, a perfect archetype of gothic jeweler. He had a long, soft-looking body and wore a dark suit that hung upon his shoulders like a prayer shawl. At the moment, Geoffrey was bent over the counter, poring over something with his jeweler's loupe.

Fortunately, Nicky had found two listings for Coldicott. One was Coldicott and Crowe at the Arcade. The other was listed as Coldicott, Geoffrey D., estate appraiser, same address in the Old Arcade.

All things considered, even if he did write the story, Nicky knew he would have to go to the cops. People on a list seemed to be dying one by one, and the police had to be made aware of that fact, if they weren't on it already. But before he made that move, he simply had to know what the hell was going on here. He had to know if any of these people knew any of the others. If they had all received this poem in the mail, if this poem meant anything to them. It was simply too good to give up.

He downed his coffee, grabbed a quarter, and headed to the pay phones.

"Mr. Coldicott?" Nicky said. He was standing at the pay phones next to the food court at the Superior side of the Arcade. He could see Geoffrey Coldicott through a thin panel of glass in the store next to Coldicott and Crowe, some kind of herb boutique.

"Yes, this is Geoffrey Coldicott. How may I help you?"

"Mr. Coldicott, my name is Nicholas Stella, and I'm a writer here in Cleveland, working on a story for *Esquire* magazine." A tiny lie, and no one had checked yet. Not once. "Are you familiar with that publication, Mr. Coldicott?"

"Certainly."

"I was wondering if you might have a few minutes to talk to me today."

"Can I ask what this is about first?"

"Well, it's a matter of some importance, so I'd rather we did it face-to-face. When would be convenient for you? I'm right downtown now, so anytime would be good for me."

Nicky knew he was pushing. Geoffrey Coldicott pushed back. Nicky saw him straighten up through the windows, his praying-mantis body taking on a defensive posture.

"I'll have to know what this is about, Mr. Stella. I'm a very busy man."

"It involves an e-mail message you may have received, Mr. Coldicott," Nicky said, wondering just how you were supposed to tell a total stranger that he might be in danger. "A graphic file that, I'm afraid, might be important."

Geoffrey Coldicott was silent for a few moments. "I don't know what you're talking about."

"Would it be okay if I stopped by your house later and we talked?" Nicky asked, reading a little anxiety in Coldicott's voice. "Maybe this is nothing at all."

At that moment, Nicky saw four or five people walk into Coldicott and Crowe. Perfect timing.

"Yes, yes, I don't care," Coldicott said. "I have to go now."

"What's your address, Mr. Coldicott?"

"I'm in the Golden Gate Villas," he said. "They're at—"

"I know where they are," Nicky said. "What time?"

"Six o'clock," Geoffrey Coldicott said. "Now, good-*bye*, Mr. Stella."

"Okay," Nicky said. "And I really do appreciate your—"

But Geoffrey Coldicott had already hung up, which surprised Nicky. Businessmen, especially retail businessmen, didn't usually hang up on people. Unless, of course, they had something to hide.

Which opened up a whole new box of animal crackers, Nicky thought. Maybe the wacko here is one of the names on the list. Maybe Geoffrey Coldicott was the Norman Fucking Bates in this equation and he had just made an appointment to meet him at the motel.

29•It was the end. Truly the end of it all.

He caught his reflection in the cab window and shook a dangerous fist at the translucent half image he found there. Since childhood, it had always been his way of threatening himself with violent abuse if he didn't carry out his own orders, saving the actual pain of self-flagellation for later, relegating the deep degradations to the wee hours of the morning.

And Geoffrey Coldicott knew something about pain.

He had told the reporter, or whatever he was, that he would be home by six. He looked at his watch. Five-ten. At least time was on his side.

Because he had always wondered two things more than any other in his life, or that part which began when, as a small child, after his father's suicide, his mother moved him from Bristol, England, to Painseville, Ohio. Two questions he was certain he was going to live his entire adult life—the part that began five years ago when he had the nerve to move out of the house and into the big city—without ever having answered.

One: What would he do if his little collection was threatened?

Two: What would he do if he found himself alone with a man who wanted to have sex with him?

Somehow, through some strange jog of serendipity, through some violent rip in the fabric of his rather imaginative fantasy life, he had managed to answer both questions within the past twenty-four hours.

When he had sat down at the bar at the Shenanigans night-

147

club on the west side the day before, deliberately far from his neighborhood, purposely out of his work environment, he hadn't any real plan in mind. He'd heard they had recently revamped the club and he really *did* want to see what they'd done with the place, so he had frequented the establishment a few times in the previous weeks. But that, he knew, was only secondary to his underlying purpose. He was there to be someone else. Geoffrey Coldicott the swinger. Geoffrey Coldicott the libertine. Geoffrey Coldicott the brash hedonist.

Just a few moments after he had entered and taken a stool at the far end of the enormous bar, a stranger had entered the nightclub and, it appeared, Geoffrey's life. The man took a stool immediately to his left and ordered a Rob Roy.

Then he turned and smiled at Geoffrey.

The man was handsome and athletic, well dressed in a casual, collegiate way. Witty in a deliciously *sarcastic* way. He said he was in Cleveland on business and was flying out in a few hours. He called himself Tom Macarty. Or McCartney. Or McIlvainey. Or something Irish like that. The music was loud and Geoffrey hadn't heard him well, so he decided to just call him Tom. Tom was fine. He really didn't need to know more.

Yet there was something about Tom that was familiar, as if he had come into the store once, or they had met at a house sale or a liquidation sale or . . . No. It went further back than that, much further. College? Geoffrey was usually good with faces, so the idea that he couldn't place Tom gnawed at him.

"Filthy habit. Going to quit next week," Tom said, offering Geoffrey a cigarette. Geoffrey accepted, Tom lighted it.

Geoffrey kept avoiding the man's eyes as they chatted, eyes that were boyish, the color of milk chocolate, now ringed with the gold of the neon beer signs behind the bar. Geoffrey smoked, sipped his drink, tried to think of something clever and urbane to say. Instead, he offered: "So what brings you to Cleveland, Tom?"

"Business first, I suppose," Tom said, turning to face Geoffrey fully. "But I'm always open to pleasure."

He smiled when he said this, and it both chilled and warmed

Geoffrey, who was already into his third gin and tonic, no longer feeling the barstool beneath him, no longer feeling the inhibitions of an overeducated rural kid gone to the city.

Was Tom trying to pick him up?

After two more cocktails, Tom said that he had to leave. Something about a meeting, a plane, something about returning a rental car. He asked Geoffrey if he might point out the nearest entry to the airport, and Geoffrey said that he would. He paid the check, walked out to the parking lot, then on to the far end of the lot, the dark end. Geoffrey was pleased they had to walk a bit, he felt that it gave them time to . . . what?

Geoffrey was painfully unsure.

But halfway across the deserted, moonlit parking lot, Tom supplied him with his answer. He stopped and placed a hand on Geoffrey's chest, halting him just inches away, staring into his eyes.

And then Tom kissed him on the cheek.

The sensation, at first, repulsed Geoffrey, although he would have been hard-pressed to explain why. Perhaps it was the slight scratch of whisker, or the musk of the unquestionably male cologne. The kiss was brief, gentle, but it ultimately sent shock waves through Geoffrey's mind and body and libido.

Then, just as unexpectedly, Tom withdrew across the parking lot, toward his car, and then on to Hopkins airport and beyond.

Geoffrey Coldicott had not slept since that moment.

And although he had not officially pulled the trigger on a bona fide homosexual encounter, not to his mind anyway, he *had* found out what he needed to know about himself.

He was, indeed, willing.

That was last night. And now, today, some reporter wanted to take a look at his computer!

It was *way* too much.

Because he was pretty sure this guy wasn't a reporter at all. He was a cop of some sort. Definitely. FBI or postal inspector or Internet cop, something like that. Regardless, he didn't buy this business about a mysterious e-mail document. Not for a moment. He had always suspected that somebody, somewhere, knew the sorts of things he was downloading into his computer. The photographs. He knew that one day they would catch him and there would be a half-hour special on CNN during which they would show his high-school photos next to the shot of him being dragged up Mayfield Road. They would display some of his naughtier computer graphics files (certain bits obscured, of course), and then they would—

The cab turned off Mayfield Road onto Golden Gate, then pulled over to the curb.

As Geoffrey scaled the steps, he knew that what he was about to do might be unnecessary—the erasure of his small but very specialized collection of digital porn—but he also knew that he couldn't take the chance. What would it do to his mother? he mused for a moment. It would kill Mina Coldicott, that's what it would do. Mina Coldicott would curl up on her creaky bentwood rocker back there in Painesville. Mina Coldicott would evaporate from shame. All eighty-one years and ninety-nine puritanical pounds of her.

Geoffrey, a bit winded now, reached his door and inserted the key in the lock. But before the first tumbler fell, a shadow darkened the wall beside him.

He spun around, more than a bit startled, and saw that it was Tom.

"H-hi," Geoffrey managed.

"Hello," Tom said softly, taking the key from Geoffrey's now-shaking hand. Tom reinserted the key and opened the door. He gestured to Geoffrey to enter the apartment. Tom wore a black wool turtleneck, tan trousers, camel-hair blazer. Very smart, Geoffrey thought. Very Ralph Lauren. He seemed taller to Geoffrey than he had the day before, broader through the shoulders and chest. But Geoffrey saw that he had not been mistaken about the aristocratic line of the man's jaw, the rueful eyes.

Tom closed the door, turned the dead bolt. "Here," he began, reaching out, "let me help you with your coat."

Geoffrey turned slowly around, unbuttoning his coat, and noticed that his pulse had begun to race, his heart had begun

to thrum a little too loudly in his chest. Geoffrey took a deep
breath and let Tom peel his coat from his shoulders.

"How did you . . . um . . . know where I lived?" Geoffrey
asked, fumbling with his pack of Salems. He was blowing it.
He wanted this man to stay, to leave, to get in and out of his
life as soon as possible.

"You told me last night, Geoffrey."

"I did?"

Tom laughed and it threw a shiver down Geoffrey's spine.
"*Some*body was into the Pimm's before they went to the pub,
eh?" Tom said as he walked over to the hall closet, seeming
to know where that was located, as well. He hung up the
raincoat and returned to the small front room. "You mean you
really don't remember telling me all about yourself last night,
Geoffrey?"

"Well, I—"

"About how you *really* don't read very much anymore and
how you *really* don't like going to the movies as much as you
used to because the films are just *so* silly nowadays," Tom
continued, moving forward, now just a few feet away. "Don't
you remember, Geoffrey?"

Geoffrey tried to strike a calm, affable pose. He failed.

"And how you *really* only care about one thing these days.
Your computer."

Geoffrey glanced at his computer, which sat in an alcove
off his living room. He looked back at Tom and the dominoes
began to tumble. He remembered now. The graphic of the
poem, the T.S. Eliot poem he had received on his e-mail account and had summarily erased as so much cyber junk mail,
now drew itself in his mind, the fluid strokes, the jet black
ink. . . .

T.S. Eliot. Julia Raines.

My God. All . . . these . . . *years*.

Geoffrey touched his cheek, understanding, now, the twisted
perversion of that kiss in the parking lot. How he fucking
knew. He felt a black gorge rise within him.

"We have business to do, and we have pleasure to do,"

Tom said, reaching into his coat pocket, retrieving a pair of thin rubber gloves.

Geoffrey stared at the gloves, his eyes widening. "We d-do?"

"*Oh* yes," Tom said, his voice affecting a thick British accent. "Which do you fancy first, love?"

30 The Golden Gate Villas were directly across Mayfield Road from Golden Gate Shopping Center, a strip center anchored by an OfficeMax and a Friday's.

Nicky arrived in the Heights at five-thirty, a half hour early, so he stopped at Ferrara's Imported Foods. It was physically impossible to drive past the Italian food store without grabbing a few slices of prosciutto and a warm bread. As Louie Stella always said, if you can't read a newspaper through it, the prosciutto's too thick. Ferrara's always did it right.

Nicky continued up Mayfield Road, pulled into the lot at Golden Gate, looked at his watch. Five-*forty*.

Okay, he said to himself, in solemn, almost liturgical tones, ten minutes, that's it. Or ten bucks. Ten minutes or ten bucks. That was his credo, although he had never been able to uphold either of those commandments in the past.

He parked the car and stepped into Half Price Books.

31 Geoffrey sat very still, his trousers around his ankles, his penis in his right hand, but for some reason, he could not seem to achieve an erection. Perhaps, more than the debilitating fear itself, it was the humiliation of having to go through his computer files, photo by photo, with another human being in the room, looking over his shoulder. Tom, who seemed to be extremely knowledgeable about computers, had set the software to run them automatically, in succession, like a slide show at a degenerates' convention.

Geoffrey stared at the screen and wondered how he ever found them so thoroughly arousing. Photographs depicting acts in which he would never dare partake. Now they were making him sick.

Another photo appeared. This one a trio of Asian girls, urinating onto a very thin, very erect black man.

"Tell me what happened that night," Tom said softly. "Tell me in your own words."

Geoffrey said it again. It seemed as if he'd said it a thousand times already. He was nearing his ballast of tears. "I swear to *God* I can't remember. I can't remember twenty *minutes* ago. Wh-why won't you believe me?"

Tom stepped around front and snapped another photograph with the Polaroid camera. *Bloosh!* went the flash. "Tell me what happened that night. Tell me in your own words."

"I don't know...." Geoffrey replied wearily. "I don't know...."

Tom stepped behind Geoffrey and stood there for a few moments, watching the slide show on the computer monitor.

Geoffrey felt his presence, but he could not turn around in the chair.

The monitor now showed a blond girl in pigtails fellating a pair of sailors.

Now a young white man in a penis clamp and a leather mask.

Tom had been very clear about what he intended to do with the Polaroid photographs of the naked, masturbating Geoffrey if Geoffrey didn't tell him what he wanted to hear. He said he was going to take the photographs and place them on the scanner, converting them to binary files. Then he was going to upload them onto the Internet. The Internet, where they would be available to the whole world.

It was unthinkable.

Tom snapped the shutter on the Polaroid once again, the flash blinding Geoffrey momentarily. He pulled the exposed film from the camera and laid it on the desk. Five pictures now. Five glossy squares reflecting the ceiling light fixture like tiny solar panels—clear, clearer, clearest.

Tom hunkered down on one knee, just to Geoffrey's right, and looked through the viewfinder. "Tell me what happened that night," he said. "Tell me in your own words."

"I don't—"

Bloosh! Then the mechanical whine of the camera's motor drive.

The computer now showed a tangle of naked bodies on red satin sheets.

Tom stepped back, looking at the screen once again. Then he leaned in front of Geoffrey, hitting a few keystrokes, setting the modem in motion. Within moments they were connected to the Net.

"Wait!" Geoffrey shouted. "Okay . . . uh . . . I remember something. . . ."

"Go on."

"It . . . it was Halloween and we were all h-hanging out at . . . uh . . . Ben Crane's apartment on Bellflower and—"

"Wrong." Tom placed the photographs facedown on the flatbed scanner and closed the lid. Tom hit a few more keystrokes, named the files, and within moments, the binary file photos of Geoffrey Coldicott's twig-thin, incandescently white body were complete.

"Last time," Tom said. "Tell me what happened that night."

Geoffrey was sobbing now, his tears flowing freely. "Please . . . why are you duh-doing this to me?"

"You selected yourself, Geoffrey. You and the others."

"But we were kids. . . ."

"We were *all* kids."

"Yes, but none of us knew how you felt about her," Geoffrey said. "Not really. We never would have, you know . . ."

"Who was the pirate in the mask that night?"

"Well," Geoffrey began, sitting a percent or two straighter in his chair. "I'm not sure about that, but—"

"And why don't you remember?"

"I was loaded!" Geoffrey said. "I was ripped by eight o'clock that night. You remember those days . . . reds for sleeping, whites for cramming, coke for parties, 'ludes for sex. And always with those stupid fucking Algonquin drinks. Come on. I was fucked *up*. We were *all* fucked up. Ask Sebastian, if he's still around. You can't hold what happened that night against us. Especially not after so many years. Julia was *willing*. You have to—"

The look that Geoffrey received at that moment froze the words on his tongue. He had said the wrong thing. He had gone too far.

"And you were just starting to make sense," Tom said, leaning over and pressing a few keys on the computer's keyboard. "And as for Dr. Keller, I'll be seeing him soon. He has a grade coming, too."

Geoffrey shifted gears. "But you c-can't upload those ph-photographs. People can see my face. My . . . my . . . *apartment*. People will know it's *me*. It will ruh-*ruin* me!"

Tom squared himself in front of Geoffrey. "Well, then. That leads us to one overwhelming question, as Mr. J. Alfred Prufrock might have put it."

A thin ray of hope skittered across Geoffrey's face. "What?"

"What happened that night?"

"I don't fucking remember! I don't fucking remember!" Geoffrey screamed. *"I don't fucking remember fucking remember fucking remember fucking remember. . . ."*

Tom hit the Enter key and began uploading the files, sending the photographs of Geoffrey Coldicott to more than a dozen sites worldwide. Geoffrey struggled for a few moments against the rubber bungee cords that secured him to the chair, but it was fruitless. Within a minute the files were uploaded, gone. His professional life with them.

"Now," Tom began, removing a hypodermic needle from his coat pocket. "Tell me what happened that night, Mr. Geoffrey Drake Coldicott, class of 1978." He placed the syringe on the desk. "Tell me in your own words."

It wasn't until ten minutes later that Tom reached into his coat pocket and removed a pair of newspaper clippings. One spoke of the death of a Dr. Bennett Marc Crane, forty-three, of Erie, Pennsylvania. The other, of the death of a Father John Angelino, forty-two, of Highland Heights, Ohio. He placed them in Geoffrey's lap.

Geoffrey glanced down at them, his mind racing, his stomach a vile torrent of nausea. Words jumped up to meet him. Names. Names he knew. Johnny Angelino. Ben Crane.

"Tell me if you remember this," Tom said.

He placed a typewritten sheet of paper in front of Geoffrey's face. On it was a poem Geoffrey knew well, a poem by T.S. Eliot entitled "Whispers of Immortality." Just the title alone hurled Geoffrey back to those heady nights in college at CWRU: Albee plays at Eldred Theater, staying up until three and four and five in the morning, all-night Fellini at Strosacker, breakfast at Howard Johnson's on the Circle, arguing until dawn about Kerouac, Kafka, Kierkegaard. His eye began to move down the page of poetry, and the newspaper clippings on his lap began to make a clear, horrifying sense.

*Webster was much possessed by death and saw the skull
beneath the skin,* the poem began. . . .

No, Geoffrey thought. This cannot be happening.

*And breastless creatures underground leaned backward in
a lipless grin.*

My God. *No.*

*Daffodil bulbs instead of balls stared from the sockets of
the eyes!*

Geoffrey slumped in his chair, a thoroughly vanquished
man, a man who could no longer fashion his features into even
a veil of terror. But he could still see. Oh, yes. His eyes were
a bit blurred with tears, but they still worked fine. Tom had
made sure of that. Because the Polaroid photograph that
dropped into Geoffrey's lap at that moment was not to be
missed. Not if you were a male child who had ever suckled
at his mother's breast, not if you'd ever stood on a silky beach
at Blackpool while the waves receded and your mother
splashed water over your legs and you laughed until it felt like
there was a knitting needle in your side; not if you'd ever put
in hour after hour in wood shop, standing at the lathe, turning
a pair of salt and pepper shakers that to this day served a
function on her table. It was not one of the photos his tor-
mentor had just taken, that was for sure, yet it took Geoffrey
a moment to realize just what he *was* looking at, because it
wasn't that often that one got to see an eighty-year-old woman
nude, especially if she was sprawled in a makeshift grave, her
face made up like an ancient streetwalker, especially if there
was something wrong, terribly wrong with her fragile anat-
omy—

And breastless creatures underground . . .

"What do you think of *her*?" Tom asked, both hands on
Geoffrey's shoulders now, gently massaging them. "Sexy? Or
don't you like older women?"

"Ah . . ." was all that Geoffrey could manage now, low and
gruff.

"Shall we upload this photo to the Net, too? Let the world
get a glimpse of Mum in her wrinkled old birthday suit? What
do you think?"

Tom walked around to face Geoffrey. He put his hand under Geoffrey's chin, lifted his head. "No . . ." Geoffrey said.

Tom picked up the Polaroid, pored over it for a moment. "Let me tell you about having sex with a woman of her advanced years, though, Geoffrey old boy," he said. "It is *not* a pleasurable experience." He looked into Geoffrey's eyes. "Ever fuck a woman this old, Geoffrey?"

Geoffrey just stared.

"It's like fucking a mattress," Tom said. "Swear to God. Like sticking your dick in fucking *hay*. Dry and loose and scratchy. And the *smell*. Smells like a goddamn kennel."

Geoffrey Coldicott began to urinate, to sob, each function liberating the other, a man now in search of a single reason to draw even one more breath of this earth.

When he looked up and saw Tom's eyes—dead copper eyes that fronted no soul, offered no quarter—he suddenly found thousands.

32 Nicky was so preoccupied when he stepped out of the Half Price Books across the street from Geoffrey Coldicott's apartment that he almost didn't recognize his cousin. The fact that Father Joseph LaCazio was wearing street clothes didn't help.

They saw each other and, as was their custom, threw their hands into the air with surprise, then embraced. "So what brings you out here?" Nicky asked. "Buying half-price Bibles?"

Father LaCazio ignored the shot, pointed at the window of the bookstore, at the boxes on the floor by the entrance. The boxes held signs that said *Free Books!* "Whenever I'm at Golden Gate, I stop here and grab a few boxes of the free books," he said. "We put them on the shelves at the church's thrift store."

Nicky smiled. "You are one scheming priest."

"Hey," Joseph said. "Every little bit, eh?"

Joseph looked tired, overworked, overwrought by the scandal in his parish. He studied Nicky for a moment, then said: "You want to know who Johnny Angelino was?"

"Yeah," Nicky said. "I do."

"One time, in Chicago, Johnny and I went out to dinner at the Szechuan House on Michigan Avenue. Now, keep in mind, we're in divinity school at this time, okay? But we have about four or five Tsing Tao beers anyway. And we're feeling it. Meanwhile, there's a table next to us with two of the most beautiful women we'd ever seen—twenty-eight or so, one redhead, one blonde. They're making eyes, we're making eyes.

We're kind of loaded, they're kind of loaded."

"I get the picture, cuz," Nicky said, hoping his cousin wasn't leading up to some kind of a sex story. Although they had swapped *Playboy*s and *Hustler*s when they were younger, Joseph LaCazio wasn't a priest then. Now it was, well, *different*.

"Anyway, our food finally comes, and instead of plates we have these sort of curved, elongated bowls. The bad news is that Johnny, in an effort to impress these girls, decides he's going to use chopsticks, no matter what. Halfway through the Kung Pao chicken he catches an edge on the bowl and launches it ten, twelve feet. It hits the floor like a shotgun blast and covers the redhead's legs with sauce. Well, Johnny's up like a shot, helping clean up, apologizing to the young woman. Within five minutes, he has her laughing. Within ten, he has her phone number. Johnny could dump garbage on a woman, then get her number. The women *always* went for Johnny."

"He was a pretty cool guy," Nicky said.

"He could charm a fucking whore."

The word, coming out of Joseph's mouth, was a shock to Nicky. He hadn't heard his cousin use anything more caustic than the occasional "shit" or the Bible-approved "damn" over the past ten or fifteen years. But *fuck*? Father Joseph?

"Anyway," Joseph said. "Gotta run. Keep me posted on your story. Call me if I can help."

"Thanks, Joseph," Nicky said, as they embraced again.

"Gil come by for the canned goods yet?"

"Not yet," Nicky said.

"He will . . . he's making the rounds."

"Cool."

"God bless you, Nicky."

"Thanks." Nicky watched his cousin enter the store, talk to the young lady behind the counter. From behind, in those clothes—stylish blazer and slacks—you'd never know he was a priest, Nicky thought. Without the vestments he looked a lot less like Spencer Tracy.

A lot more like Sal Mineo.

33• It was around the third cup of coffee that Amelia confessed.

"And you *made out*?" Paige asked, her hand over her mouth.

"Oh my God," Amelia said, burying her head in her hands. "I *did* make out, didn't I? I *necked*."

Paige had stopped by, ostensibly to drop off an adorable white cardigan for Maddie that she had found on sale at Value City. She had also shocked Amelia by coloring her hair a deep auburn, no more than a shade or two away from Amelia's. It suited her.

The *real* reason Paige had stopped by, of course, was to tell Amelia that Garth had come by the store, and that she and Garth had a date. But Paige knew the open book that was Amelia's face, and in it she read something was up. First things first.

She asked.

Amelia spilled.

"How old is he?" Paige asked.

"I don't know."

"Thirty? Thirty-five? Forty?"

"I don't know."

"*Jesus*. Twenty?"

"*No.*"

"Eyes?"

"Brown."

"Hair?"

"Brown."

"Long?"

"Ish," Amelia replied.

"What does he do?"

"I don't know."

"How tall is he?" Paige asked, Joe Friday on a roll.

Amelia put her hand in the vicinity of five eleven, six feet.

"What was he wearing?"

"Tight jeans. Leather jacket. Boots," Amelia said.

"Hiking boots? Work boots?"

"*Cowboy* boots."

"Was the leather jacket scuffed?"

"Yep."

"Yeow," Paige said, closing her eyes for a moment, conjuring up her best friend's fantasy boy. "What's his name?"

"I don't know."

"*What?*"

"So I don't know his name. What's so—"

"Not even his *first* name?" Paige yelled, then covered her mouth and looked around, even though they were in Amelia's kitchen and Amelia's husband was three hundred miles away.

"Nope."

"You *harlot*," Paige said with a smile.

"Hey, I was pissed, okay? I had a couple of shots of schnapps and I thought I was a wild woman. I guess I was looking for a zipless, you know, *something*."

"But what were you so pissed about?"

"I don't know. You know . . . *things*."

Paige wasn't buying it. "Come on, Sparky."

Amelia thought about it. She'd come this far. But it was so embarrassing to talk about, even to your best friend. "Shelley Roth stopped by last night."

"Whoa."

"She said she's pregnant."

Paige did not react to the news in the fashion that her dearest friend might have predicted. Amelia thought that she might have reacted the way *she* had, flinging ceramic like a skeet machine gone berserk. "What did you do?"

"Well, the first thing I did was throw her out," Amelia

said. "Then I came in here and played some wall hockey with the dinnerware, I'm afraid."

"You're kidding."

"Why do you think you're drinking that coffee out of a Styrofoam cup?"

Paige had to stifle a laugh while she thought about Amelia winging bowls and cups and plates around the kitchen. "Well, okay," she began, her optimism machine reaching full rattle and thrum. "Here's the way I see it. When is your next class?"

"Tomorrow. It was scheduled for Monday, but the teacher has to be out of town."

"Okay. Tomorrow I'll go with you to the class, and you can introduce me to this guy."

"*Okay . . .*" Amelia said, a little skeptically. "Then what?"

"Then nothing. Then I can have him. You're *married,* girl-friend. Remember?"

"You're right," Amelia said. "Of course, you're right."

Paige laughed, grabbed Amelia's hand. "Look, she said, sliding off the stool at the counter. "I gotta get back to the store. Call me there. We'll talk all night."

"Thanks for Maddie's sweater, honey," Amelia said, giving her best friend a hug. "And for, you know . . ."

"Yes, I know," Paige said, returning the hug. "Just put it on my tab." She walked to the door, opened it, stepped through, turned. "But just to be on the safe side, I'm keeping tomorrow night open."

"Smart-ass," Amelia said.

"I've always wanted to be a writer," Paige said. "Did I ever tell you that?"

"Go to work," Amelia said. "And *hey!*"

"What?" Paige asked.

Amelia smiled. "Love your hair."

Paige walked to her car, feeling a chill through her thick sweater. It was almost November and northeastern Ohio had decided to remind her.

Poor Amelia, she thought. Here she had it made—good-looking husband, the daughter of all daughters, a great house, great legs. Then Roger the Artful Dodger had to go and pull this shit.

As she headed west, toward Falls Road, Paige thought of Maddie and Amelia's future, and had a feeling that everything was going to change for them soon.

What the feeling could not tell her at that moment was that, within the next twenty-four hours, death, and its minion grief, would walk hand in hand down the center of Wyckamore Lane.

34•Nicky pressed the button next to Geoffrey Coldicott's name, but got no immediate response. He tried again. Nothing. He hoped Geoffrey hadn't left. He tried again.

Finally the speaker offered, weakly: "Yes?"

"Is this Geoffrey?"

"Who is this?" came the disembodied voice.

Once again, Nicky thought, this man likes to answer questions with questions. "Mr. Coldicott," Nicky began, not knowing if he was indeed speaking to Geoffrey Coldicott at all. "It's Nicholas Stella. With the *Cleveland Chronicle*." Shit. "I mean, you know, *Esquire*."

Nothing.

"From this *morning*?" Nicky continued.

Silence.

"We spoke on the phone?"

More silence.

Nicky plodded on, starting to get irritated. Here he was trying to save this man's life and all he was getting was resistance. "And I just happened to be in Cleveland this week on a Bobbing for Walleye package tour and I was wondering if I could—"

The arm that encircled Nicky's throat was massive. Thick and muscular. In an instant Nicky was yanked from his feet and slammed roughly to the hardwood floor of the vestibule, the force of the blow pummeling the air from his lungs. He then felt the crushing weight of two huge knees on his chest and four strong hands pinning his arms to the ground. He also felt a sharp, purely intentional elbow to his groin. The bright orange pain shot to the center of his brain, blinding him momentarily.

"Now . . . I'm gonna count to *three*," said a raspy voice, just inches away from Nicky's face, the sound drifting in on a moist cloud of onions, garlic, and tobacco. "And you're gonna tell me what the fuck your business is with the man in three eighteen."

Nicky looked around the room, at the handful of forensic scientists working the scene—dusting for prints, bagging the cigarette butts, Band-Aids, coffee cups. His back throbbed, his head hurt, felt oversized. The sharp pain in his loins had now settled into a dull, pulsating ache he knew would be there for a day or two, seriously curtailing any romantic prospects for the near future. Maybe ever.

The primate who had slammed him to the ground was a huge uniformed cop named Sykes, a somber Goliath who now filled the doorway to the apartment, essentially becoming a six-foot-five security door between the crime scene and the outside world. He still looked at Nicky as if he were one hundred seventy-five pounds of fresh Genoa salami.

Geoffrey Coldicott's apartment was a four-room affair— living room, bedroom, pullman kitchen, bathroom. In spite of Geoffrey's occupation, in spite of the fact that he probably spent half his time at estate sales, all the furnishings looked like items purchased by a man who couldn't be bothered to make even a passing acquaintance with the world of interior design. Cheap chrome-and-glass tables, leather-look love seats, all barely functional. Mall art on the walls. A huge mirror over the mantel. It was easy to tell just what was central to Geoffrey Coldicott's life, such as it was. Geoffrey clearly loved his computer. It was the only area of the apartment that was truly clean and tidy. Books organized, pencils sharpened, tabletop shining. Nicky knew enough computer nerds to know the look of a true propeller-head's nook.

The big cop had said that he could sit in the corner and wait, far away from the victim—who looked to be sitting upright on the couch, covered with a sheet—until the detective in charge got there. Nicky had dutifully obeyed.

From where he sat, Geoffrey Coldicott's body looked like a museum piece, draped with a white cotton cloth. The only things that clued Nicky in to the fact that this was not statuary were the red smudges near the top of the head, the erratic scarlet line that ran laterally across where the forehead should be, then down into what was beginning to look like a nose, a mouth.

The door to Geoffrey's apartment, Nicky overheard, had been left ajar, and when Geoffrey's neighbor stopped by to borrow a couple of tea bags, she had found the body. The neighbor, an elderly woman named Sadie Pultz, was sedated, Nicky heard, and resting in her own apartment next door.

That was an hour ago, they said. Right around the time Nicky was stepping inside Half Price Books.

Then, from the hallway, came a voice that sounded vaguely familiar.

Nicky got to his feet as the owner of the voice turned the corner, ducked under the yellow crime-scene tape, and entered the apartment. The man was white, clean-shaven, about Nicky's height and weight, a few years older. He wore a dark overcoat, tailored, and tinted glasses; a badge was pinned to his lapel.

"Hi. Nicholas Stella. *Esquire* magazine," he introduced himself.

The man looked him up and down before extending his own hand. "Ivan Kral," he said. "Detective Ivan Kral, Cleveland Homicide Task Force."

They shook hands and Nicky noticed how strong the man's grip was. He tried, and failed, to match it. "Cleveland? What are you doing out here in the 'burbs, if I might ask?"

"Sorry about the mix-up downstairs," Kral continued, ignoring the question.

"No problem," Nicky lied, knowing that the Homicide Unit of the Cleveland Police Department usually worked exclusively within city limits. "And I'd just like to say how much I—"

"But I'm still going to call them."

"What?" Nicky replied. "Who?"

"*Esquire*. I'm going to call them. Right now. If you lied to me, you're going to fucking jail."

The big cop, Sykes, burst out laughing, then covered his mouth.

And Nicky knew.

Detective Ivan Kral was the Birdman.

"And you only met him this morning?" Kral asked.

"No," Nicky said. "I *talked* to him this morning. On the phone."

"At his place of business."

"Yes."

"And how did you come to call Mr. Coldicott in the first place?"

Nicky had to tread lightly here. "Well, it's kind of a long story."

"I have a great deal of time," Kral said.

They were sitting at Geoffrey Coldicott's small dinette table, a gray and white Formica job that he had probably picked up at a Garfield Heights garage sale. They were drinking Geoffrey's instant coffee, too. "Am I a suspect?" Nicky asked.

"Of course not," Kral said. "You're a witness, Nicky. A very important one. You spoke to the deceased on the day he was murdered. Very important."

Nicky's mind began to sprint. How was he going to tell them the manner in which he got Geoffrey Coldicott's name? Did Kral know of his recent meeting with Willie T? Had they talked? Because if they could prove that he had prior knowledge of a conspiracy, or that he had knowledge that a crime was imminent and he did nothing to prevent it, couldn't they put him away for a lot of years?

He was certain of it. So he lied to a cop. "I'm doing a story on antique jewelry for a *Cleveland Today* supplement. I called Mr. Coldicott this morning, at his place of business, and asked for an interview. He told me to meet him here at six. That's the whole thing."

Kral held his gaze for a few moments. "That's your long story?"

"Well, that's the nutshell. You don't want to hear about all my research into the fascinating world of antique jewelry, do you?" Nicky tried a half smile, but it was not returned.

"And who's your editor over there at *Cleveland Today*?" Kral said, his pen poised over his notebook.

Fucking cops, Nicky thought. It was one of the reasons he never got away with shit when he was a kid. "Okay, it's not an assigned piece I was going to do it on spec."

"A spec piece on antique jewelry."

"Yes."

"You?"

"Hey . . . a man's gotta make a living, you know?"

Due to the thousands of times that the teenaged Nicholas Stella had been grilled by his father, one of the most decorated cops ever to work out of the Third District, Nicky knew that Kral wasn't buying what he was selling, and that Kral wasn't done with him. But he also knew that now was the time to strike, if he was going to strike at all.

"So . . . how about an exclusive on this, Birdman?"

Kral studied him, not reacting to the "Birdman" familiarity, which was a good sign for Nicky. So Nicky continued.

"C'mon, man. I'll write it up like the 'Crack Alley Blues' piece, except this time we go national. Think about it. *Esquire, GQ, Vanity Fair*. A homicide investigation from the inside. What do you say? You could be the new Popeye Doyle."

"You want to write about this?"

"Yes."

"You're sure?"

"Yes," Nicky said. "Beats the crap out of a story on antique jewelry. What do you say?"

Instead of answering him, Kral stood up and walked over to where Geoffrey Coldicott's body was slumped on the love seat, just a few feet from where they were sitting. Next to the body was a hypodermic needle and a GemPac.

Kral removed the sheet.

And Nicky vomited on the table.

*   *   *

The skin, the assistant coroner said, had been removed from Geoffrey Coldicott's face in one piece, and quite expertly at that. Whoever had done this, Dr. Vikram Raj went on to say, had made an incision starting at the hairline in the middle of the forehead, down one side, in front of the ear, under the chin, then back up the other side. Incisions were also made around the eyes, nose, and lips. Then the skin was gently, slowly peeled away.

What remained, at least to Nicky's eyes, looked like the bloody negative of a picture of a goalie, or maybe of Jason in the *Friday the 13th* series; a reddish brown hockey mask that glistened under the explosion of the flashbulbs.

While the photographers were at it, Kral asked for a picture of Nicky.

A half hour later, as the forensic activity died down, Detective Kral directed his pen flashlight at Geoffrey Coldicott's blood-clotted cheek, at the small patch of grayish fluid near the corner of his mouth, fluid that looked to be drying semen. A slight parting of the dead man's lips revealed more semen, the viscous liquid forming thin, sticky bars between his upper and lower lips.

Kral took his pen and began to probe around Coldicott's clothing. The man's belt was fastened, his trousers zipped. Instinctively Nicky and Kral simultaneously glanced over at the bed, which was still made, untouched.

Nicky wasn't all that interested in Geoffrey Coldicott's sexual proclivities. What he really wanted was a look at the computer. "Did anyone check his computer?" he asked no one in particular, knowing he was pushing it, knowing he was only in this room as long as Kral allowed him to be. "Might be some clues in there. His itinerary for today, appointment book, calendar, stuff like that."

Kral looked at one of the forensic team, a tall black woman named Billings.

"Nothing there," Billings said.

"What do you mean?" Nicky asked.

"Just what I said. '*Drive C* not found.' Nothing there."

*   *   *

When Nicky turned the corner onto the landing in front of his door and saw the figure sitting there, he nearly screamed. He was sure it was Frank Corso, and he was sure there was a gun pointed at him.

"Hi, Nick," the man said.

"Jesus, I was just gonna call you and—" Nicky managed, but stopped when he realized that it wasn't Frank Corso after all. It was Gil Strauss. Gil was there to pick up the canned goods for the food drive.

"Hey . . . *hi*, Gil," Nicky said, finally exhaling.

Gil stood up, looking a little embarrassed. "Did I scare you? I'm sorry. Door was open downstairs."

Gil had always struck Nicky as the kind of guy who would apologize for getting hit by a car. Always dressed in workman fatigues, he wore thick glasses that gave him the appearance of a bookworm, although Nicky believed him to be a lot better with a pair of vise grips than a volume of Marcel Proust. "I can take a look at this, you know," Gil said, pointing to the skewed hinge on Nicky's door. "Got the tools downstairs."

"No, that's okay," Nicky replied, unlocking his door. "That's what the landlord gets paid to avoid."

Gil laughed as they mounted the steps, then stepped into Nicky's tiny kitchen.

"Always wanted to ask you," Nicky said, opening some cupboards. "What's Gil short for?"

"Gillian."

"Oh," Nicky said. "I guess that's better than Gilbert, no?"

"Not when you're ten," Gil said. "I was pretty fat when I was a kid. I got 'Gillian weighs a million' all the time."

"Ouch," Nicky replied.

Gil looked around, as if remodeling the small apartment in his mind. Dormer here. Skylight here. Perhaps a direct-vent fireplace against that outside wall. He walked into the living room, picked up the picture of Meg. "Was this your wife, Nick?"

Was? Nicky thought. After being startled by the question at first—he didn't know Gil Strauss nearly well enough to discuss his personal life—then realizing that Joseph must have told him about Meg, Nicky stepped into the living room, looked over Gil's shoulder. "Yes. That's Meg."

"She's very pretty," Gil said.

"That she is." He took the photo from Gil and, for the thousandth time, tried to brush that fine wisp of hair from Meg's forehead. "She would've been thirty-two this year. Thirty-*two*. She used to think *thirty* was ancient."

"Didn't we all," Gil answered. "Didn't we all."

Nicky placed the photo back into its easel. He looked up, into Gil's eyes, eyes refracted in a dozen directions by the thick lenses. He asked, "Have you ever been in love, Gil?"

For a moment it looked as if the question had been a whip crack in the room. It looked as if Gil might turn and run. Then, just as suddenly, he began to smile, to redden. "It's just that I never ... you know ..." he began, giving what sounded to Nicky like the stock answer. Nicky helped him out.

"Never met the right girl?"

"Well ..."

The reddening deepened. Nicky looked for a way out. "There's still plenty of time," Nicky said, sounding way too fatherly, considering he was talking to a guy a few years older.

"I don't know. . . ." Gil said. "I'm pretty busy most of the time."

"Gotta take time out for life, though, Gil," Nicky said, wondering if this wasn't advice he should be taking instead of giving.

Gil took it as a cue. He clapped his hands once and said: "Well, what do you say we take time out for the hungry right now? Point me toward the canned goods, my friend."

"Right this way," Nicky said.

Nicky hadn't prepared any canned foods for the drive, so what Gil's visit amounted to, as it had for three years, was an emptying of Nicky's cupboards. And he had *just* gone shopping at the Finast at Severance. He grabbed a pair of empty cardboard boxes from under the sink and indicated to Gil that he should help himself. He did.

"You know, your cousin thinks the world of you," Gil said, filling a box. "Talks about you all the time. Talks about when you were growing up. I love those stories."

Nicky didn't know if this was small talk or not, but Gil sounded sincere. "Yeah, well, Joseph's the best." He winced, watching Gil put a sealed jar of Folger's crystals into the box. It was all the coffee in the house.

"*Father LaCazio* talks about your writing to everyone, too. He's very proud. Keeps three copies of everything you write. I especially like that story you did about the boxers."

"Oh, uh, thanks," Nicky said, standing corrected. "I'm pretty proud of that one myself."

They finished filling the boxes and Nicky placed them near the head of the stairs. "Did you know that I was writing a story about Father Angelino?"

Gil stopped what he was doing, looked up. "No, I didn't. But anything the rectory can do to help, you let me know."

Nicky smiled. Gil sounded like a priest. "Thanks." He grabbed a box and headed for the stairs. "There's cold Pepsi in the fridge. Help yourself."

By the time Nicky reached the bottom of the stairs, the phrase came back to him with full force, a cold declaration of fact that frightened him: *Drive C not found.*

They missed John Angelino's laptop, though, didn't they? Nicky thought.

Whoever was doing this had missed the fucking laptop.

Nicky watched Gil load the last of the boxes into the St. Francis station wagon. Gil got behind the wheel, rolled down the window.

"Thanks, Nicky."

"No sweat. Happy to do it." They shook hands again.

"I have two more stops to make," Gil said. "I'll be back in an hour or so. We'll go over to the food bank together, okay?"

It was the last thing Nicky wanted to do, but he had made a promise to help out on the docks. And you don't stiff the church. Ask any Catholic. "Sure," he said. "See you in an hour."

What did he know? He knew this. People were being shot full of dope and having parts of their bodies removed. Parts they were still young enough to need. Things like lips, facial skin, eyes.

So far, Nicky thought, he had been lucky to get out of this with his life. Four other people hadn't, and the guilt of not having brought this straight to the police was weighing on him. There was some crazy shit going on here; it had something to do with poetry and dope and dead people, and that was about all he needed to know to get the fuck out of the way. Who was he kidding? He would talk Erique Mars into a story on something else. Christmas in Collinwood. Christmas with the Cleveland Indians. Something that didn't involve scalpels and heroin, if you don't mind. If not, then he'd have to get a job.

Sorry, Grampa.

Gil's visit had left him without any food, so over soup at Sol's he decided to do the wise thing. The moment he got back to his apartment he would call Kral and give him everything he had.

"Fuck you, asshole."

The fist attached to that greeting seemed to hurtle out of the darkness that led to the basement, shrieking through space, growing in size and velocity, catching Nicky high on his left cheek, slamming him back into the door. Luckily, it was a glancing blow because the fist was enormous and wrapped in some sort of hard leather.

But still Nicky visited an entire galaxy of yellow and orange stars; his legs felt *al dente*.

"You think I'm fuckin' stupid?" the owner of the fist barked into his face as he pushed Nicky up the stairs. "Huh? You think you can play me night after fuckin' night? I been *lenient* with you, asshole. Lee-nee-yent. Now I'm going to kick your fuckin' ass."

This time it was, of course, Frank Corso, but Nicky's vision was so blurred at the moment that it could've been anyone. Anyone the size and shape of Pittsburgh.

With incredible ease, Frank shoved Nicky up the remaining six steps to his door.

They stood in Nicky's cramped living room, five feet apart, and Nicky gave him all the money he had. Frank pulled his own huge roll of bills kept together in a rubber band, put it under his left armpit, and began to count Nicky's money. He finished, looked Nicky in the eye. "It's only three hundred."

"What are you talking about?" Nicky said, his face throbbing, swelling. "That's my payment."

"What did I fuckin' tell you last week? I want the four large." He retrieved the roll from under his arm, unbanded it, added Nicky's money. "Man, I thought you was hipper than that." He raised the gun—a .38 police special—and pointed it at Nicky. "Where's the rest?"

"What, are you *kidding* me?"

"No," Frank said. "Drop down."

Nicky pretended to be incredulous. "You were serious about that?"

"Like skin cancer. Gimme my fuckin' money."

Nicky's mind was reeling. He knew he had something like ten dollars available to him, and half of *that* was probably in dimes and quarters. He doubted if Frank Corso would take a check. It would only bounce and they'd have to do this all over again.

So Nicky, standing near the doorway to his bedroom, figured he had two options. One, to dive into his bedroom, slam the door, turn the key, and buy himself just enough time to jump out the window and fall thirty feet. Or try to bluff.

Okay, *one* option.

"I gotta go to the ATM then. I can get maybe fifteen hundred," Nicky said, hoping Frank Corso was too stupid to know that you can't withdraw that much from an ATM machine.

Thankfully, he was.

"Show me the card," Frank said, keeping the gun on him. "Slow."

Nicky reached into his back pocket slowly, retrieved his wallet, keeping his eye on the barrel of the gun the whole time. Then, suddenly, a shadow appeared on the wall behind Frank, a steadily creeping shadow that grew in size for a moment, then narrowed into a human form.

And somehow, the Birdman was standing right behind Frank.

At first Nicky feared the worst. A flashback. Some kind of drug he had ingested once had just decided to kick in and he was hallucinating things. Cops showing up in the nick of time to save his life. Was this a dad thing? he wondered.

But the Birdman was real.

"Don't fucking move," Kral said coolly, putting the barrel of his nine-millimeter pistol to the back of Frank Corso's head. He cocked his weapon and continued: "Now, I'm assuming you got through the third grade, but I'll go slow anyway, just in case. We're gonna count to three now. Okay?"

Nobody said a word. Nicky stole a glance at Frank Corso's face. His eyes were darting from side to side, a rivulet of sweat was working its way down his forehead, over the bridge of his nose. But still he kept his revolver pointed at Nicky.

"Nicky, you count with me, okay? I'm going to shoot him in the head on three."

"*What?*"

"One . . ."

"Un," Nicky said, coming in halfway through the word. The gun in Corso's hand began to shake.

"Two . . ." Kral and Nicky said in perfect unison, drawing a breath afterward. On that upbeat of air, Nicky knew he was going to live through this. He saw the break in Frank Corso's resolve. He also saw Frank mouth the words *you are fucking dead, asshole* as he slowly lowered the gun to his side and let it drop to the floor.

Nicky figured that Kral would now reach behind his back, grab a pair of cuffs, and slip them on Corso. What Nicky didn't expect was what actually happened. The moment that

Frank Corso's gun hit the carpet, Kral leaned to his left, putting all of his weight on his left foot, spun in place, and slammed his right foot into Frank Corso's liver. Hard. Frank Corso folded to the floor like an accordion pleat.

The banded roll of bills, which Frank still had in his left hand when the impact occurred, went flying across the room and rolled under the couch. Incredibly, Kral didn't see it, and Frank Corso was far too busy puking to care. Nicky backed to the couch slowly, sat down, not having to feign relief at all. Kral spoke into his two-way radio, and within a few minutes two uniformed officers came up the stairs and took the folded-up version of Frank Corso into custody. While everyone's back was turned, Nicky reached under the couch, grabbed the roll, and shoved it into his pocket.

He sat there, his pulse racing, waiting, the roll of bills against his leg like a big green erection. His heart began to thrum in his chest.

Five minutes later, he got the shock of his life.

"You've got two choices, Nicky," Kral said. "Downtown or here. But I will tell you that we have a policy at the Homicide Unit. Your first trip is always an overnighter."

Shit, Nicky thought. "You gonna tell me what this is all about first?" he asked, although he knew his bargaining power was nil.

"Yeah, I'll tell you," Kral said, as he put the handcuffs on Nicky. "Ronnie Choi is dead."

Nicky, of course, told them everything. Rolled like a fat guy down Granger Road hill. This had gotten so out of control, so fast, that it had begun to teach him one of those indelible lessons that you carry with you the rest of your life. Never lie to a cop. Stay away from the crazy shit. He explained about Frank Corso and the loan, but not about the roll. It appeared that Kral believed him, and that there was nothing prosecutable about Nicky's end of the matter. So Kral moved on.

"The girl at the drug house identified you, Nicky. Two narcotics cops showed her your picture and she tossed."

Nicky recalled the pretty young hostess at Elegant Linda's. The one with the small butterfly tattoo by her right eye. "Okay . . ."

"Said you came in with a black he/she. A hooker."

"She's not a hooker."

"And you asked for Ronnie Choi."

Nicky figured he'd save the argument regarding Beverly Ahn's virtue for another time. "That's right."

"And you just saw Ronnie Choi that one time. At the drug house."

"Yes."

"With this Beverly Ahn."

"Yes. But there's no way she's involved in any of this," Nicky said. "I mean . . . there's just no way."

"You made her involved, Nicky. You dropped her right in the middle of it, didn't you?"

"She's a trans*vestite*. A show girl. The only things she's interested in are makeup and magazines. She's not a killer."

"She a user?"

Nicky knew he would have to lie again to stop this particular line of questioning. "Well, you know what kind of lifestyle she leads. I'm sure she smokes. Little toot now and then. But I'm sure she doesn't—"

"What exactly did she want to talk to Ronnie Choi about that day?" Kral asked.

"I told you. She was trying to get an interview with him. Talk him into it for me. I figured if he was selling the killer smack, I would ask him how he felt about it. But I wouldn't have even *known* about him if it wasn't for you guys. Ask Willie T. He's the one who told me where Rat Boy was going to be that morning. Talk to him."

"I have," Kral said.

"And what did he say?" Nicky asked.

"He said what you said."

"Well, there you go. As to all this other shit . . . I had no idea. The doctor in Erie, this Coldicott guy . . ."

The cuffs were off, but they were sitting on Nicky's coffee table. Alongside Nicky's collection of bright green floppy disks, about a dozen. For some reason, the dark blue disk with the poem and the e-mail was nowhere in sight.

It looked as if he might not be making that trip downtown after all, but the Birdman's face, now that Nicky had gotten to look at it sans disguise for much longer than he liked, was nothing if not inscrutable. It still could go either way. But still Nicky pushed. "And let me ask *you* something now," he said.

"What is it?"

"Do I have a shot at an exclusive here? I mean, there are three murders here that seem to be related, right? Four, with the girl. I've got the rest of the names. What do you say?"

"We had most of this, Nicky."

Nicky was stunned for a moment. "What?"

"The FBI is already looking into the connection between the Crane murder in Erie and the death of John Angelino. The jaguar and marmoset stamps—that is a marmoset, by the way, not a monkey—are being run through VICAP now. What we didn't have was the poem and the list. And for that the people of the states of Ohio and Pennsylvania are grateful to you."

"It's a marmoset?"

"Yes."

"Got any idea what it means?" Nicky asked.

"Not yet," Kral said, rising to his feet. "But the bad news for us is that the feds are here already and they're going to take this away from us. Needless to say, we want this asshole *bad*."

"Then let me help," Nicky said, remembering his father's great disdain for the attitude of the FBI agents he had worked with. He reached over to the end table and opened a drawer. He pulled out the half of the hundred-dollar bill, held it up. "Let me have the story, Detective Kral. Look at my face. I've earned it."

Kral studied him. He didn't take the half C note. "We'll see."

Yes, Nicky thought. He put the bill in his pocket.

"Now," Kral continued, "do you have that computer disk with the names here?"

"Yeah. It must be in my car, though." Before he stood up,

he looked to Kral for permission. Some things just rub off when you're a policeman's kid. Kral nodded and Nicky walked into his bedroom, retrieved his keys, ran down the steps and out the back door. As he was going through the papers on the passenger seat he noticed that Frank Corso's Firebird was still parked out front. Then he remembered the roll. He took it out of his pocket and gave it a quick count.

It looked like fifteen hundred dollars!

Hang on, Grampa. We're going to Atlantic City.

He put it in an empty McDonald's bag, crumpled it, stuffed it under the seat. Except for the swelling on the left side of his face, and the fact that he had just narrowly avoided being booked for first-degree murder, it was turning out to be a fairly decent day.

But the disk was nowhere to be found.

He generally kept his floppy disks in a box in the glove compartment when he did any mobile computing, but the only things in there now were a dozen or so foil packets of ketchup and a hairbrush with a masking-taped handle.

Kral wrote down the name and address of a place called the Caprice Lounge.

"You meet me here in an hour, Nicky. Bring the disk."

"No problem," Nicky answered, hoping he could put his hands on it. Where the hell had it gotten to? "I'll be there."

Kral held his gaze for a few moments before speaking. "Don't fuck with me, Nicky. I'm giving you a pass here. I'm trusting you. You hear me?"

"I hear you," Nicky said.

Kral gave Nicky a few more volts of attitude, then headed for the steps.

Twenty minutes later, when Gil returned to Nicky's apartment, the two men tore the place apart. The disk was gone.

Nicky remembered copying the e-mail addresses into his notebook—but now that was missing too.

Shit.

*   *   *

Happy Hour at the Caprice Lounge was a jumble of seventies rock, shouted obscenities, and boisterous retellings of near-death encounters with the city's vilest desperadoes. As cop bars go, Nicky had once heard from his father, the beer at the Caprice was cold enough, the food was edible, and the blondes didn't steal your wallet.

Nicky and Gil slipped into a back booth, ordered two Michelobs. The bar was dark, half-full. The waitress arrived, served, left.

"I appreciate you doing this," Nicky said. He hadn't told Gil much, and to Gil's credit, he hadn't asked. All that was said was that Nicky had to meet a cop and give him something. "This shouldn't take too long."

"This is police business, Nick. I respect the police."

They went silent for a few minutes, listening to the music. It was R. Dean Taylor's "Indiana Wants Me" on the jukebox now. Nicky looked at Gil—khaki chinos, Michelob in hand—and thought he looked rather at home in a blue-collar setting like this.

"So you're a beer drinker, eh?" Nicky said with a smile.

Gil blushed a little, looked guilty. "I like it just fine, Nick. Needless to say, we don't usually have it sitting around the rectory much."

"No keg parties with the St. Francis nuns?"

"Not too often," Gil replied, playing along, but reddening further.

"Well, drink up," Nicky said, figuring Gil was probably not too comfortable with nun jokes. "Beers are on me."

They clinked bottles, sipped. "Thanks, Nick."

He took another sip of his beer, slipped out of the booth.

"You can stay," Nicky said.

"It's okay," Gil replied, zipping his jacket. "I'm sure this is private. I'll be in the car out front. Take as long as you need."

Before Nicky could object, Gil turned on his heels and headed for the door.

Five minutes later there came a loud burst of laughter at the front of the bar. Nicky looked up and saw Kral standing by the front door with a stocky blond woman. He was telling her an animated story, one that ended with another thunderous cackle of boozy laughter. After a minute or two, the blonde hugged him, left. Kral wobbled a bit, then began glad-handing his way around the horseshoe-shaped bar.

Within seconds, Kral noticed Nicky, finished his story to the big uniformed cop at the end of the bar, and headed to the booth.

The second thing Nicky noticed about Kral was the huge grin across his face. The first thing he noticed was probably the reason for the second thing.

Detective Ivan Kral was shit-face drunk.

"Nicky. How are ya?" Kral said, putting his jigger of whiskey carefully on the table, then sliding clumsily into the booth opposite Nicky.

"I'm okay," Nicky said, cautiously. "You look like you're feeling no pain. Not on duty, are ya, Birdman?"

"I've never been better," Kral said. "Been off since six."

Nicky glanced at the wall clock. It was six-ten. Nobody got this loaded that fast.

"Well," Nicky began, "you're not going to believe this, but—"

Kral held up his hand, interrupting him. "Whatever it is, I don't want to hear it."

"Well, let me at least—"

"What I'm saying is . . . I don't want to fucking *hear* it. Capeesh?"

Nicky's heart sank. Was he going to jail? "What are you talking about?"

"I'm talking about how it isn't my case anymore, see? The feds are treating this as a serial murder. We've got G-men up the fucking wazoo down at the Justice Center."

Nicky figured it was now or never. "It's gone. The disk is gone. Can't find my notebook either."

Kral looked at him for a few moments, focusing a bit drunkenly. He smirked. "Feds will want your laptop. Give them something to do. They're really good at finding shit where shit don't grow." Kral grabbed Nicky's Michelob, took a long, hard swallow. "But *we* gave them the fact that all the victims went to CWRU. Right under their fuckin' noses."

He said it so casually. Nicky thought for a moment he had misunderstood. Geoffrey, too? Geoffrey went to Case, too? *"What?"*

"Yeah. Angelino, Coldicott, Crane," Kral said, slurring his words a little now. "They all went to CWRU in the late seventies. It was the one thing that popped up on all their sheets. As soon as that surfaced, the feds pounced. Interstate homicide, too. So it's their case now. I'm out of it."

"No shit."

"None," Kral replied. "And what's more, I don't give a fuck." He threw back his shot of whiskey, looked for the waitress.

"Case Western Reserve," Nicky said, softly, new wheels beginning to spin. His cousin Joseph had gone to CWRU, too. "Well, would it be okay if I talked to people down at Case for background?"

Kral laughed, raised his hand, called the waitress. He looked at Nicky, his tinted glasses reflecting the neon beer signs scattered around the room. "As long as you keep it out of print until the feds close the case, I don't care if you talk to the pope."

"Thanks," Nicky said with a smile, grateful for Kral's inebriated mood, glad to be leaving the Caprice Lounge without handcuffs. Kral had given him inside cop stuff with the CWRU lead. He knew what was expected of him. "Are we square now, Birdman?" Nicky asked, sliding his half of the hundred across the table.

This time Kral pocketed the bill without even looking at it. "Like Pat Fuckin' Boone."

five

The AdVerse Society

35° Sebastian Keller stared at the newspaper, the type running together in a miasma of floating black and white dots: a pointillist response caused by the painkillers.

Two dead now. At least, two that he knew of. And how many more to go? Two? Three? Four? That is, if they weren't already gone.

Geoffrey Coldicott, a victim of heroin.

He thought about the strange, spindly Mr. Coldicott, his fey manners and lascivious leers. He had thought Mr. Coldicott gay in those years, or perhaps even bisexual, but either sexuality seemed to be denied within the man. Or at least that was how it seemed from the vantage point of his arm's-length acquaintance with him.

Because the first thing Sebastian Keller had learned as an English teacher at Brush High School, in his mid-twenties, was that you cannot *really* become friends with your students. Especially at the high-school level.

But in college, everything changes. In college a young professor can score big with the undergraduate women.

Sebastian Keller really thought he had penetrated their little group, but on twenty years of reflection, he had concluded that he had not. Five or even ten years difference in age was probably surmountable at the college level, but twenty? He didn't think so. He had certainly thought so *then,* but he had been wrong. He had just been a middle-aged guy with bridgework and a burgeoning paunch who had dressed and acted embarrassingly young.

He had taken them all to dinner one evening after a particularly lively afternoon session of his 300-level poetry class. There had been seven or eight of them, the AdVerse Society in its totality plus a few hangers-on, freshmen who got a literary contact high from being in the same room with people, like themselves, who had actually *read* books such as *Catcher in the Rye* or *Naked Lunch* or *Steppenwolf.*

One of the freshmen who tagged along to the Boarding House that night was a delicately beautiful girl named Julia Raines, a transfer student from Bowling Green who had come over midsemester because the restrictions that living at home near BGU put on her had denied her the campus experience of college. Even though she was not all that far from her home in Haskins, Ohio, she said she felt quite liberated.

Julia was the quintessential waif, he had thought that night, provincial in manner, slender and pale, a sweet Cossette in her peasant dresses and sandals. She was beautiful in the sense that a languid willow is beautiful; sky blue eyes that squinted at the slightest change in light, soft brown hair that seemed to always be fighting the thinnest of breezes.

By nine-thirty that night they had eaten dinner, and subsequently consumed a half dozen pitchers of beer, along with the ubiquitous Algonquin cocktails. Soon the conversation among the ten or so people at the table became both insufferably lofty and cacophonous; so much so that he remembered they had, at times, even drowned out the three-piece combo in the corner of the upstairs level at the Boarding House.

"Emily Dickinson," John Angelino said, "is the only woman who could even hold a candle to her male contemporaries."

There was a brief moment of silence before John Angelino was pelted with a hurricane of balled-up napkins, swizzle sticks, and bits of onion ring by the handful of women at the table.

"Sylvia Plath," one of them hurled.

"Gwendolyn Brooks," said another.

"Sara Teasdale, Marianne Moore," said yet another.

Then, as if their heads were all tied together with string, they all looked to Julia to get in her lick, but instead, Julia

smiled and blushed, a little off guard and, it appeared, woefully underread on the subject. She looked at her shoes.

A few more halfhearted projectiles came sailing John Angelino's way as Julia excused herself from the table.

A few moments later, Sebastian Keller followed.

There was a pay phone at the dark end of the corridor in those
days, directly across from the ladies' room entrance. Sebastian
picked up the phone but didn't insert any coins, didn't dial a
number. He just stood there, silently, the cold, quiet plastic to
his ear. He did this because he knew that, from that angle, one
could see the slightest wedge of the anteroom to the ladies'
toilet, the room that held the couch and the stand-up ashtrays
and one long wall with a succession of round, art deco mirrors.
He also knew that sometimes, when the door was propped
open in the manner in which it was that night, one could see
inside that room, could covertly watch whoever was standing
in front of the very last mirror by the door, could observe her
from the cover of darkness.

A minute or two into his voyeuristic deception, Sebastian
Keller was rewarded. Julia Raines stopped at the last mirror,
and he watched her do something that he had thought about
a thousand times since. Something that would make Julia
Raines live in his mind for what he now knew to be the rest
of his life.

He watched her speak to the mirror.

She seemed to be rehearsing what she was going to say
when she returned to the table. She practiced her laugh, the
brief, courteous laugh of the cognoscenti, the laugh that lets
everyone at the table know that you've gotten the joke, or
nailed down the reference. She flicked her hair over her shoulder, cocked her head at an angle, as if rapt, listening to a story.
Then, quite dramatically, she had burst into laughter, covering
her mouth in response to what quite possibly had been the
funniest story she had ever heard. Robert Benchley said *that*?
Dorothy Parker wrote *that*?

He'd known at that moment that he would never forget her.
Just as he knew that someone in that group had to have been

head over heels in love with Julia Raines, as he had been himself, and that someone in that group, or near that group, had blamed the rest of them for what happened to her that night.

Sebastian Keller picked up the phone on his desk, punched the number nine, waited, dialed the number, waited. When someone answered, he said: "May I have the homicide division, please?"

"One moment."

More than a *few* moments later (Sebastian Keller was getting very precise with his time, even the indiscernible depth and breadth of a few moments), the phone was picked up.

"Homicide, Detective Paris."

"Detective Paris, my name is Sebastian Keller, I'm the head of the English Department at Case Western Reserve University."

"What can I do for you, Mr. Keller?"

A bright red rope of pain snuck under the pain medication for a moment, encircling his bowels, knotting tightly, causing him to grip the arms of his chairs. After a moment, it submerged to its tolerable intolerable level. "I have some information for you."

36• On the way out of the back door, the phone rang. Amelia picked up the cordless and continued out onto the deck, the seven or eight million leaves that needed to be raked denying her the luxury of a chair and a cup of coffee for this conversation, whoever it was.

"Hello?"

"Mrs. Saintsbury?"

"Yes."

"Hi . . . uh . . . it's Eddie."

Eddie? Amelia wondered. Who's Eddie? "I'm sorry. Who is this?"

"Eddie. Eddie Pankow. From Cybernauts."

Cybernauts, Amelia thought. What the hell was a cyber— "Oh, right, right, the computer guys."

"Yes, exactly."

"Eddie and . . ."

"Andy," she heard, spoken in a different voice. They were both on the line.

"Well . . . how are you guys?" Amelia asked, smiling. They were, in their way, kind of cute. The fact that they got flustered around her made her feel good. Like she was still in there pitching.

"Good," Eddie said.

"Both of us," Andy added. "We're both . . . you know . . . *good*."

"That's great," Amelia said, eyeing the leaves. Maddie was home from school, and even with what little help she might provide, it was good to have some assistance. She was anxious to get to it. "What can I do for you?"

"Well," Eddie began, "the reason we're calling is . . . you remember that .tif file you brought in?"

"Tiff file?" Amelia asked.

"Yeah . . . the graphic file of that poem?"

"Yes," Amelia said, a little more interested now. "Sure. What about it?"

"Well," Andy said, taking the ball from Eddie. "We found out what it's from. Or *who* it's from. I mean, like, who wrote it and everything. The poem. Not the e-mail."

"Great," Amelia said. "I kind of struck out looking for it."

"Well, it turns out that we got a couple freebie CD-ROMs in the mail the next day, promo stuff. We're in the industry, so we get stuff like that all the time," Andy said, obviously trying to sound as corporate as possible.

"I see," Amelia said. She stole a glance at Maddie, who was halfway to the back of the yard, already working on a small pile of leaves with her bright red plastic rake. Amelia climbed the steps onto the deck, then stepped through the sliding glass door and inside. The reception improved a little as she entered the computer room and clicked open her Notepad program.

Handoff to Eddie. "Anyway, one of them was called *Poets: 1900–1950*, and this morning we were, well, it got a little slow up front, so we started cruising the CD-ROM and, just for laughs, we keyed in the four lines of poetry that you had and . . . *voilà*. It was there."

"Wow," Amelia said, cradling the phone to her shoulder. She sat down at the computer. "You guys are amazing."

"Thanks," one of them said. It was getting hard to distinguish. "The lines are from a poem called 'Preludes.' "

Amelia typed it in.

The other one said: "And it was written by T.S. Eliot."

"This is just great, guys," she said. "You've been very helpful."

"Right. No problem. Our pleasure. By the way . . . do you have a fax machine?"

"Yes," Amelia said.

"We could fax you a hard copy of the poem if you want. Or we could send it e-mail. Either way."

"Uh . . . okay," Amelia said. She gave them the fax number and e-mail address.

"Cool," Andy said. "We'll get right on it."

"Thanks," Amelia answered.

"Both of us," Eddie added.

Amelia hung up the phone, walked to the window, checked on Maddie. Her daughter was now pinning leaves to the fence at the back of the yard with white pushpins. It looked like a heart pattern from the house.

It was then that she remembered that she hadn't put the receipt for the LilyWorks software into the proper pocket of the accordion file that Roger had made her set aside for her home-office expenditures. She took the receipt from the bag, walked into the kitchen, poured herself some juice. She opened the cardboard file envelope, dropped in the receipt, and noticed a half dozen bright blue invoices stuffed in the household section. She pulled them out. They were sales slips from an Elsner Hardware at 5600 Euclid.

Fifty-sixth and Euclid? Why would Roger go to a hardware store at Fifty-sixth and Euclid? Wasn't it mostly abandoned warehouses around there?

She looked at the invoices. Standard items—nails, screws, washers, masking tape. But there were also three invoices for space heaters. Four hundred dollars each! Cash! Were those the heaters Roger put in the garage last year, so he could work on the cars? Amelia wondered. She'd had no idea they were that expensive. Why hadn't he charged them? She put it on the list of things to yell at him about.

She returned to the computer room. No fax yet. She dialed Paige at the store and told her that she had left her leather coat behind when she had stopped by with Maddie's sweater.

She picked up the cordless, stuck it in her sweatshirt pocket, and stepped onto the deck, just as the wind flattened the three piles of leaves she had spent the last hour raking together.

37• It seemed a bit incongruous—perhaps even illegal in some sense, although he was not a lawyer—to talk to a writer while a murder investigation was ongoing. But, he thought, all he was actually doing was providing background on three people who were already dead, so on reflection, it probably was both legal and ethical. Morbid and exploitative perhaps, but not against the law. The young man—Nicholas Stella, his name—called and arranged to meet him in front of Thwing Hall.

The voice came from behind him.

"Dr. Keller?"

He spun around, startled. "Yes. Mr. Stella?"

"Yes."

They had met before, Keller was sure of it. "You frightened me."

"Oh . . . sorry."

"Sebastian Keller," he finally said, extending his hand.

"Nick Stella."

Keller held the young man's grip for a few extra moments. "Have we met before, Mr. Stella?" he asked. "You look familiar."

"I don't think so."

They sat down on a bench, fell silent for a while. The younger man took out a pencil and pad, and Sebastian Keller knew he was finally going to tell the truth. A truth he had carried for twenty years like a deadweight. "You wouldn't happen to have a cigarette, would you?" Keller asked.

"No. Sorry."

"Funny," Keller began. "I haven't wanted one in nearly fifteen years. Now that I'm dying of cancer, it really doesn't matter, does it? A little cancer here, a little cancer there . . ." He looked at the ground, arranging his thoughts, his words, his courage.

"Tell me what happened that night," the younger man said. "Tell me in your own words."

Keller knew it was time. He began.

"It was Halloween night, 1978. . . ."

38• Amelia was at the back end of the yard, surrounded by a half dozen piles of brightly hued leaves. Beneath one of the piles lurked the allegedly invisible, yet still giggling, Madeleine Saintsbury.

"Don't get dirty," Amelia said to her daughter who wasn't there.

Maddie remained silent.

"Oh . . ." Amelia began, as she heaped more leaves on Maddie's pile, "I guess Maddie already went back inside the house. I guess I can call city hall and tell them to bring that huge vacuum cleaner back here . . . have them vacuum up all these leaves."

Leaf Girl laughed.

Amelia had the cordless telephone in the pocket of her hooded sweatshirt and had been so far out on a daydreaming voyage as she raked leaves—a bizarre escapade that included Roger, Paige, Garth, Shelley Roth, Dag and Martha Randolph, her as-yet-unwritten antihero Gaspar Sencio, and the enigmatic Mr. Curls—that the sound, emanating from somewhere on her body, nearly made her jump. It was almost an electronic whine instead of a ring, a sure sign that the batteries needed replacing. She removed the phone from the pocket, feeling a little silly, and answered. She was about a hundred fifty feet from the house and the reception was terrible. "Hello?"

Through a barrage of static, it sounded like: "Izz Miz Sainesree?" The batteries, she could tell, were going and going fast. ". . . 'lo?"

A man. Barely audible. "You'll have to speak up. I'm on a cordless and the, uh . . ."

"Sainseree?"

No better. It still sounded as if the man were speaking through a yard of cheesecloth. Sounded like a salesman. "I'm sorry . . . I can't . . . uh . . ."

Then there came another burst of static, a crack of electronic thunder beneath which Amelia could hear the man talking.

"Hang on . . . let me . . ." Amelia said as she walked toward the house and closer to the telephone's base station. Another burst of static, then she heard the line begin to clear.

". . . e-mail . . ."

"Just a minute . . . hold on. . . ." Amelia said. She was halfway to the house now and she began to pick up bits and pieces of what the man was saying, but the phone bouncing at her ear didn't help in assessing the who and what of it all.

". . . of the police . . ." the man said.

Amelia stopped in her tracks. "What? What's this about the police?" The word had come in loud and clear and it frightened her. "Hello?"

Silence.

"*Hello?*"

Nothing.

The batteries were dead.

When she stepped into the house and picked up the telephone in the kitchen, all she heard was the steady drone of a dial tone.

The doorbell rang.

Or *did* it? Amelia shut off the vacuum cleaner. She hit the switch on the side of the upright, listened for a few moments as the motor ground to silence. Molson was out back, so she didn't have the dog to tip her off as to whether or not someone had rung the bell. Ever since the phone call, the call that had mentioned the word *police*, she had been edgy, vigilant. This was the third time she had shut off the vacuum cleaner. The first two times she thought she heard the phone. She was just about to continue when the doorbell clanged, loud and resonant. She looked out the front window, at the driveway, her hand over her heart, but whoever it was must've pulled up tight against the garage. She could only see the rear bumper. She couldn't tell if it was a car, a van, a truck.

As she moved to the front door she found that her heart was beginning to race, her mind was beginning to fill with a million dark vignettes: Roger's plane had crashed, something was wrong with Maddie, something had happened to Dag or Martha or both. Fire. Plague. Pestilence. Murder. She expected to open the door and be confronted with a grim-faced man in a policeman's uniform, there to roughly remove her heart and soul, her very life.

But she opened the front door anyway, and came face-to-face with the last person on earth she would've expected to be standing on her front porch at that moment.

It was Dark Curls.

39. "Hi," he said, his face seeming to register as much shock as her own.

"Hi," Amelia replied, but made no immediate effort to open the door. Roger usually left the screen in the front storm door until after Halloween, so she and Mr. Curls weren't shouting at each other through glass. Still, their postures were about as awkward as possible, considering what they had done the last time they had been together. What was he doing here? Amelia wondered. How did he know where she lived? Had he followed her?

Did he have something to do with the phone call?

Immediately her mind went to Maddie and her whereabouts. Maddie was bundled off to Karen McGregor's. Everything was fine.

"Mrs. *Saintsbury*?" he asked.

"Yes," Amelia said before she could stop herself, although she wasn't sure why. They had made out in a parking lot already; why couldn't he know her name? This was *very* bizarre, she thought. Very unnerving. For a few moments she felt every bit the penitent adulterer.

"Mrs. *Roger* Saintsbury?"

"Yes. But how did you . . . what are you . . . ."

Dark Curls held up his hand, stopping her. He looked at the ground for a moment, as if he were processing a great deal of data at once, bringing together a few thousand pieces of a jigsaw puzzle in just a few seconds. When he looked up, fixing her with his soulful brown eyes, he told her a story. A chilling

story that seemed to have, at its center, the destruction of
everything on earth she cherished.

When he was finished, when she was once again able to
move, Amelia opened the front door to her home.

And Nicholas Stella stepped inside.

40 Sappho Nova was a drag. But it was packed and, as lesbian nightclubs go—at least the downtown clubs—the clientele was, for the most part, well dressed and generally civilized. Jennifer Schumann sat at the bar, ordered her usual. The music raged, thunderous and unrelenting. She scanned the corners of the room, saw all the usual suspects.

Jennifer had been twenty-seven years old before she had mustered the emotional courage to come out, although all of that seemed like another era altogether. With all the experimenting she had done in college, with all the flirtations during her sham live-in relationship with a man in her mid-twenties, she never really came to terms with the fact that she was probably a lesbian. Unfortunately, she had no gay friends at the time, or anyone else to talk to about it. All of her friends thought she was straight in those days, as did all of her coworkers at Blue Cross. Although it didn't surprise her that they had their suspicions. The one person she could confide in was her younger sister Greta. Unfortunately, Greta had cerebral palsy and, because the insurance had finally run out, lived in Jennifer's tiny house now. Jennifer wasn't sure that Greta had understood much of anything she had told her for years.

Still, contrary to the image the straight world had of homosexuals, Jennifer was anything but promiscuous. The fact was, at least romance-wise, that she had yet to have a relationship with a woman that lasted more than six weeks, and it had now been more than three years since she had even had a one-nighter.

Maybe that'll change tonight, she thought as she spun on

her barstool, checking out the new arrivals near the door.

And that was when she saw her. Out on the dance floor. She wore very tight black jeans and a thin yellow tank top. Her hair was pinned up in the back and as she moved to the music, her earrings, in the shape of small silver lightning bolts, slashed about her face and neck.

She had a small butterfly tattoo near her right eye.

Her name was Taffy and she had flirted with Jennifer mercilessly a few nights earlier. In the back of Jennifer's mind, she supposed there lurked the notion, the hope, that Taffy might be at Sappho Nova tonight. And there she was. Jennifer had written the previous flirtation off as the exuberance of a pretty young woman who simply didn't realize what simple conversation and the occasional touch on the leg might mean to a woman of Jennifer's age and position.

But tonight, Jennifer thought, ordering the drink she knew would put her over the edge of inebriated false confidence, if she comes over and talks to me tonight . . .

Jennifer knew it was stupid to be playing a game like this at her age, but she just couldn't stop herself. She was over forty now, more than a few pounds overweight. But she was a little drunk, she was horny as hell, and the game seemed to have taken over her body, her mind, her will.

Cat and mouse.

Kitty, kitty, kitty.

Taffy had left the club, making her departure extremely obvious to Jennifer, lingering at the door, lingering in the lobby, lingering on the street corner at West Third. She walked slowly up the now-deserted street, toward Lakeside, swinging her hips a bit drunkenly, driving Jennifer a bit mad with desire.

Then she turned down the alley, opened a rusted steel door, and stepped inside one of the warehouses. The fluorescent lights from inside the building painted a wedge of white onto the dark alleyway, and after a few moments, Jennifer followed. But by the time she did, by the time she opened the door and looked down the long, narrow paneled hallway, the girl was gone.

A little spooked, a lot aroused, Jennifer stepped inside the building, closed the door behind her, and inched forward.

She found Taffy behind the last door on the left, in an abandoned office. There was a large wooden desk in the center of the room, a few fifty-gallon drums, and a small table lamp on the floor in one corner that provided perhaps twenty-five watts of light. The girl had taken her coat off and was sitting on the desk. Her feet were up on a dusty but rather substantial-looking oak executive chair, and from the index finger of her right hand dangled a gleaming pair of handcuffs.

Without saying a word, Jennifer looked back down the hallway, toward the alley, then stepped into the room. She removed her coat, letting it slip to the floor, and crossed the office. She sat in the chair and, for a moment, scrutinized the girl's face in the dim orange light from the lamp. She was so pretty, so fresh. Did I ever look that young? Jennifer wondered.

The girl wound the cuffs through the spokes of the chair, then clicked them closed over Jennifer's wrists. She stepped back, spun Jennifer around so that she was facing the door. She unplugged the lamp. The only illumination in the office now was the slanted column of yellowish light from the hallway. "What?" Jennifer said. "What's wrong?"

The girl grabbed her coat and stepped toward the door, then waited.

After a few moments, the silhouette of a man filled the doorway, a man in a dark overcoat. He stepped inside the room, into the shadows. The young girl walked up to him, kissed him lightly on the cheek, glanced back in Jennifer's direction, then walked down the hallway, her heels clicking hard on the grimy linoleum. A few seconds later, Jennifer heard the door to the alley open and close.

They were alone.

"Hello, Jennifer," the man said.

"What's going on here? Who the hell are *you*?"

The man didn't answer, but seemed to study her for a few moments from the darkness instead. After a full minute, he reached into his pocket, retrieving, Jennifer was certain, what was to be the instrument of her death—gun, knife, straight razor, bludgeon. Instead, it turned out to be an instrument of her imminent madness.

A microcassette recorder.

The man pressed a button and placed the recorder on top of one of the fifty-gallon drums next to him. The tape began to play. *"Webster was much possessed by death and saw the skull beneath the skin,"* came the recorder, a rendition read by someone English. Jeremy Irons, Jennifer thought. *"And breastless creatures underground leaned backward in a lipless grin. . . ."*

"Got a question for you," the man said, still in shadow. "I want you to think back, now. Way back. I want you to recall a night about twenty years ago. Back when you were in college, Jenny. The others did."

"Others?" Against her will, her voice had already begun to shake.

"Yes. Friends of ours. Geoffrey Coldicott. Johnny Angelino."

The names threw a cold shudder through Jennifer. The night came fluttering back, as it had so many times before. She remembered the Halloween party . . . the people in and out of dorm rooms . . . the heroin . . . Julia Raines . . . her hands on Julia's hips . . . Julia's breasts. As much as she fought them, tears began to well in Jennifer's eyes.

"Tell me what happened that night, Jenny. Tell me in your own words."

"I'm not going to tell you a damn thing," Jennifer said, emboldened by her growing anger. "Now, take these cuffs off me."

"No."

The poem continued in the background, the sound echoing in Jennifer's head, dodging the thrumming pulse in her ears. *"The couched Brazilian jaguar compels the scampering marmoset with subtle effluence of cat. . . ."*

"Subtle effluence of cat," the man repeated. "Is that what brought you back here, Jenny? The smell of that young girl?"

"Fuck . . . your . . . *mother*."

The man laughed. "Speaking of family . . ." he said.

The microcassette recorder, which had fallen silent, hissed and popped a few times. Then a new recording started. At first, to Jennifer, it sounded like someone was recording a memo on a train. The steady click-click-click of the tracks lulled her. Then she heard a familiar voice.

"No . . . no . . . no . . ." came the recorder.

Jennifer was ten years old now, cowering in the corner after watching Greta break one of her mother's figurines, waiting for the punishment. Whenever Greta broke something, which was very often, it was Jennifer who took the punishment. It was her sister's voice on the tape.

The *tape* . . .

She heard the squeak of the bed, the pounding of the headboard against the wall. It wasn't a train after all. Jennifer closed her eyes for a moment and saw the institutional steel headboard in her sister's room, the Lalique figures rattling on the nightstand. The vitriol rose within her, hot and fluid.

"Nooooo . . ." Greta Schumann moaned. *"Nooooo."*

"Had to do a little computer work at your place today," the man said. "Your primary caregiver on duty wasn't much of a challenge, I'm afraid."

Jennifer exploded, the nausea falling away, liquidated by rage. "My *sister* . . . you cocksucker . . . my *sister* . . ."

"You didn't think about it twenty years ago, did you, Jenny?" the man screamed, now just a few inches from her face. He seemed to have crossed the room in a single step. "Twenty years ago you didn't care about family, did you? Julia and I were going to have children. Did you know that? Did you? Julia was going to experience motherhood and you fucking stole it from her. You stole it from *me*, you cunt. Now I steal everything from you. *Everything*."

He crossed the office, flipped on the overhead lights, and lifted the lid of the fifty-gallon can next to him. There, amid the deadfall of arms and legs, bent at unnatural angles, Jennifer saw the sprig of graying hair, the skinny wrist bearing the cheap watch with the big numbers on the face. She also saw something dangling from her sister's hand that looked as out of place as anything else this horror show had produced so far.

Her sister held a rosary.

Mein Greta.

"I have an idea," the man said brightly. And that's when Jennifer knew exactly who stood before her. He removed a hypodermic needle from his coat pocket. "Let's get high."

Jennifer Schumann opened her mouth to scream. But it was too late.

Somewhere, she imagined as he wrapped a tourniquet around her arm, in the vicinity of twenty years too late.

41• It had been a toss-up whether to tell her about the gory details. He decided against it for the time being. Somehow, when he looked into her eyes, he couldn't do it. The words sort of bottlenecked in his throat and he found that, when real people were involved, when real murder was involved, everything changed. This wasn't an Andrew Vachss novel. Amelia Saintsbury was flesh and blood and she had a house and a car and a husband and a daughter, and everything he rehearsed on the way over (before he knew that she was the woman from his writing class) sort of dissipated like steam from a sidewalk grate when he looked into her eyes.

Although he still couldn't find his notebook, he had remembered the name Saintsbury from the e-mail list. Not a common name. He had found it immediately in the directory. The other name, the last name on the list, wasn't so clear. Schubert. Schunemann. Something like that.

He told Amelia that he was writing a story for the *Chronicle* and that three people on the list that came with the poem had died from an overdose of heroin, and that the police were investigating.

When they had kissed that night in the school's parking lot, he had, of course, noticed the ring—and he sure as hell had no intention of dating a married woman—but she had been right there, dammit, with her schnapps and her soft lips and her little black dress and . . .

She was married.

After Nicky's initial nervous spiel, Amelia had told him about her efforts to decode the e-mail message, about the young men at Cybernauts, how the whole process had been kind of an obsession with her. Unfortunately, she, too, could not seem to put her hands on the list or the poem of late. Somehow she must have thrown it out.

Every so often, as they sat on opposing love seats, realizing how they had been pursuing the same thing, Nicholas Stella and Amelia Saintsbury shook their heads in blank wonderment.

Amelia made a few phone calls, one to her husband's voice mail, one to Karen McGregor's house, one to the two young men at Cybernauts, hoping they still had a copy of the e-mail. She got their answering machine, left a message. Within a few minutes, headlights washed the front windows of the house as Karen pulled up in her station wagon and Maddie got out.

Up the steps, through the door, in the house, safe.

Amelia felt 50 percent better already. She dead-bolted the door as Maddie wandered into the living room, dropped her jacket on the couch, and walked over to where Nicky sat.

"Hi," Maddie said.

"Hi," Nicky replied.

The two studied each other for a few moments. Maddie twirled a curl with an index finger; Nicky smoothed his hair, fixed the collar of his shirt. Finally: "My name's Nicky." He extended his hand.

"My name's Madeleine. Everybody calls me Maddie, though."

They shook hands. Nicky was more than a little charmed by the girl's forthright, businesslike manner. She had her mother's green eyes, eyes for which Italian men have tumbled for centuries. Meg's eyes. "Can *I* call you Maddie?" he asked.

"Yes," Maddie said. "It's okay. Are you a friend of my dad's?"

Nicky glanced at Amelia, who suddenly got interested in arranging the magazines on the coffee table. "Uh, well, no," Nicky said. "Not yet. I'm more a friend of your mom's. I'm in her writing class."

Maddie wrinkled her nose. "You don't write *romance* books, do you?"

Nicky laughed. "What's wrong with romance books?"

"I don't know for sure," Maddie said. "I guess they're okay."

"I write . . ." Nicky began, "I write all kinds of stuff."

"Do you like dogs?"

"Yes. I like dogs a lot, in fact," Nicky said, glancing at the huge golden retriever that was napping under the dining room table.

"That's Molson. He's kind of a sissy," Maddie added. "He runs from hummingbirds."

"Oh, he'll toughen up," Nicky said. "He looks like a big puppy to me."

"Maddie, it's time for bed," Amelia said. "Go get ready, hon."

" 'Kay," Maddie said, heading for the stairs. When she got to the foot of the steps, she turned and added, " 'Bye, Nicky."

" 'Bye, Maddie. Sleep good."

With what looked a little like a blush—was her little girl flirting? Amelia wondered—Maddie raced up the stairs.

"She's a doll," Nicky said.

"Thanks," Amelia said. She sat down on the love seat, across from Nicky, then immediately sprang back up. "My husband should've called back by now."

Amelia crossed the room, picked up the phone, replaced it.

"I'm sure he'll call soon. I'm sure everything's okay," Nicky said, rising to his feet. He edged toward the front door. "I really didn't mean to freak you out."

"It's okay," Amelia said. She walked Nicky to the front door, tried to strike a casual pose against the jamb. She failed. "We'll be okay."

"Before I leave, though, I need a favor," Nicky said.

"What's that?"

"Does your husband have any yearbooks from Case Western Reserve?"

"I think so," Amelia said. "Let me look." She returned in a few moments.

"This is the only year he has," she said, holding up an embossed 1977 CWRU yearbook. "But there's two of them for some reason."

"Would it be okay if I borrowed it?"

"Sure," Amelia said, handing it to him. "But why do you need it?"

"Background stuff." Nicky opened the door. Still no G-men. "Thanks."

"You're welcome."

Nicky was halfway through the door. He turned, studied her for a moment, and said, "About the other night . . ."

"Yeah?" Amelia said. She felt she might be nervous if the subject came up. She was right. "What about it?"

"I realize now that it isn't going to happen, okay?" Nicky said.

"Okay . . ."

"But I just want you to know that, at least for a few days, thinking that it might happen was, well, really wonderful." Nicky stepped onto the porch.

Amelia began to color, fought it. "Thanks, Nicky."

"You'll be okay?"

"Yes, I'm fine," Amelia said. "But what about you? You going to tell me what happened to your face?"

"Little disagreement over a past-due account," Nicky said. He reached out, touched her hand gently. When she turned her hand over, he placed his business card in it. "If you need anything, or if you want to talk about this, call me. Okay?"

Amelia nodded.

A minute later, as Nicky turned onto Falls Road, a dark blue van made the turn behind him, then kept a safe distance as the two vehicles headed north, into the darkness of the MetroPark.

42 He couldn't stop thinking about her. Amelia. He even liked her name. Sounded so . . . Jane Austen or something.

Nicky stood in his boxer shorts, looked out the front window of his apartment, through the small Palladian window right under the peak of the gable, and pondered the very strange scenario that was his life of late. In the past few days he had been punched out by a gypsy, threatened with a gun, suspected—albeit briefly—of the murder of a Chinese drug dealer. And he'd gotten a crush on a married woman whose husband was involved in a bizarre murder plot that seemed to stretch back twenty years, to the Case Western Reserve University campus of 1978, a plot that somehow included his cousin Joseph's old friend Johnny Angel.

The strange, frightening part of it all, Nicky thought, was that the one thing that seemed to be at the center of it all, the one cog in the wheel that allowed this bizarre juggernaut to roll, was him.

Okay. How had he come to join the writer's class where he met Amelia? When had he started getting those flyers for the class out in Collier Falls? Hadn't he got a dozen or so in just a few months? Had somebody *wanted* him to join the class?

Nicky walked over to the TV, grabbed the remote, flipped it on, fell into his big recliner. He cruised the channels: exercise equipment, *Gilligan*, a southern preacher asking for money, Al Sharpton bitching about something, more exercise equipment, the C-SPAN bus. He stopped at a local station. It was a news wrap-up.

"*. . . of our top stories. Once again, NewsFinder Five has*

*learned that the FBI may have uncovered new evidence in the
recent death of Father John Angelino of the St. Francis of
Assisi parish on the city's east side. You'll recall that Father
Angelino's body was found in an apartment on Cedar Road,
apparently the victim of an accidental heroin overdose, but
police have since learned that there may have been foul play.
Although FBI spokesmen would neither confirm or deny it, our
sources tell us that they are now treating it as a homicide,
and that this may not be an isolated incident. Stay tuned to
Channel Five for more details as they develop. . . . "*

Nicky sprinted to the phone and put in a call to Kral, who
was out. He left a message with the desk sergeant.

As he took off his shorts and started the shower, he found
that he was shaking a bit. He was on the cutting edge of one
of the biggest stories of the year. This could easily make the
national magazines. Even a movie of the week. He had an in
with the cops. He had an in with Amelia. Which he hoped
would mean an in with her husband.

And the answer, he thought as he stepped into the hot, pulsating stream of water, was in that yearbook.

It had to be.

After his shower he dried himself, checked his messages,
slipped into black sweatpants and sweatshirt. He sat at his
desk, opened the CWRU yearbook, and was instantly dragged
down a long corridor of memory, courtesy of the hairstyles,
the clothing, the outlandish fads of the era. He had been a
teenager himself then and he remembered well the wide lapels,
skinny ties, long-collared shirts, fluffy hair, tinted shades. And,
of course, the ubiquitous white three-piece knockoffs of the
suit Travolta wore in *Saturday Night Fever.*

He riffled some more pages and came to a page devoted to
something called *Poetica '78.* It appeared to be a poetry fes-
tival that was held in Clark Hall, the building that housed the
English Department. The photograph showed a group of
maybe twenty students, standing on the steps of the building,
loosely posed for the photograph. Nicky immediately recognized the tall, bony student in front, the guy with the barber-

college haircut and protruding ears. It was Geoffrey Coldicott.
His mind flashed on the skinless death mask he had seen in
Geoffrey's apartment. Next to Geoffrey—in fact, with his arm
on Geoffrey's shoulder—was John Angelino.

Nicky searched the sea of faces, looking for somebody,
something. His eyes were soon drawn to the back row where
he saw a dark-haired young man leaning against a sandstone
pillar, smiling, his arm very tentatively around a beautiful
young woman. Nicky thought he looked a little familiar, but
couldn't place him. Was it Bennett Crane? He flipped through
the seniors and found Ben Crane, confirming the fact that he
was *not* the man by the pillar.

Nicky was just about to give up when he spotted the young
man from the steps. Page 154, lower right. G. Daniel Woltz.
Next to the picture was printed *Computer Club, Poetry Club,
Audiovisual Club*. G. Daniel was slender, had dark eyes, dark
hair swept over his forehead in the standard collegiate cut.

Nicky moved on, flipping the pages into the freshman section, and saw the young woman around whom G. Daniel had
his arm; a beautiful girl who caught Nicky's breath for a moment. Julia Ann Raines was her name. Soft hair, delicate features, innocent eyes. What struck him most, what drew his eye
to the photo to begin with, besides the girl's beauty, was the
fact that Julia Ann Raines had signed her small picture in the
freshman section. Beneath her photo, in a tiny but well-
calligraphed hand, she had written, simply:

Oh do not ask what is it, let us go and make our visit!

Nicky recognized it. T.S. Eliot, from "The Lovesong of J.
Alfred Prufrock."

More friggin' poetry.

He had an Eliot anthology somewhere, he'd have to scan
it. He then tried to remember the e-mail addresses from the
disk. He could only recall one, probably because it just didn't
seem to fit the man. Geoffrey Coldicott: hardman@ttk.net.

Nicky clicked open his communications program, dialed
into the Net. After checking his e-mail and finding nothing,
he opened his UseNet program. UseNet was the Internet's version of a worldwide collection of bulletin boards, with nearly

twenty thousand boards devoted to every imaginable subject. Most were rather benign, pruriently speaking, but with the advent of digitized graphics, it didn't take the Net long to discover that one could post binary files of photographs and illustrations that could be downloaded, decoded, and viewed on computers worldwide.

He started a keyword search of *hardman@ttk.net* and hit Enter. Theoretically, if Geoffrey Coldicott had recently posted something to a news group, under his own name, this search should yield the whereabouts of those files. Nicky knew it was a long shot, but within seconds, the search found something.

As he looked at the screen, Nicky's heart stammered. He had to read it three times before it would sink in.

There was an upload from Geoffrey Coldicott.

The address of the uploader was *hardman@ttk.net*, and it was cross-posted to a few groups: alt.sex.male, alt.-binaries.exhibitionism, alt.binaries.voyeurism. Nicky looked at the time of the upload. Five thirty-four P.M. on the day of Geoffrey's murder.

The file was uploaded at the moment of Geoffrey Coldicott's death.

As he downloaded the photographs of Geoffrey Coldicott, as the graphics revealed themselves on his screen, slowly, from top to bottom, Nicky found that he was holding his breath. He could see that it was a number of pictures, a series of color shots arranged like a contact sheet. The five photographs were all of Geoffrey Coldicott sitting in a chair, his dinette chair—the chair Nicky had just occupied himself while being questioned by the cops. The main difference, of course, was that Geoffrey was naked.

He remembered seeing Geoffrey's face, briefly, through the storefront at the Arcade, but now his face was a tortured canvas of pain and humiliation.

The person who had taken these pictures was probably the person who had killed him, Nicky thought.

And that person, Nicky could see as he looked a little more closely at one of the photos, the one in the upper right-hand corner of the screen, was reflected in the mirror over Geoffrey's mantel.

Nicky enlarged the section of the photograph that held the mirror, found that he was right. You could clearly see that it was a man, and that he was taking Geoffrey's picture. He hit the Enter button again and doubled the size of the enlargement. Now he could see more of the man's face and shoulders. The man had dark hair and wore a gold watch. But beyond that, he couldn't make out much.

He closed his laptop, grabbed the yearbook and his keys, and headed for the back steps. On the way he stopped at his bookshelf and found the T.S. Eliot anthology, brought that, too.

There was no coffee or cigarettes in the house and there was no way he could do any of this without them. He would catch a pack and a few cups on the way down to the Justice Center, figuring that there would definitely be someone downtown who could improve the quality of the digital image of Geoffrey and his visitor.

This was no career-making article, Nicky thought, beside himself with excitement.

This was a career-making *book*.

It had started to rain, but Nicky couldn't be bothered to run back upstairs for a raincoat. He sprinted to the car, started it, and drove to Denny's.

On the inside back cover of Roger Saintsbury's yearbook, on the fancy green endpaper, were a dozen or so signatures, accompanied by the standard yearbook repartee. There was an inscription from John Angelino. "May God smile on your every endeavor," it read, portending, perhaps, Father John's life in the clergy. There were more than a few from women, mostly suggestive. At the bottom left, written in a precise block style, was an inscription from a "GD." G. Daniel? Nicky wondered. The inscription read: "Remember, always, the infinitely suffering things."

The *poem*.

He opened the T.S. Eliot book to the appendix, found the
section that listed the contents in reference to opening lines.
There was no poem that began with "I am moved by fancies . . ."

He flipped through the pages of the book of poetry, and
when he turned to the page bearing the poem "Preludes," he
didn't have to scan at all to find what he was looking for. The
passage was right there, halfway down the page. "*I am moved
by fancies that are curled around these images, and
cling. . . .*" it read. But what was more remarkable than the
fact that he had managed to find it so quickly was another,
now indelible image.

The passage was circled.

What?

When the hell had he done that? Hadn't he bought the book
new? He didn't know the answer to either question, but the
evidence was right in front of his eyes. The same four lines
of poetry that had been sent to these people—these *dead* people, he reminded himself—was circled in a book he owned.

In the nick of time, he lowered the lid of his laptop as his
waitress approached him with her coffee pot held high. That's
all I need, Nicky thought, to have some waitress catch me
looking at naked guys on my laptop at Denny's.

She poured, oblivious, smiled, left.

Nicky looked back at the photo, at the face in the mirror.
The man's dark hair was parted on the left. He held up the
various yearbook photos of the people involved. G. Daniel was
almost a perfect match to the man in the mirror. The hairline
had receded, but as he held the yearbook photo up to the
laptop, as he placed the paper over the bright screen, he found
that the images were about the same size, the basic shape of
the two faces was identical.

Nicky shot to his feet, dropped a dollar on the table, paid
his tab at the register by the door. He decided to stop home
and make a copy of the Geoffrey Coldicott photos on a floppy
disk. He didn't want to risk a hard drive crash and lose everything. He also had a pretty good idea that the cops would want
the whole laptop, anyway.

But for the second time in two days, when he turned onto Normandy Road he saw something odd. It immediately reminded him of the time he saw The Electric Light Orchestra at the old Allen Theater on Euclid Avenue—blue and red swirls, a gouache of violet in the crooked rain-rivers that streaked the windshield. He slammed on the brakes and counted.

There were a half dozen police cars around his house.

43 What a night, Amelia thought. What a crazy, scary night. And it wasn't even Halloween yet. Although a quick glance at the bedside clock proved her wrong. It was now twelve-thirty.

Regardless, she hadn't been able to sleep a wink.

Roger had called back and put her mind somewhat at ease. He recalled all the people on the list, made a few excuses for their lifestyle, but also added that he was not surprised that they were still doing hard drugs. He also said he'd be home in time to trick-or-treat with Maddie, and that he'd meet them at Dag and Martha's. That, Amelia thought, in light of the evening's rather spooky turn, was the best news of all.

She got up, checked on Maddie for what had to have been the twentieth time, found her sleeping, dreaming, perhaps, of Snickers bars and Mallo cups and Twizzler strawberry licorice.

She sat down at her computer and dialed into World Online. And, for the second time in her life, she heard the cheerful cyber-voice say: "You've got mail!"

This time she didn't jump. She was getting good at this. She clicked the appropriate buttons and found that it was mail from the Cybernauts, Eddie and Andy. She had forgotten that they had promised to send her the poem they had found on their CD-ROM. What they hadn't told her was that they were going to send her the complete poetical works of T.S. Eliot.

The file was huge and took a few minutes to download, but once it arrived and Amelia began to read the poetry, she found herself moved, astounded, confused. She read "The Lovesong of J. Alfred Prufrock," something she had heard about for years, but never had actually read. She read the poems about cats.

But the poem that frightened her was one called "Whispers of Immortality." There were lines about mutilation, it seemed. Something about replacing someone's eyes with daffodil bulbs, something about lipless grins. She didn't finish that one. She didn't need to be any more spooked than she was.

She printed out some of the file, made a pot of tea, took them both to the bedroom, got under the comforter, and began to read.

44. Nicky turned around in Joe Metzger's driveway, five houses north of his own, and hightailed it back to Chagrin. What the hell was *this* about? The fact that he had seen at least three guns drawn meant it was no social call.

They were there to *arrest* him.

They were ready to *shoot* him.

He drove downtown in a fog, checked into the Holiday Inn Lakeside, under the name Louie Starr. He used sixty-five dollars from the roll he had acquired courtesy of Frank Corso.

He hadn't officially run from the police, had he? It's not like any of them had seen him and told him to stop. He simply hadn't gotten home yet.

Right?

As he rode the elevator he felt like a child making up excuses as to why the basement window was lying in a dozen pieces. This was serious business. Nobody was going to buy that shit. And his roiling stomach confirmed it.

He checked into his room, then took the stairs back down, exited a side door. He drove across the bridge, where he parked near a pay phone, across from St. Malachi's. He dialed his home phone number, feeling certain that there would be some kind of message from the police. Instead, on the third ring, someone answered.

It was Kral. And Nicky's silence gave him away. "Nicky?" Kral said. "Nicky . . . listen to me. You've got to come in. Hear me?"

"I don't . . . Are you going to tell me what this is about?"

"We'll talk about it when you come in."

"I-I thought the Rat Boy thing had been settled. I thought you believed me."

"This isn't about Rat Boy, Nicky. Just drive to the Justice Center now, walk in the front door like a man. We'll talk. Every second that goes by, the fucking hole gets deeper for you. Don't you realize that?"

"But I swear to God I don't—"

"Sebastian Keller, Nicky."

"Who?"

"We just found his body in the Art Museum lagoon."

"But I don't—"

"Where's his fucking hands, Nicky?"

Nicky's stomach did a pirouette. He was speechless with horror.

"What did you do with his goddamn *hands*, you sick fuck?"

"I swear to God I—"

"Your name is on his appointment calendar," Kral continued. "His secretary remembers the call."

Nicky's mind reeled. "I don't even—"

"Come on, Nicky. Who the fuck do you think you're dealing with?" Kral said, his voice picking up volume. "The office has Caller ID. We checked."

"What do you mean, checked? Checked what?"

"The call came from your apartment."

"What?" Nicky screamed, loud enough for the parking lot attendant across the street to raise his eyes from his paper for a moment.

"On the other hand, *don't* come in," Kral said. "Let me find you, Nicky. Okay? Do me a favor. Let me find you, and when you see me, I want you to make a move."

"What are you—"

"I want you to make a move for your pocket. Okay? Because you know what's in there, Nicky? Do you know what's in that pocket? I'll tell you. It's the twenty-five-caliber semi-automatic pistol I have in my hand right now. I've carried it for ten years, just waiting for the right piece of shit. You qualify. You hear me?" Ivan Kral began to scream. He sounded unhinged. "You made a *fucking asshole out of me, Nicky.*"

"I . . . I can't hear you," Nicky began as he tore out a few pages from the telephone book, put them near the mouth of the phone, and began to crumple them. Old trick. Sounded like static at the other end. Kral, he knew, wouldn't buy it. But he couldn't think of anything else to do at the moment.

They had not had time to trace the call, he thought, as long as real technology had not exceeded what he saw in the movies. Besides, that's why he had driven over the bridge to make the call in the first place. But just to be on the safe side, he reached into a tiny patch of mud that bordered the parking lot and smeared it over his rear license plate.

The man in the yearbook picture. He had to find him.

And there was only one place to begin.

After only two rings, Amelia answered. She sounded wide-awake. It also sounded like she was on a cordless phone.

"Hello?"

"Amelia, it's Nicky."

"Hi. Are you—"

"Listen," Nicky began, not knowing how much he should say on the phone. He had checked the phone book, found no listings for Woltz. He continued. "You have a World Online account, right?"

"Yes. It's my husband's account, but I've—"

"Do you know your way around it?"

"Well, somewhat. In fact, I was just on-line a little while ago."

"Great," Nicky said. "Do you know about the chat rooms there?"

"Kind of. Although I've never actually—"

"Do you remember our teacher's name?"

"Our teacher?"

"Our writing teacher."

"Oh . . . yes, sure." It was Mr. Price he was talking about, Amelia thought. "It was—"

"I'll name the chat room after him and I'll be there in ten minutes. Have that other yearbook with you."

Mac listened in with his scanner. Amelia was on the cordless.

He heard chat rooms. He heard ten minutes. He heard *yearbook*.

This was not good.

He jacked the cellular modem into his laptop and dialed into World Online.

In room 616 of the Holiday Inn Lakeside, Nicky plugged his laptop into the wall jack, dialed World Online, created the chat room—PriceIsRight, he called it—and waited. Within a few minutes Amelia confirmed what he had suspected. She was very sharp. The screen showed:

RAS has entered the room.

"RAS" must have been her husband's default on-line nickname at World Online. STARR99 was Nicky's.

    STARR99>   Hi. U there?

He waited a few seconds. Nothing. He typed:

    STARR99>   Type your response . . . then
                    hit Enter.
    RAS>   I'n here . . .
    RAS>   I'm, I mean . . . sorry
    STARR99>   Have the yearbook?
    RAS>   Yes. But are you going to
                    tell me what this is all
                    about?
    STARR99>   I will. I promise. Go to page
                    154.
    RAS>   Promise?
    STARR99>   Yes. 154.
    RAS>   Okay. hangf on.
    RAS>   hang
    RAS>   Okay. I'm there now.

| STARR99> | Do you know the guy in the bottom row, second from the right? |
| RAS> | No. G. Daniel? No. |

At that moment Nicky decided he would tell Amelia the whole truth. Everything. Because, he thought, if the police thought *he* was guilty of these killings, it meant they weren't looking for the real killer. And that meant that Amelia might be in danger.

He couldn't risk talking about it on the phone, but the chat room was safe, he imagined. He glanced at the upper right corner of the screen, the corner that lists who is in the room. RAS and STARR99. It was safe to talk here.

But before he could even begin to type, there came two system messages in succession. Standard messages for chat rooms, but two messages that troubled Nicky.

| RAS> | has left the room. |
| PRUFROCK> | has entered the room. |

This can't be a coincidence, Nicky thought. Plus, he knew that you can't change nicknames on the fly on World Online. You had to log off. He reached out.

| STARR99> | Hi pruf |

It was a standard chat-room greeting. Nicky waited a full minute. Nothing. No response. Nicky glanced at the upper right-hand corner of the screen again and saw their two nicknames. RAS was definitely gone. PRUFROCK was still in the room.

Then, with two words, the intruder responded:

PRUFROCK>	Walk away.
STARR99>	What do you mean?
PRUFROCK>	Walk away.

STARR99>	I'm not sure I know what you mean. Walk away from what?
PRUFROCK>	Walk away. Speak to no police officers. Not one.
STARR99>	Police?
PRUFROCK>	Or I will hurt you every day for the rest of your life.
STARR99>	Who is this???
PRUFROCK>	Okay. Then *I'll* go. Maybe I'll send you a postcard.
STARR99>	A postcard?
PRUFROCK>	I can mail it at any time. Remember that.
STARR99>	A postcard from where?

There was a pause of nearly thirty seconds before Nicky saw a response.

PRUFROCK>	The front of the card will show a brilliant blue sky, a red brick building, green trees.
PRUFROCK>	And at the top . . .
PRUFROCK>	In festive yellow . . .
PRUFROCK>	Greetings from Villa Corelli.
PRUFROCK>	Walk away, Nick.

By the time Nicky reached 105th Street he was driving nearly seventy miles an hour.

Jimmy Corelli's face changed completely when Nicky put the ten one-hundred-dollar bills on the desk. In fact, his entire body suddenly assumed the posture of a friendly, drunken uncle, in spite of the fact that he had not five seconds earlier threatened to throw Nicky bodily into the street. Jimmy was the youngest of the brothers and still maintained a suite on the top floor of Villa Corelli, was still point man for any problems that would occur at the home. Nicky knew that if he made enough noise at the front desk, he would get Jimmy out of bed. He also knew what the sight of the cash would do to Jimmy Corelli's demeanor. Jimmy could mess around with his grandfather's account and the grand would never show up in the Corelli Brothers, Inc., ledger.

The money disappeared from the desk in a motion almost too quick for the human eye to scan.

Jimmy Corelli, clad in a ridiculous bright red paisley ki-mono and eel-skin slippers, then picked up the receiver from one of the three phones on the desk and punched a few num-bers, gleefully throwing his considerable bulk around in the middle of the night, setting Nicky's plan in motion.

After Nicky watched them wheel his grandfather's bed onto the elevator and then down the second-floor hallway, he found an empty room, where he flipped on the TV, scanned the chan-nels. No all-points bulletin on him yet. No shots of his high-school senior picture. He turned off the TV and walked to the orderlies' station at the end of the hall, where he found his first talisman of good luck. Sandy McCall was black, in his late twenties, lean and muscular. And, best of all, he was on duty. He and Nicky had spent more than a few nights in the basement at Villa Corelli, playing poker with the other order-lies, swigging Kentucky bourbon. Sandy McCall made sure that Louie Stella always had plenty of blankets, plenty of ice water.

"Sandy . . . mah man."

"Nicky!" Sandy offered in a loud whisper; his trained, in-stitutional, late-night voice.

"How's everything?"

"You got it," Sandy said. "What's goin' on, Nicky? What you doin' here in the wee hours? Louie all right?"

"Yeah, he's fine. But I need a favor from you," Nicky replied, slipping a hundred-dollar bill into Sandy's palm as they shook hands. "Big time."

Sandy looked up and down the hallway, then glanced at his hand. He thrust the bill into his pocket. "Lay it out, man."

Twenty minutes later, as Nicky drove back into town in Sandy's Olds 88, Sandy McCall slid a fresh nameplate into the door of room 220, Louie Stella's new digs at Villa Corelli.

The nameplate read: Henry K. Piunno.

She came around the corner at six-fifteen, her makeup still in place. She looked like a Kabuki actress in a miniskirt, leather jacket, and high heels. In the morning light, Nicky could see that the butterfly tattoo near her right eye was a vibrant yellow.

Gumball colors, Nicky thought, crazily. Her skirt was red, her jacket a royal blue. She was very young and she was partial to gumball colors.

Nicky, on the other hand, realized that when he stepped in front of her on the corner of St. Clair and East Thirtieth Street, he must have looked like a wino—two-day beard, a big purple bruise where Frank Corso had punched him. Mickey Rourke in *Barfly*.

But something registered in the girl's eyes when she looked into his. Something that said "I know who you are, I know what this is about, I had a feeling I would see you soon." All of that in a single second.

Still, they played the street games as they knew them.

"Hi," Nicky said. "Could I—"

"Get lost, asshole. It's late."

She skirted him, kept walking up St. Clair. He drew up to her right side.

"Actually, it's really early," Nicky said, trying, and failing, to float some charm.

Taffy stopped, grimaced. "Wow. Haven't heard that one in about nine seconds. You think you're the first to come up with that?"

Nicky had to suppress a laugh. "You think you're the first woman to call me an asshole?"

A half smile. Partial victory.

"I bet I'm not," Taffy said.

"But I bet I'm the most *desperate* asshole to come up with that line, all things considered."

And consider him, Taffy did. But only for a few seconds

before her resolve, and ice, broke. "Oh yeah? You're in big trouble, then? A desperado of some sort?"

"You don't know who I am, do you?"

She stopped, looked him up and down. "Okay . . . you look familiar. That's the only reason I'm talking to you. Maybe we've met before. If you had roughed me up, I'd remember. So that puts you in the safe-guy category."

"Gee, thanks," Nicky said.

"But only temporarily."

"I see," Nicky replied. "Like purgatory?"

She smiled at him. "You're a Catholic? Me too."

Nicky nodded.

Then told her the whole story.

"You've got to help me."

"Why? Why do I have to help you?"

They were sitting at a booth at the McDonald's near Fourteenth Street. Nicky had scanned the morning's *Plain Dealer* and was pleased to see that his picture wasn't displayed prominently anywhere inside.

Within ten minutes of sitting down he had heard Taffy's whole life story. Her father was a long-haul trucker who took a permanent run to the coast when she was three. Mom was a boozer, slept around the entire corporation limit of East McKeesport, Pennsylvania. She said she met a man named Jimmy Woo at the bus station on Chester. Jimmy and his family owned Elegant Linda's. She said the cops had talked to her after Rat Boy had turned up dead, asked if anyone had owed him a large sum of money, or if anybody had asked about him lately. They showed her pictures and she had picked out Nicky. No reason to lie.

But she had no idea where the trail led from there.

"Someone is setting me up here, Taffy. You can see that, right? Someone who is willing to get to my grandfather, just to make a point. And it somehow began with me trying to interview Rat Boy. I've been thinking all along I was working a story. I think the story's been working me."

"Yeah," Taffy began, "but that doesn't exactly answer the 'why me' end of things."

Nicky shifted gears. "Look, you know Willie T, don't you? Black, forties, narcotics cop."

"Yeah," Taffy said. "I know him. Everybody in my business knows Willie T."

"Well, all I want you to do is call him for me. Tell him I want to come in, but I'm not going to turn myself in to Kral. He wants to fucking kill me right now."

"Don't know Kral, don't wanna know him," Taffy said. "But I still don't understand why you don't call Willie yourself."

"Because they tape everything, Taffy. If I call him, I'll be on tape for the rest of my life. Things like that have a nasty way of turning into evidence. Plus, I need a little time. And I don't need to be looking over my shoulder while I try to clear myself."

Taffy thought about it, seemed to understand. "Okay, then. If I call Willie T for you, what's in it for me?" She looked at him as if he were having a garage sale and she was trying to negotiate over a stack of used dinnerware. He hauled out the last smile in his arsenal, hoping there wasn't a piece of McMuffin hanging from his teeth. Either this one worked or he was fucked.

"A hundred bucks. And you'll be a big part of the book I'm going to write about this."

Taffy studied him for a full minute, the word "Hollywood" seeming to pass through her mind, slowly, like a banner trailing a small plane. "You want me to call him now?"

"No," Nicky said, relieved. "But soon. There's a few things I have to do first that I'm not going to be able to do with handcuffs on."

"Like what?" Taffy asked.

"Like find the guy in the yearbook."

Taffy held up the 1977 CWRU yearbook. "He's in this?"

"Yeah," Nicky replied. He took the book from her, riffled some pages, found page 154. He spun the book on the table, pointed to the small picture of G. Daniel Woltz.

Taffy's face drained of all color. Her skin turned an ashen gray. "*This* is the guy you're talking about?"

"Yes."

"Oh my God."

six

Halloween

45. He was on the second floor when he heard the noise.

It was the front door. A key, the sound of the hinge, hard soles on the quarry tile of the foyer. A woman's step, light and purposeful. He had tuned in to her cordless phone conversations from the corner of Bendemeer Lane and Sharpe Road, and what he had heard was that Amelia had had a full morning. She had put Maddie on the bus at seven-forty, then had left the house herself at five past nine. She had said on the phone that she would not be back until eleven, and he had been counting on this two-hour window of opportunity to do what he needed to do.

But now it seemed she was back. And he wasn't nearly ready for her.

If she did not come upstairs, he might be able to pull it off. If she did, and she saw the pile of objects on the bed, he would kill her. He would kill her, bury her, and move on with his day.

And Taffy would take her place at the party.

It was just outside the powder blue bathroom on the second floor that he took the chloroformed rag out of the zippered plastic bag and put it over her nose and mouth, held it there tightly. She struggled for a few moments, thrashing her body against him, filling him with an urge he did not have time to salve. Not at the moment, anyway. Not here.

Then her body fell limp in his arms.

He picked her up, brought her downstairs, and crossed the kitchen. He laid her body by the door to the garage. A short while later, he backed the van into the garage and closed the door behind him. No one would see him loading his cargo: the woman and all the props they would need later that night.

She didn't stir until forty-five minutes later.

But by then, they were already deep into the woods.

When he depressed the plunger on the hypodermic needle, releasing the cloudy liquid mixed with blood into her system, her eyelids fluttered once, twice, then slowly floated shut, her head now drifting downward with the debilitating rush of the heroin speeding through her veins. From where she stood— tied at the feet, waist, and neck, propped against a maple tree—it was nearly three hundred feet to the road, and even the loudest, most blood-chilling scream, were she capable of such a noise, would not be heard by any human being. Faintly, ever so faintly, one could hear the occasional passing of a car on Sperry Road.

In spite of the slight chill in the air, he removed his shirt.

And for the first time in days, felt as if he could fly, as if he could smell the worms boring through the earth beneath the sod, luxuriating in the flesh, fur, and faeces.

A fine thread of spittle trailed out of the corner of her mouth, coming to rest in a small puddle on the top of her right breast.

He stepped very close.

"So . . . tell me . . . is Maddie going to be Pocahontas for Halloween again this year?"

Silence. He thought for the moment that he had given her a fatal dose, but when he lifted an eyelid he saw movement. He checked her pulse. Steady, slow.

He placed his hand beneath her chin, lifted her head.

"What time does she get out of school?"

The question seemed to energize her for a moment, allowing her to crawl through the haze that had descended over her world. She struggled against the ropes.

"Oh, you don't have to answer. It was a trick question. The Montgomery School on Fairmount. Her last class lets out at three-ten and then she takes the three-fifty bus. Today she's

wearing an orange ribbon in her hair. Today she'll have some
kind of construction-paper cutout pumpkin with her when she
gets off the bus. Or maybe she'll have one of those black cats
with its back arched high.'' He stepped away, examined the
blade of the scalpel for a moment, holding it up to the morning
sunlight. "Which cat do you think it will be?'' he continued.
"Mungojerrie? Griddlebone? Skimbleshanks? Gus?''

He reached out, unbuttoned her jacket.

"Well,'' he said. "I'll tell you who'll be *watching* little
Madeleine today. Macavity. That's who.'' He turned and ran
the scalpel, slowly, over the front of her blouse, popping the
buttons, one by one. "And what time is trick-or-treating tonight? Six? Six-thirty? Let's see. Will you head up Edgefield
Road toward Huron? Or will you go the other way, towards
Meadowood Road?''

He popped the last button and, in one expert motion, ran
the blade back up, slitting her bra. The front of her clothing
fell open. He stepped back, admired her for a few moments,
then turned his back to her and looked skyward, extending his
arms straight out to his sides, flexing his muscles. He faced
her again. Through the thin ocher mist of the drug, in the
morning sunlight, he hoped she could see the tattoo that
stretched across his chest, the finely etched outline of a hawk.

He studied her for a while, then began to spin in a circle,
slowly at first, then faster, faster, churning leaves and rich,
black earth, a dervish of muscle and flesh and sinew in front
of her.

Another line of heroin in her arm. Time and matter evaporated
with the rush.

Naked now. Hot. Still standing, still tied. A waft of cinnamon-
sweet breath against her face . . . then he was inside her . . .
but only for a moment . . . then more of his hypnotic voice . . .
the poetry . . . behind her now . . . the crunch of leaves and
branches . . . his warm saliva . . . and then he was inside her
again.

Hard. Angry. Big.

But painless . . .

Soon after, a pinch at the side of her neck. A paper-cut feeling, but deeper, followed by the icy rush of wind on her throat, the magma of her being running thick between her breasts, over her womb, her legs, down to the damp, disapproving earth. . . .

And as the last of the loam and leaves were tamped on her grave, as she lay motionless, deep in the putrefaction of Mina Coldicott's frigid, eternal embrace, the earth, as once promised, accepted her fully.

46• They spent the day at Taffy's apartment on Hampshire, a two-room efficiency a few blocks from Coventry Village, Cleveland's bohemian answer to Greenwich Village. Her apartment was not that much smaller than Nicky's third floor, but he found himself thinking: She's nineteen or so. I'm pushing forty. What's wrong with this picture?

But the decor was secondary to what Taffy Kilbane was going through. Taffy had cried for three hours straight. Two packs of cigarettes, four boxes of tissue. Three . . . continuous . . . hours.

She was only sobbing slightly when she told Nicky about the guy who called himself Mac, the guy she said was a ringer for G. Daniel. She told him how they met and how Mac had told her he was from a small Ohio town called Fostoria, and that Rat Boy Choi and this woman had taken him for a lot of money. All she did was make a call. All she did was lure this woman to a deserted office. Mac had said no rough stuff.

More tissue.

Nicky began to pace the small apartment. He picked up Taffy's cordless phone, called Amelia's number, got the machine, hung up. He called his own number, but this time no one answered. There were no messages either. He dialed a third number.

"Villa Corelli," the switchboard operator said.

"Second-floor station please."

"Lemme tell you 'bout Louie," the black voice said. "Fuckin' Louie wakes up this morning, looks around the room like he on fuckin' *Mars*, man.'' The black man laughed. ''I mean, we moved alla his shit, put it right where it go. All the rooms look *exactly* the same, but still he knew. Unnerstand 'm sayin'? He *knew*. Muhfuh's *sharp*, man. Don't let that old-man shit fool ya.''

Mac sat at the corner of Hampshire and Coventry. The signal from Taffy's cordless phone was weak, but his scanner was very sensitive. He had been able to pick up Amelia's conversations from almost a quarter mile away that morning, and now he listened to Nicky talk to the orderly at Villa Corelli.

''But everybody who needs to know already knows, right?'' Nicky said. ''I mean, Louie isn't gonna get Hank's medicine, is he?''

''You took care of Sandy McCall, Nicky. Everything's cool in two-two-oh.''

''So I don't have to worry?''

'' 'Bout nothin' at all, man,'' Sandy McCall said. '' 'Bout nothin' at all.''

At three-thirty Taffy walked up to Tommy's on Coventry and sprang for lunch—French onion soup and falafel. Nicky wolfed down the food, his Italian appetite overruling his nervous stomach. Taffy picked at her sandwich, lit another cigarette.

''It all makes sense now,'' Taffy said. ''All of it.''

''What does?'' Nicky said.

''The fucking dorm room, all the seventies stuff. This guy is stuck in 1978.''

''You say it was definitely a dorm room?''

''Definitely. The furniture, the books, the posters. None of the albums were any newer than 1978. And he called me Julia.''

''Jesus. This has something to do with the girl on the steps. Julia Ann Raines.'' Nicky flipped to Julia Raines's picture, showed it to Taffy. She shook her head, shrugged.

''But . . after twenty years, though?'' Taffy asked.

"Hey," Nicky said. "The heart has no statute of limitations."

Then the phone rang. Taffy answered.

Nicky took the opportunity to look around the small apartment—junk-store lamps with gauzy scarves draped over them, apple-crate end tables, hard-rock posters on the walls. At least I've got some real furniture, he thought, although it supplied only a morsel of solace.

"Hi," she said. "Uh-huh, yeah . . ."

Nicky looked at her bookshelves. Stephen King. Dean Koontz. Peter Straub. Scary stuff, he thought. But it's so different when it's real, isn't it?

"What time tonight?" Taffy asked.

Then Nicky realized something was moving in the room. Flailing, like a pink pennant in the breeze. Then a bright blue fuzzy slipper hit him in the head.

He looked at Taffy. She was desperately trying to get his attention. She pointed to the phone and mouthed the words "It's . . . *him*!"

"Okay . . . okay . . ." Taffy continued, a little unsteadily. "Okay . . . I'll be there. Should I wear a costume or anything?"

Nicky stood up, crossed the room, sat on the edge of the small dinette table.

"Okay, then. Okay. 'Bye." She clicked off the phone and dropped it as if it were riddled with disease. "Sorry, Nicky. I can't do this. Too fucking weird," she said as she began to pace. "Too fucking weird. Sorry. No. Uh-uh."

She sat down, lit a cigarette, stood up, sat back down, drew hard, blew the smoke out in a thin, seething ribbon. She began to shake.

"What's going on, Taffy?"

"He said he's having a Halloween party tonight. He wants me to come."

"At the—"

"Yeah. At the warehouse. He told me not to bother with a costume. Said he'd have one for me."

He picked up the phone, handed it to Taffy. ''Call Willie T,'' he said. ''Tell him what I told you.''

Taffy took the phone, clicked it back on, listened for a dial tone. ''And what else?''

Nicky looked at his watch. ''Tell him to meet me at the warehouse at nine.''

47•Doughnuts. There had been chocolate-iced doughnuts, covered with orange and black sprinkles, at the party. There had also been, of course, every drug and alcoholic beverage known to humankind there as well. Reefer, cocaine, pills, hashish, bourbon, scotch, gin, vodka. Even mushrooms. Someone made a cocktail of magic mushrooms and Japanese tea: frothy green madness in a primitive earthen bowl.

He had been in charge of the doughnuts that night, so this night he dutifully pulled into the Amy Joy's at Richmond and Mayfield Roads and parked in a dark corner, in a space farthest from the scorchingly bright fluorescence of the doughnut shop.

He got out, checked all the doors, crossed the parking lot.

There were two uniformed police officers in the doughnut shop, both in their early thirties. Suburban, veteran cops on a Halloween night. He nodded to them, they returned the greeting, the knowing nod of worldly men, men who knew the score, the dirty realities of modern urban life. He pitied them, feared them, of course. Probable cause was an ever-widening thoroughfare these days.

He bought two dozen assorted Halloween-themed doughnuts and quickly left the shop, not making any further eye contact with the officers. He had come so far, and although the notion of all of this drawing to an end, a violent end, was a distinct possibility, it would be criminal to have it end before the party. A wrong, furtive glance in a doughnut shop. A stop sign not totally obeyed.

He got in, started the van, pulled back onto Mayfield Road, and, obeying all traffic laws, headed east.

* * *

Julia.

She would not, of course, be at the party tonight. Not this one. Not any one, ever. The love of his life would not be in attendance because she had been hypnotized somehow into taking part in a sick, twisted orgy twenty years ago, twenty years to the day, an orgy of hard sex and hard drugs and the night had taken her away from him.

The *pirate* had taken her away from him.

The pharmaceuticals and booze had been consumed at a frivolous, furious rate. They had smoked and drank and popped and snorted like savages, all in the name of collegiate freedom, all in the name of youthful, academic excess, the hubris of the physically strong, the mentally acute.

He had gotten stoned a few times with the general group—having been brought into the intellectual fold by Julia, who shared a poetry class with John Angelino—but he did not know them well. It was only because of Julia that they tolerated him. He always felt unclever around them, constantly challenged, as if he were required to be witty all the time, to get every single literary reference, no matter how obscure.

But if they tolerated him for Julia, he tolerated them for the same reason. He had to be where she was, to breathe the same air, to feel the same rain on his face, to smell the same smells.

The party began to degenerate at around eleven-thirty, with couples moving drunkenly off to their respective dorm rooms to party one on one. By midnight the only people left were the core of the AdVerse Society and the usual gang of misfits, hangers-on. The still frame of that moment was burned into his mind, a dark acid etching that had formed the backdrop to his every thought for two decades.

He turned onto Edgefield Road, closed his eyes, saw it again: Julia was on the floor at the foot of the bed when Jenny turned off the table lamps and lit the candles. Geoffrey flipped through the box of albums, finally picking out the Rolling Stones' *Get Yer Ya-Yas Out*. A standard frat party scene, but something was wrong. As he sat there, on the floor, unable to move, the edges of his vision vibrated and waved. Formerly straight lines doing a cartoon hula dance in front of him. And he knew why. An hour earlier, The Saint had given him the two pink pills, and now they were kicking in. "What are these?" he had asked.

"Ups," The Saint had said. "Amphetamines. You don't want to miss the witching hour, do you?"

"No. Wouldn't want to do that," he'd replied, once again seeing the need to best the man with some sort of *bon mot*, but once again failing.

"The shank of the evening, my good man," The Saint had added, dropping the pills into his hand. "The shank of the evening."

The Saint always said things like *my good man* and *precisely*. As if he were Michael York or someone, which he clearly was not.

But why hadn't he refused the pills? How high was high enough? Why hadn't he simply said that, while he was happy to smoke pot with them, to speak pretentiously about dead poets, to drink cocktails that even their parents considered ancient, he was not about to pop a pair of insufficiently identified pink pills into his mouth at the behest of this self-annointed guru of the AdVerse Society.

But he'd taken them anyway.

And they were not amphetamines.

He found this out at around eleven-thirty, the moment his legs ceased to hold his weight and he found himself on the floor, propped against the large speaker under the window. Right across from Julia, who sat at the foot of the bed, a book of T.S. Eliot on her lap, a joint held clumsily in her small, delicate hand.

But now, in his frosted vision, she was a Degas painting: lithe, beautiful, sheathed in liquid light.

As the drug pinned him to the floor, time welded itself together, people came and went, faces and bodies drifted into his tunnel. The echo of the music at times was deafening, but he couldn't even bring his hands to his ears. He saw Dr. Keller of all people lean in, smile, ask if he was okay. He tried to answer, couldn't.

Moments of clarity came, lingered briefly, dissipated. At one point he saw someone he didn't recognize leave the room, then return with a pile of clothing. It looked like costume material, with sequins and satin and feathers poking out. Geoffrey looked through them. Benny Crane, too. Much laughter, loud music. The Groundhogs were playing now. . . .

Benny had sobered up somewhat and seemed to be taking charge of the party, holding up various costumes to various people, dictating who should wear what. There was a pirate costume, a vampire's cape, a set of GI fatigues, a flapper's dress and boa. Lots of masks.

But none of that mattered to him because he couldn't move, couldn't select a costume if he wanted to. And when he saw Julia having a grand, theatrical time with her new friends, he wanted to.

Losing her to these people, these phonies, was his ultimate nightmare, a cancerous fear that had eaten at him all semester. And now it seemed to be happening right in front of him.

Julia looked over at him and smiled. A stoned, country-girl openness that flicked at his heart.

Don't, he thought, weakly.

Don't, Julia. . . .

48 By six-thirty the streets of Lyndhurst, Ohio, were over-run with ghosts, goblins, and superheroes of every conceivable stripe and pedigree. From the porch at 1728 Edgefield Road she could see Superman, Spiderman, the Terminator, Batman. The sky was clear and black, dotted with stars; the breeze held the promise of cider, cinnamon, caramel apples.

It was every Halloween of her youth.

She tried the knob on the front door, found it locked. A rarity when she was expected at her parents' house. She looked up and down the street, at the cars parked along the curb. She didn't see Paige's red Mazda. Paige had said that if she could get away from the store by six, she'd go trick-or-treating with them.

But Paige hadn't opened the store today.

Amelia had tried calling three times, kept getting the store's machine. And Paige's leather coat was still hanging over the back of the kitchen stool. Paige had a key. She'd said she would stop by in the morning to get her coat, but there it hung. And now Amelia was a little worried.

She rang the bell just as a handful of kids across the street chanted, "Trigger-treeeeeeee!" in unison. The dog next door started barking. After a moment, the door swung wide and Amelia and Maddie were confronted with a tall, swashbuckling pirate, complete with eye patch, scimitar, black boots, and golden earring.

"Ahoy, ye two beauties!" the pirate said.

"Ahoy!" Maddie exclaimed.

"And who might ye be?"

"I'm Pocahontas," Maddie said.

The pirate then looked at Amelia. "And ye?"

"Ye?" Amelia replied, raising a solitary eyebrow. "I'm, um, *Mrs.* Hontas. Her mother."

The pirate laughed. "And what brings ye out on such a night as this?"

Maddie looked at her mother—who smiled and shrugged her shoulders—then back at the pirate. "Candy?"

"Yes! Booty! Treasure! *Swag!*" the pirate said, stepping to the side. "Ye may now come aboard the brigantine *Randolph*!"

Amelia, after getting over the initial shock of seeing someone other than her mother or father open the door to her parents' house, shook a finger at her older brother and ushered her daughter inside.

"Roger here?"

"Not yet," Garth said. "He called from the airport. Half hour ago, maybe. Should be here any minute."

"How is he getting here?"

"What?" Garth replied, that tiny vein making its appearance on the left side of his forehead, the way it always did when he stalled for time. Amelia had read that vein for more than thirty years.

"Did I stutter or something? I asked how Roger was getting here from the airport."

"Oh," Garth began, pouring himself some cider, stretching it. "I guess he's cabbing it. Or maybe somebody from the company was meeting him. I didn't ask." Then Garth's face registered understanding. "Oh, please, Meelie. It's not the bimbo. I thought *you* said that *he* said it's over."

"He also told me he'd never do it in the first place, remember? You were there. Remember that 'forsaking all others' line?"

Garth smiled, defeated. "He's taking a cab. I'm sure of it. In fact, that's what he said, and I just forgot it."

Amelia looked at him skeptically for a few moments, then

let him off the hook. "If I ever find out you're keeping something from me . . ."

Garth drew his plastic sword, smiled. "Then I would have to do the right thing and hoist myself on my own petard," he said. "Or something along those lines."

Amelia let it go for the moment. "What about Paige?" she asked. "Has she called?"

"No. Why? Was she supposed to?"

"She said she might go with us tonight, but I haven't been able to get ahold of her."

"Well, this morning she said she—"

"Wait," Amelia said. "You saw her this morning?"

"Yeah. We had coffee. Amy Joy's."

"And what did she say?"

"She didn't say anything. Said she was gonna stop by and get her coat, but that's about it," Garth replied. "But I'll tell you, when she walked in, I almost did a double take."

"What do you mean?"

"I mean it could've been you. She cut her hair, dyed it. Seriously. Could've been you."

"I knew she colored it," Amelia said, feeling a slight shiver. "I didn't know—"

"Except for, you know . . ." Garth grinned, raised his hands, indicating breasts.

"Funny," Amelia said. "Really hysterical."

At that moment Maddie raced around the corner, into the living room, and came to a halt in front of Amelia, waiting for inspection. Everything was somewhat off center—her wig, her fringed skirt, her mask. Fine Maddie Saintsbury form.

Amelia and Garth looked at each other, laughed.

She was, of course, being silly. Paige was fine, Roger was fine. Her husband would be there any minute—delivered safely by a big yellow taxi—and life would mercifully get back to normal.

The foursome walked north on Edgefield Road, toward Huron Road, slowly, with Dag and Maddie on point about five houses ahead, Amelia and Garth bringing up the rear. Just about every

house on the street was lit up, decorated with tree-swinging
ghosts, bright jack-o'-lanterns, phony spiderwebs strung along
night blue hedges. Maddie took full advantage of this bounty,
shuttling up to the porches while Dag stood at the end of the
driveways, inspecting his granddaughter's take before dropping it into the bag. Fortunately, after the yearly battle over
the wearing of a coat over her costume, Maddie had given in
and put on her Little Mermaid jacket. At least it was in the
Pocahontas extended family of products, Amelia thought.

She located her father in this scene, halfway up the Maslars'
drive. He looked rather trim in his beige golf jacket, she
thought. And because he was Dag Randolph, he had a Freddie
the Freeloader mask on.

For a moment, Amelia froze this tableau in her mind. It
didn't get any more Norman Rockwell than this. And that was
good. Except . . .

Except for the fact that Roger was late. So they had started
without him.

"Is that Garth *Randolph*?" came a voice from a blue compact car trolling along the curb behind them.

Amelia recognized the nasal whine immediately. Debbie
Panzarella. Technically, Debbie Jean Panzarella Martucci Lanzini. Twice married, twice divorced, much henna-ed. Debbie
had a voice like a Cuisinart full of shotgun pellets.

"Who's that?" Garth asked, moving his eye patch over.

"Debbie *Lanzini*, silly," Debbie answered.

As Garth swaggered over to the passenger window, Amelia
saw Debbie conduct a lightning-quick inventory of her face in
the visor mirror. She looked back out and smiled her big,
phony smile.

"And is that A-me-li-a?" Debbie singsonged.

"Yes it is," Amelia said. "How are you, Debbie?"

"Goodnyou?" she answered, her cashier charms rushing to
the fore.

"Still married," Amelia answered, hoping the sarcasm
dripped through. Her petty feuds with Debbie Panzarella went
back twenty-some years and showed no signs of ever abating.

She pulled her brother closer, whispered, "You're not seriously—"

"Go ahead," Garth said. "I'll catch up."

Amelia made her best sour-lemon face.

"Come on, Meelie. I spent fifty-six bucks on this freakin' outfit. Let me get some value, eh?" He smiled at her and the conversation was over.

"Okay," Amelia said. "We're going left on Huron, then over to Sunview."

"Right," Garth replied without a modicum of interest. "Okay."

Amelia gave Debbie a half smile, then continued up Edgefield Road, scanning the horizon in front of her. At first she couldn't see her father or her daughter, and a pang of fear caromed around her stomach. She looked at the next few houses, at the porches, driveways, tree lawns. No Maddie or Dag. She was just about to go back and get Garth when she saw her father and daughter rounding the corner onto Sunview Road, hand in hand.

Easy, Meelie, she thought. Don't need to make Halloween any scarier than it already is.

Still, she doubled her pace.

When she turned the corner onto Sunview Road, she noticed that far fewer of the houses were lit up with Halloween decorations. She could see some kids scurrying along the sidewalks, but once again, she could not see her father or Maddie. They couldn't have gotten far, she thought. Eight of the first ten houses on this side of the street were lit up and had their front doors wide open. Surely Maddie had run up to them. Amelia looked at the porches.

No little Indian girls.

Why would they have passed them up? she wondered.

She looked at the other side of the street. Only two houses had their porch lights on. Maybe they had decided to get those out of the way and tackle the east side of the street all at once. It sounded like a Dag Randolph plan.

Amelia crossed to the dark side of the street, passing a

stretch of five or six darkened houses, stopping, once, when she heard a rustling in the hedges in front of a gray and white colonial, a rustling that turned out to be a beagle puppy, enthralled to suddenly be on the loose, following some primordial path of its own. When she reached 1749 Sunview Road—a house she knew as the Cameron house growing up, a house long since sold and resold—she caught a glimpse of something moving in the backyard. At first she thought it may have been a towel hanging on a line, or perhaps a T-shirt.

She stopped, looked up the driveway, tried to focus.

After a few moments, her eyes adjusted and she saw that it was her father's jacket she had seen moving in the dark backyard. He was now standing next to a trellis and appeared to be examining a bulging burlap sack on the ground in front of him. It was too dark to tell much else, though, except that he was still wearing his hobo mask. He looked up, spotted Amelia, waved, beckoned her to come to the backyard.

"What, Dad?" she said in a gruff whisper, as loud as she dared between two dark houses. "What's going on?"

Instead of answering, he waved her in again.

Now what has he gone and done? Amelia wondered. Did he get himself invited to a party? As she walked up the driveway, she realized that it couldn't be a party. At least, not an outdoor party, because there were no lights on in the backyard. Nor were there any lights on in the house, for that matter. The only illumination she could see were the interior lights of the van that was idling in the driveway.

She approached the trellis.

Her father waved again, his beige jacket and the white highlights in the mask catching the moonlight, creating a bizarre effect that gave the appearance of a floating head and torso in the darkness, an effect that—

Amelia stopped a few feet away. Something was wrong. It was her father's jacket and mask, but somehow, it wasn't her father. Dag Randolph was five nine on a good day.

The man who stood in front of her now was six feet tall.

She turned to run, but a hand shot out of the blackness,

webbing her face with ironlike fingers. A strong arm encircled her waist. Then, in an instant, a thick brown fog enveloped her.

A mist that smelled like medicine.

49. Nicky looked at his now meager roll of cash. When he stepped into the Army Navy Store on Prospect he had every intention of buying a simple overcoat, maybe a pair of gloves. He had left the house wearing only his sweats the night before—a night that now seemed at least a month ago—and the temperature was dropping fast.

He was lucky that the store was open late, and after he had picked out a basic pea coat, he was caught by the selection of defensive sprays under glass by the front door. He pointed to the small can of pepper spray, with no idea how he would use it. It just seemed like the right thing to have in his pocket.

By the time Nicky stepped back out onto Prospect Avenue, Frank Corso's fifteen-hundred-dollar roll had been reduced to eighty-eight dollars and twenty cents.

The corner of East Fifty-first Street and Euclid Avenue was deserted, a blasted scape of rusting, blocked-up cars and empty stores with whitewashed windows. At night, nothing human stirred here. On the northwest corner stood a crumbling four-story redbrick building that at one time had housed the Acme Retail Supply company, long since defunct. The first-floor windows were covered with plywood, their surfaces coated three gangs deep in brightly hued graffiti.

The building on the northeast corner was imposing, monstrous. Ten stories high, a half block deep, a monolithic cube of soot-blackened stone and brick. The first few floors had tall, narrow windows, covered with decades of grime and exhaust, jailed by thick black bars. From there on up, at least as far as

Nicky could see, the windows were bricked in, the color in those squares only slightly less gray than the older brick.

The top floor, the floor Taffy had told him about, was a mystery. Nicky would have to stand across the street, fully exposed, to see anything above the sixth or seventh floor. He decided to wait until Willie T arrived to check it out.

There was only one entrance on the west side of the building. The alcove was at least fifty feet from the nearest streetlamp, and the angle allowed a wedge of welcome darkness in the doorway. Nicky glanced at his watch. Nine-fifty. He had slept a few hours in Sandy's car and awakened to two flat tires. Luckily, Sandy had had two bald but serviceable spares in the trunk. The delay had cost him nearly an hour.

He stepped into the doorway, lit a cigarette, then cupped it in his hand. It was a trick he learned from Vic Morrow on the old *Combat!* television series.

At just after ten o'clock a car slowed down in front of the doorway where Nicky stood. It wasn't Willie T's car, at least not the car Nicky had seen at the Burger King. This was a late-model red Mazda. He couldn't see inside, but he could hear the pulsing bass of the stereo.

Nicky flattened himself against the rusted steel door of the warehouse, trying to lose himself in the shadows, but knowing that the occupants of the car had probably seen him. Maybe Willie T had borrowed a car, he thought. Maybe some of his homeboys had come along to kick this crazy fucker's ass. Bunch of drunk, off-duty cops with AK-47s and shit.

But nobody made a move. For what seemed like an hour but was in reality no more than a few minutes, the car idled, Nicky idled. There was no sign of life or commerce for three full blocks in any direction. The occupants of the car weren't there to pick up a forty-ounce. They were there for Nicky.

He was just about to run when, incredibly, the car started rolling again, slowly, toward the avenue. After a few seconds, Nicky leaned forward slightly, daring the light. The red Mazda made a right turn onto Euclid Avenue and disappeared into the night.

He leaned back and found that he had been holding his breath the whole time. And that his sweat-slicked hand was wrapped tightly, almost painfully, around the can of pepper spray in his pocket.

They had seen the power, he thought crazily. Wacko white boy waiting in an alcove. Bernhard Goetz and Charlie Starkweather rolled into one, baby. Don't fuck with us. You never know what we might do, see. You never—

Suddenly the rusty hinge of the door behind him screeched like a wounded animal.

And Nicky fell, backwards, downwards, into the cold, lightless warehouse.

50 Mac rewound all three tapes on all three VCRs. They were the big, old three-fourths-inch U-Matic tapes that universities and electronic news-gathering organizations swore by in the early days of video, even long after the VHS revolution had begun. He had taped so much junk when he ran the Audiovisual Department at Case Western Reserve, yet so much of it had served to keep that time alive for him. Just to see the faces on the news programs reassured him that it was still 1978, that the door might open any minute and Julia would drift into the room, take his hand, laugh at one of his terrible jokes.

He had once offered a research assistant at NBC a thousand dollars for the original broadcast tape of the nightly news from October 31, 1978. A thousand dollars. And that was back when a thousand dollars could buy a pretty good used car, or about the best stereo there was. But the young man had refused. He'd refused and one day met an untimely death when his car accidentally backed off the Ninth Street pier after dinner and drinks at Captain Frank's.

When the tapes were fully rewound, he hit the Play button on all three machines, starting the evening's television schedule, sending the signals through the coax cable to the TVs in the dorm rooms.

Everything was coming together nicely, he thought, although he hadn't anticipated Amelia's friend Paige cutting and dying her hair. Or Johnny Angel's laptop. He had erased the desktop at St. Michael's—no doubt sending the parish finances into a vortex of confusion—but he had missed

Johnny's laptop. The two mistakes had nearly cost him everything. He would not make another.

He took out the small vial of PCP, prepared a syringe.

He cooked a few hits of heroin, too.

Now that all of his friends had arrived, he could change his clothes, start the festivities. He picked out a disco greatest-hits album, started the turntable, and poured himself a glass of Spanada.

51 She was in Donna Turley's bedroom. Donna was playing "Le Freak" for the eight millionth time and was probably dancing like a palsied chicken around the room in her green velvet hip-huggers and white patent leather telephone-platform shoes that made her look about six feet tall. Amelia could smell patchouli incense and the slightest hint of reefer. Donna the pothead.

She couldn't open her eyes for some reason, but for some reason, that was okay. She felt good, warm. *Young.* Warm and cozy and . . . well . . . sexy, kind of. But why can't I move? she thought. She opened her eyes and saw Al Pacino, his big, brown, Michael Corleone eyes staring down from the wall.

Al. Baby.

How ya doin'?

How come I can't—

Maddie, she thought. Her body was suddenly wracked by a wave of fear and guilt. *I'm drunk and I don't know where Maddie is.*

Not drunk but . . .

"Hello." The voice came from right in front of her. Just a few feet away. She squinted, trapped a shadow or two, but still couldn't bring the man's face into focus. He tapped her gently on the forehead, as if knocking on the door to her mind. "Question for you," he said. "You up for a question?"

Amelia stirred, tried to gather her wits, her bearings. Where *was* she? Why did her shoulders suddenly feel so heavy? Why couldn't she move? Was she tied up?

Jesus Christ, was she *tied up*?

"How does it look from the inside?" he continued. "I mean . . . from inside the buzz? Can you see me?"

She could. Sort of. But why did he sound so weird? And why was he dressed like that? She hadn't seen anyone dressed like that in years, had she? And why was he wearing a black sequined mask?

Was it Halloween?

She remembered, vaguely, the hum of the car, the thrum of the freeway. Slam. Slam. Slam. Then: loud, oily machinery. A pinch in her arm. That's it. Her memory in toto. Five more minutes, Mom. It's *soooo* warm.

"Because this is what it looked like to Julia, see?" the man in the white suit and black mask said. "This is what it looked like that night. From the inside. All fuzzy around the edges, that good/bad feeling in your stomach."

The bad part of whatever he was talking about reached her, made her feel sick. But only for a few seconds. Then it was gone. Floating again . . .

Amelia decided to take a little nap.

Somewhere, in the distance, Rod Stewart asked if she thought he was sexy.

52 Blackness. The blackness of the dead.

The floor where he fell was wet, concrete, smooth. Luckily he didn't hit his head, but he was nonetheless robbed of his air for a good minute and a half, which didn't help him in the scrambling-to-his-feet department.

Now he was fine, he had his wind back.

Just fine enough to be scared shitless.

He cocked his head to the stillness, listened. A thick black blanket of nothing. Then the nearby rumble of a truck. Euclid was to his right; that meant the door was behind him. He began to spin, slowly, his hands extended out in front of him. He turned a full one hundred eighty degrees, leaned forward. Nothing. He took a tentative step, groped with his fingertips. Still nothing. He took another step and his foot came to rest against a curb of some sort, a curb that seemed to angle outward, upward. Not a curb, a concrete ramp. He got down on his knees, felt along the surface. Slick. Oily. He must've slid down the ramp when he'd fallen in, although he couldn't recall it. He tried mounting the ramp, but as expected, he kept sliding back down.

He wasn't getting back out that way.

"Shit," he said aloud.

And was rewarded with the sound of his voice boomeranging back to him, as if he were enclosed in a big cedar chest.

What? If I'm in a warehouse, why does it sound like I'm in a closet? "Hey," he tried, a little louder. Same thing. A soft finish to the sound. No echo.

He turned back to the expanse of the room, squinted. Nothing. He had never been in a darker place than this. There *was* no darker place than this. He stepped forward and to the right, groped the air in front of him, feeling a little bit like Audrey Hepburn in *Wait Until Dark*. But before he had taken five full steps, he hit a wall. A wood-paneled wall, by the feel. He pushed on it, felt it give slightly, but still hold firm.

He put his back to the door that adjoined East Fifty-first Street and began to feel his way along the wall, moving farther into the ink black warehouse.

He lost track of the number of steps he had taken at around the hundred mark, right around the time he began to get the sinking feeling that he was in a makeshift maze, cutting across the expanse of the warehouse, a maze created exclusively for him.

But before he could let that paranoia wash over him fully, he barked his shin on something cold and unforgivingly hard.

Steps. Steps leading upward.

When the pain in his leg subsided a bit he started up the stairs, his hand sliding up a rusted iron railing. Forty-three steps later, at the top, was a door, closed but unlocked. He opened it and the sound of the hinge echoed throughout the warehouse. He was now above the paneled walls. It *was* some sort of makeshift rat maze.

He stepped through the door and found himself in another hallway, this one wider, brick walls. He knew this because there was a window to his left, and the light, even the thin nicotine stain of yellow struggling through the grime, filled him with joy. He was over the alley in the back of the warehouse now, clearly on the second floor. He had his bearings.

He climbed onto the massive sill, pressed his face against the pane, looked down.

Willie T's big Ford was in the alley.

The cavalry had arrived.

53 She sat upright in her chair, nauseous, filled with dread, but wide-awake now. Her vague sense of uncertainty, that buoyant unpleasantness, had now become a razor-sharp panic. She may not have known where she was, or what time it was, but she sure as hell knew *who* she was. She was Amelia Saintsbury and it was 1998 and she had been trick-or-treating at Mom and Dad's and someone had jumped her in Pete Cameron's backyard.

And she didn't know where Maddie was.

She felt ill, powerless, terrified.

She was in a dorm room of some sort. An impromptu dorm room, made out of canvas walls. There were two windows, through which she could see the top of an office building. There was a blue lava lamp, some votive candles lit. A desk and chair. She smelled Ambush cologne. She remembered Ambush well. By Dana. It was the woman's perfume answer to Canoe. Cologne? Why was she—

She had to focus. But her head felt light. Her stomach was on fire.

She looked to her right, beneath the window. A student desk with a turntable and eight-track combo on it. Makeup and brushes. There was also a bottle of wine, a pair of goblets. Everything looked dated, as if they were museum exhibits dedicated to 1970s collegiate life.

Except that *she* was part of the exhibit. She was tied to a chair, there was duct tape around her mouth, and she did not know where she was.

She struggled against the ropes that bound her hands. They

were very tight. She tried to move her feet, but found them to
be part of the chair itself, well lashed with nylon cord. She
tried to rock forward, but the moment she did she heard a
sound behind her, inches away.

A footfall.

Amelia froze.

Then she felt another pinch on her arm, a slight nick that
was followed by a warm, wet feeling all over. And soon after
that, nothing mattered.

Nothing at all.

Moving now. Rolling. She was being wheeled across a dark
room. Cold, drafty, damp like a basement. Something in her
mouth, soft and spongy. Had to breathe through her nose.
Head *so* heavy. Music. Bad smells nearby. Rotting meat?
Gotta clean the kitchen, gotta get the garbage out. Still tied.
Hands, feet. Her stomach leapt, spun, settled.

Maddie? Where was—

Then came a flash of white from the man's suit as he
stepped in front of her. A fisheye view now. He was still
wearing his sequined mask. Then reality, or what she could
conceive of as reality in her present state, came shrieking back.
Along with some *very* loud music. Loud and scratchy. The
Rolling Stones' "Sympathy for the Devil."

The man in white parted the curtains to a new room, another
dormitory cubicle out of the seventies. A roomful of candles.
He stepped behind her and they continued forward, slowly.
The first thing she saw was the slide projector on the shelf
near the desk, the huge images being projected onto the canvas
wall over the bed. A city street scene. Then Roger's college
yearbook picture. Then a picture of Molson, sitting in the park.

They were fully inside the room now. The music roared like
an angry monster. The maracas slashed at her ears. The chorus
pounded.

*"Please   t'meet'choo . . . hope   you   guess . . . mah . . .
name . . ."*

As she was wheeled inside, as the music became her world
and the rancid smells filled that world, her first reaction was

that it was some sort of documentary film freeze-frame of a horror scene. A concentration camp, perhaps. The killing fields of Cambodia.

Bodies, everywhere, strewn at unhealthy angles. Broken forms. Former people. The candlelight danced over the musculature, the smooth curves of flesh over bone.

She fought her tears, lost.

My God.

Not bodies. No. Please God, not bodies. Not Maddie. Not Dad.

"Just as ev'ry cop is a criminal . . . an' awwwwl the sinners . . . saints . . ."

The tears obscured her vision for a few moments, but soon her chair came to rest. Her eyes cleared somewhat, and she tried to take another visual inventory. A masculine room. Pennants, pinup posters, a couple of trophies. There was a desk and chair against the wall opposite her, placed beneath a pair of windows. A number of photos in frames sat on top. Family shots.

She stared at the pictures and felt her heart jump in her chest. Roger's family. Roger's family pictures from the den. She focused on the form that was propped in the chair at the desk. And that's when it dawned on her. She looked around the room.

Mannequins.

Amelia felt an enervating wave of relief. She dared another look. Yes . . . a mannequin sat at the desk, a mannequin wearing a red dress, a flapper's dress out of the 1920s. A mannequin was also propped up on the bed, dressed like a doctor. Something dark and wet-looking was attached where its lips should be. A soldier sat on the floor, thin, rotting skin for a face. A cowboy lay nearby.

But where was Maddie? Who had Maddie?

God she couldn't think straight.

Minutes later the nausea returned in full force. She battled it back. There was still a gag in her mouth and she knew that if she brought something up from her stomach, she surely would choke. She had gone from such a warm high to such a freezing low in just minutes. She began to shake, just as another chair was wheeled into the room, coming to a stop next to her.

At first she did not have the courage to look. Then, slowly, reluctantly, she glanced to her left, moving her eyes only.

And saw that it was no mannequin.

It was Roger.

Her husband was sitting in a wheelchair, not two feet from her. But instead of a sense of relief and joy at seeing her knight in shining armor arrive, Amelia felt the bile rise in her throat, soaking the gag in her mouth with the sour taste of fear.

Roger was naked.

And he was shackled hand and foot.

A slow song now . . . a saxophone . . . "Strangers on the Shore"?

The man in the white suit put the wheelchairs back to back. Amelia was facing the bed now; Roger was behind her—at least she thought he was—silently facing the wall bearing the Farrah Fawcett poster.

Her mind was clearing by the minute. She watched the man carefully. She would find a way out of this.

More slides on the wall. Yearbook pictures of people she didn't know. Then, suddenly, one she did. A pretty young woman whose picture she once found among Roger's college papers. Julia, it was signed. She had always wondered about Julia, if she was a conquest of Roger's.

The man took a glass hypodermic needle from the desk and stepped behind her. "Do you know what this is, Roger?" Silence. He continued. "I want you to think back, Roger. Way back. Twenty years ago tonight, right about, well, right about *now*, you dropped a couple of pink pills into my hand. Do you remember?"

Instead of the slurred answer that Amelia expected, Roger's answer was clear, lucid. "Yes."

"And do you remember what you said?"

A few moments of silence, then: "No."

"Well, it's understandable. Twenty years and all. You told

me it was speed. You told me you wanted me wide-awake at
the 'witching hour.' Your words. Witching hour. Can you believe that? Well, I took them. Like the asshole I was in those
days. And do you remember what they were, Roger?''

More silence. ''I don't exactly—''

A hard slap. A pause, then Roger spoke again. ''I-I don't
remember exactly.''

''No matter,'' the man said, casually. ''I think you *do* remember. But I think you're just embarrassed, even after all
this time. I think you're embarrassed that your wife will find
out what a manipulative little cocksucker you are. As if she
didn't know, right?''

The man poked Amelia in the shoulder blade, sharing some
secret wisdom, a joke at Roger's expense. Every muscle in
her body tightened.

''But what you're not considering, Counselor, is just how
far I might go to get you to confess. So here's what's going
to happen. I'm going to inject you with this needle, you're
going to become totally incapacitated, and then I'm gonna spin
you around and you're going to watch.''

''Watch?'' Roger asked.

''Yes. You're going to watch me fuck your wife.''

''But . . . I don't—'' Roger began.

''Shut up,'' the man said. ''Just shut the fuck up.''

Then Amelia heard Roger grunt. The man in white had injected him. The used needle went flying across the room,
landed next to the wastebasket, next to the desk. The slide
show continued. Now a chunky young woman and a retarded
girl, sitting at a food court.

''So . . . tell me,'' the man began, matter-of-factly. ''Do you
think you'll enjoy it? Seeing me fuck her? Do you think you'll
get a hard-on? Some men like it, you know.'' He stepped
around, in front of Amelia. He looked at her legs, her breasts,
her mouth. Amelia had to turn away, her revulsion growing.
''Does she like it from behind?''

Her husband remained silent.

''You know I'm pretty well hung, Roger. Funny how that
happens, no? The goofy guys always getting the big dicks.

She might just like it and want to stay with me. Wouldn't that be justice? After all these years?"

All Amelia could hear now was Roger's steady inhale and exhale of breath.

"Of course, we all know how *you* like it," the man said. He reached over to the desk, picked up the remote for the slide projector, clicked ahead a few slides. The canvas wall now showed a series of telephoto shots, outdoor shots of a car. Closer, closer. A man and a woman inside the car, a naked woman, the woman sitting on the man's lap, facing him. A familiar car.

It was Roger and Shelley Roth.

The man in white sat on the edge of the bed, his elbows on the desk, cooking heroin in a spoon held over a candle. Amelia had not heard a noise out of Roger since his injection.

"I've just been giving you little tastes, Amelia," the man said. "Just enough to keep the edges ragged. You know what I mean? Enough to keep you manageable. Now it's time to rock." The liquid in the spoon began to bubble. "Those other shots were in your arm. This one is going in a vein. This one's a mainline. Whole different story." He reached over to a powder compact on the desk, patted his cheeks, his chin, his forehead above the mask. "Do you know what a full spike of heroin does to you? Especially some really good junk like this? Especially to a clean system like yours? I'll bet you don't. I'll bet that Roger never shared that savory part of his past with you."

He put the spoon down on the desk, leaned forward, tied a rubber tourniquet around her arm. She tried to see his eyes through the holes in the mask, failed. For some reason Amelia felt that if she could just make eye contact, she could reason with this man. But the holes in the mask offered nothing but darkness.

"Well, let me see if I can describe it," he continued. "Someone once said it was like taking a ride on a giant white swan. You might want to hold on to that image." He found a vein, tapped it, then took a disposable hypodermic needle out of its plastic. He dropped in a small piece of cotton, put the tip of the needle carefully into the bowl of the spoon, and drew the liquid inside. Amelia cringed, but couldn't move.

He knelt in front of her. "And God save you if you like it, Amelia. God save you indeed. Because I've seen it, you know. Working at the inner-city missions." He drew himself closer, rested his arms on her thighs, began to run his hands up and down her legs. "I knew this junkie once—white girl, maybe twenty years old. Hadn't fixed in two, three days. Well, when she was done sucking me off this one time I tossed her a dime bag, put my coat on. But she was so shaky she couldn't get the GemPac open, kept fumbling with the spoon, the matches. The last thing I remember about her, as I walked out the door, was her sitting on the edge of the bed, vibrating. And that's when she took a single-edge razor blade, slit her arm, and dumped the junk right into a vein. Can you imagine? Something having that much control over you? She couldn't even wait."

Amelia knew the feeling. Her fear was that palpable. She began to sob.

"If you understand her, you understand me," he said.

And then the liquid was inside her.

He untied the tourniquet as the top of her head seemed to peel itself away. He drew his face very close to hers and kissed her, running the tip of his tongue over her lips. "I love this part," he said, softly. "There is nothing, nothing in the world, quite as sexy as a pretty woman on heroin."

Amelia's head dropped slowly, her mind afloat on a warm, stagnant pool. She forced open her eyes one more time and saw that the man had changed her clothes the last time she had passed out. She was wearing a black miniskirt, fishnet hose, red suede high heels that were way too tight.

As the white swan bucked beneath her and took her on the ride of her life, she realized what she looked like. She looked like a whore.

54• A whore. Julia looked like a whore.

The effect on him was so startling that he could hardly believe it was Julia. She sat on the edge of Roger's bed, wearing a short skirt, her knees so primly together, nineteen years old, every man's dream. Geoffrey had noticed. Johnny, too. They couldn't take their eyes off her.

But this was not *his* Julia. His Julia had always been partial to peasant dresses, jeans, sandals. She had gone away for a weekend once with some of the girls from her dorm, and he noticed that she fit everything into a knapsack. Julia was a simple, bright girl. But not lately, not tonight, not now.

Now she sat in a black miniskirt and fishnet hose, her legs looking long and slender and perfect. Her tiny feet were stuffed into red high heels. On her head was a black beret.

She was wearing far more lipstick than he'd ever seen, far more eye makeup, too. He felt himself getting hard looking at her, but feeling nothing else. Nothing except a dark rage, tempered by this sick attraction, this all-consuming fear. The drugs Roger had given him were in full and complete control.

And so he watched. . . .

A doctor was tying a rubber tourniquet around Julia's arm. Benny Crane, of course. Had to be Benny. Benny was always in charge of things medical, things pharmaceutical.

Julia looked frightened, apprehensive. She glanced up at the pirate standing next to her, who placed a reassuring hand on her shoulder. A combat soldier sat behind her. Couldn't be sure who that was. A rather chunky flapper sat at the desk, rolling joints. Jennifer. Had to be.

His head felt as if it were in a vise, his hands a thousand pounds each.

Behind him, the Stones blared and thundered.

Everyone had changed costumes, it seemed. And everyone, except Julia, wore a mask. It was as if they knew they were going to cross the line that night. People were passed out in every corner of the room; some sat in chairs, staring blankly into space.

"Please   t'meet'choo . . . hope   you   guess . . . mah . . . name. . . ." came Jagger's voice.

But he didn't have to guess.

He knew.

A single candle now. Whorehouse light, pastel orange. Julia on the bed, kneeling, the pirate holding her from behind. Flesh, skin, muscles, hands. Julia's blouse was off.

Tunnel vision.

Yet through it, he saw so many things.

He saw the pirate look in his direction every so often, the eyes behind the mask mocking him, daring him to act, react. The pirate took Julia from behind.

He saw the cowboy kneel in front of Julia, kissing her deeply, running his hands over her breasts.

He saw Dr. Keller standing in the shadow by the door, his eyes two black marbles in the candlelight. Dr. Keller was masturbating. He was watching the fivesome on the bed—the pirate, the soldier, the cowboy, the flapper, Julia. Under the cover of the darkness, under the cover of the loud music, he stepped forward, his erect penis in one hand, and placed his other hand into the maelstrom of flesh, running it over Julia's stomach, her breasts. And then he retreated.

He saw the pirate lift Julia and place her on the windowsill. He saw the pirate push Julia's skirt up around her waist, and as the music roared, he watched the pirate fuck the woman he loved, fuck her until she came, her fingernails digging deep in his back.

And later, after more degradation, after more drugs, when the windowpane snapped, when the sound wrenched him from his coma and he saw her fall, the heel of her shoe catching on the final shard, coming off, twisting, turning, landing at his feet . . .

He saw.

To the police they were, of course, proper young collegiates, scrubbed and well lawyered, kids who'd simply had a Halloween party that went too far. The investigation was short, the inquiry shorter.

Poor Julia, they all said. She jumped.

Small-town girl. The drugs and all.

Poor, poor Julia.

55 She came drifting back to consciousness, on the bed, on her knees, her arms straight up over her head, her hands roped together and linked to a cable that rose high into the blackness of the warehouse ceiling. She was still fully dressed, her feet were untied.

The first thing she did was kick off the shoes.

Roger sat across from her now, his head straight down. He looked unconscious. A thin ribbon of drool ran from his mouth to his lap.

The man in white was not in the room.

The record player had finished whatever it was playing and the needle was stuck at the end. The *brip, brip, brip* coming through the cheap speakers was a water torture—methodical, a metronome urging her to act. But she couldn't act. Her head swam, her body was numb.

The mannequins were now arranged on the bed around her. She was able to spin a little and she saw that a mannequin dressed as a pirate was kneeling behind her, as was the flapper she had seen sitting at the desk earlier. In front of her was a soldier, on his knees, on the floor. The doctor was sitting at the desk. Standing next to Roger, propped against the wall, was the cowboy. This close, Amelia could see what it was that was causing the stench. The eyes on the cowboy. The lips on the doctor. The rotting breasts on the flapper.

Her stomach revolted.

Amelia looked straight up, away from the carnage. But soon the effort became too taxing. She lowered her eyes and tried to find a place to rest them, a place that didn't steal pieces of her mind, her sanity.

The burlap bag. It sat on the ground near the cowboy's boots, just to the left of Roger's wheelchair, just beneath the windows. Amelia ran her eyes over the shape, the size, the angles.

It was the burlap bag that had been in the Camerons' backyard.

The one that had sat at this monster's feet.

Maddie.

No.

When the man in white returned this time, he seemed manic, clearly in the grip of a drug rush of some sort, soaring. Amelia knew that he was no longer going to play with them. This was the end of her family, right here and now, and there was nothing she could do to stop it.

"Now, before I fuck your wife, I have a question for you," the man said, conversationally, lifting Roger's head. "I want you to tell me what happened that night, Roger. Tell me in your own words."

Amelia looked at the burlap bag. Please, God, just an inch, she thought, staring at the middle of the bag. Please let me see the material move up one inch, then back down. Let me see her breathe once. One. Solitary. Breath. God, if you've ever heard a mother's prayer, hear this one.

One breath.

She would not, could not, take her eyes from the bag.

Nothing.

"Who's room is this, Roger?" the man asked.

Roger lifted his eyes. "My room."

The words were slurred, thick with his tongue.

"That's right," he said. He gestured to the mannequin next to him. "You remember Johnny Angel, don't you?"

Roger looked up, his eyes wet with fear. "Yes."

"Course you do," the man said. "I always thought Johnny had the nicest eyes. Caring and honest, you know?"

Roger remained silent. The man looked at Amelia.

Amelia looked back at the burlap bag.

Breathe, Maddie.

Breathe.

Amelia had never felt as repulsed or powerless in her life.

"What do you want?" she heard Roger ask, weakly.

"I want you to tell me what happened that night. I want you to be a man and confess to your part."

Then a light next to the television lit up, a red light on a small, sophisticated-looking panel. The man walked over to the TV, punched a few buttons.

And, without a word, walked out of the room.

56 After seeing Willie T's car in the alley, Nicky found some scraps of wood, wedged a few pieces under the door, propping it open, and descended the steps. He made it back across the warehouse and over to where he had entered, still not braving the center of the maze, but rather hugging the wall he had followed the first time.

He waited by the ramp that led to the door, listening for footsteps outside, listening for Willie T. An occasional car, an occasional reverberation of gangsta rap bass, but no footsteps, no one pushing on the door.

Come on, Willie, he thought. What the fuck are you doing?

He took the time to inventory his pockets. He had a pack of matches that he had taken from the seat of Sandy's car. He opened the pack, felt inside. One match. Great. A single match and a can of pepper spray. A regular one-man SWAT team. After five minutes of brain-numbing silence, he decided to head back up to the second floor, see if Willie's car had moved.

This third trip through the darkness he walked, slowly, down the center of the hallway, his hands out in front, probing the blackness like antennae. Somehow his eyes seemed to have adjusted to this total darkness. It wasn't as if he could see in front of him, but he seemed to be able to *sense* in front of him.

But where the hell was Willie?

Maybe there was another way in, he thought. Maybe Willie had found another way inside. Or maybe he had waited a couple of minutes and taken off, only to call in an all-points bulletin on the crazy Stella fucker who thinks he can manipulate the where, when, and how of his arrest.

He began to walk a little faster, still keeping his ears attuned to anyone banging on a door or rattling a window.

And that was when the man knocked him down.

Nicky screamed, a short, guttural burst of surprise, scrambled to his feet, lashed out with a much-practiced combination of punches. Air. His heart began to race. Another left, right, left. Still nothing.

"*Who's there?*" he screamed.

No answer.

And then the man ran into him again. Except this time, something felt wrong. It felt as if the man's shoes had hit him in the chest. Nicky punched, a straight right hand, and connected with hard bone. Hard *vertical* bone. He backed up a few feet, waiting in an attack stance, his fear catching the breath in his chest.

A leg, Nicky thought. A shinbone. He had punched a shinbone. It didn't make any sense, but still his hand flared with pain, red swords that shot up his arm and across his back.

He backed up another ten feet or so, crouched down, listened. Nothing shifted or moved in front of him. Although, he thought, it would have been hard to hear over the thrumming of his heart.

When he felt confident that no one was going to lunge at him, he searched his pockets, found the pack of matches. He plucked the last match, carefully felt along the edge until he found the flint surface. He took a breath, held it, struck the match.

The flare was small and insignificant in the expanse of the maze, but it threw enough of its pale light onto the blood-splattered shoes of the man hanging in front of him. There was enough light for Nicky to see the deep red stains that had soaked through the formerly blue denim, the crimson intaglio that was the man's T-shirt.

And the wraparound shades. For that brief instant, the wraparound shades stared down at him like the eyes of a giant spider.

Willie T, Nicky thought, through the horror.
Willie T.
He skirted the body and ran toward the steps.
The cavalry was dead.

57 "They all cried. And talked. In the end. Geoffrey especially. Confessed to everything he had ever done in his life. Even told me about kicking his old dog. Then he cried like a little girl. It was pathetic."

The man in the white suit and black mask walked over to the television, turned the channels. *Love Boat*. A news break-in with Sander Vanocur. And a channel that looked like a closed-circuit shot of a long hallway.

Amelia was still tied to the cable that led to the ceiling. Her arms were numb, no longer part of her body. She was still gagged.

"Speaking of little girls," he said. He picked up the burlap sack. He handled it with ease, in spite of its weight, its bulk, brought it next to the desk, dropped it roughly. "I always wanted a little girl. Julia and I were going to have two children, you know. A boy and a girl."

He grabbed a hypodermic needle from the desk, squirted a drop or two into the air, and fixed Roger in a defiant stare. "Tell me why you fucked all that up for me, Roger. Tell me why you should have a wife and a family and I don't."

Roger lifted his head slowly. "I . . . didn't . . ."

In an instant the man brought the needle down, violently, and stabbed the burlap bag, finding purchase in flesh. He depressed the plunger, removed it, tossed it casually on the desk. He looked back at Roger, as if he had just clipped a toenail, or brushed a bit of lint from his trousers. "Of course, you might have a drug addict on your hands in the future. Plenty of product here. Plenty of time." He began to pace. "Can you imagine that, Roger? Your little Maddie a junkie? Daughter of a TRW hatchet man shooting dope like some skell? Picture it. She's eleven, twelve years old, she's sneaking out of her bedroom window, riding into town with some guy named Rasheed, scoring some smack. Imagine that. Little Maddie sucking cock in the back of some furry van, a slave to her daddy's habits.''

Amelia looked at the burlap sack, the last pieces of her heart breaking. Then, miraculously, as if she had willed it, Amelia saw the center of the bag move up and down. Once. Then twice.

Breathing . . .

The man started to rant, his voice getting louder now, clearly more agitated. ''Well, I guess Roger isn't in a talkative *mood* tonight. Odd, isn't it? If I remember correctly, you could never seem to shut him the fuck up back in college. And the smooth talk. Jesus. The man could charm the panties off a corpse. Right, Mrs. Roger?'' He moved the chair out of the way and stood next to the window that overlooked the back alley. ''Second last chance, Roger. Tell me now.'' He picked up the burlap bag, one hand holding each end. He suspended it a foot or so off the ground.

''I don't . . .'' Roger managed.

The man in the white suit began to swing the bag back and forth, side to side, slowly, knee-high. Back and forth. ''I'm going to ask you only two more times.''

Amelia struggled against the ropes. She couldn't turn her head far enough to see Roger fully, but she could see the window. Oh yes. She could see the man in white, the sparkling of his sequined mask, she could see the bag that held her daughter, her very life, being swung in an ever-increasing arc, ever nearing the windowpane. She tried to scream, but the gag caught it. Her terror tasted like wet foil.

''Tell me,'' the man said. ''You were the pirate that night, weren't you?''

Roger's head lolled on his shoulders. He didn't speak. The drugs had taken his voice, his mind, his memory. Roger, please, Amelia thought. Please come back. Fight it. Please tell him. Amelia closed her eyes, imagined the crack of the glass, the thunderclap of the pane breaking outward, the bag sailing through. She forced herself to look.

"Tell me you were the god ... damn ... PIRATE!" he screamed, the effort to swing the bag faster and faster drawing a bead of sweat on his brow. Amelia saw the droplet run down his forehead, leaving a thin white streak. The man in the white suit was wearing Pan-Cake makeup.

Roger. My God. What have you done?

"Wasn't . . . me," Roger offered, weakly.

The man grimaced, baring his teeth. "Liar," he said. "Fucking . . . *liar*."

And then it happened.

In one fluid motion, the man let go of the bag, and the weight of the sack carried it into the glass—shattering it into a thousand sparkling pieces—and out into the black night. For a moment, as the glass rained down, Amelia saw Maddie's short life unspool in her mind. Her little girl's first Christmas, her first Easter bonnet. The time she took all the hot dogs out of the fridge and left a trail of them heading upstairs to her room. Her first day of school. How she cried that day. How they *both* cried . . .

Then the horror blossomed within her, and her grief became a living thing, so powerful a force that she suddenly felt light, almost weightless, as if her insides were being bled through the pores of her skin. Every fear she had ever had, every dark scenario she had ever considered for her daughter, had just happened in a single second.

Maddie.

Maddie-bear.

Amelia Saintsbury opened her mouth.

And for a long time, her screams devoured her.

58 Nicky heard the music. And something that sounded like breaking glass. He was one floor below. He had learned on the second floor that the doors were locking behind him, but he wasn't surprised. Ever since his phone call to his cousin Joseph, ever since learning of Johnny Angel's death, he felt as if he were being drawn deeper and deeper into this core of darkness.

Willie T.

Had Willie been so far into this that the only way out for him was to end up hanging in a warehouse with his throat sliced open? And if that was what this maniac would do to a cop, what chance did *he* have? It was Willie T who had told him about Rat Boy to begin with.

Was *that* what sealed his fate?

Nicky continued up the stairwell, the music now growing in volume. Something with a disco beat. He opened the door an inch or so and found, as expected, that he had reached the top floor. But of all the things he expected to see when he edged open the door and glanced into the room, what he actually saw nearly took his legs away.

The huge room was laid out like a Sesame Street version of Main Street.

Six-foot boxes that looked like buildings were placed diagonally across the center of the room, connecting the hundred or so feet between the two canvas rooms that Taffy had told him about. He had to look twice. Yes, there really *were* replicas of streetlights, and cars along the path between the rooms. Some of the boxes were crudely painted to look like buildings with which he was familiar. The Allen Medical Library. Severance Hall. The Boarding House. Euclid Tavern.

Holy *shit*, Nicky thought. It's the Case Western Reserve University campus in 1978.

Right down to the mailboxes.

He could hear that the loud music was coming from the canvas room to his left. He could see a shadow against the wall, moving around, darting, growing in size, diminishing. Then slides projected onto the canvas. Yearbook pictures. John Angelino. Bennett Marc Crane. Julia Raines.

He stepped up to the curtains, parted them slightly, and peered inside. His mind was hardly prepared for what he saw, but he tried to take it all in. Amelia was tied up, kneeling on the bed, surrounded by department-store mannequins. There was a man, a naked man, passed out in a wheelchair, facing her.

But it was the other man in the room that filled Nicky with dread. A man who sat down at the desk, then turned to face Nicky, as if sensing his presence, and slowly removed his sequined mask, a dime-store trick that concealed a very familiar face.

This time, though, the man behind the face wasn't wearing glasses.

Yet what he *was* wearing blew Nicky's mind. A white three-piece suit with flared trousers. A black shirt, open at the neck. Gold chains. He seemed to be in full John Travolta regalia from *Saturday Night Fever*.

But he wasn't wearing his thick glasses. And it was for that simple reason that Nicky finally saw Gil Strauss's eyes. Sure, the nose was different, and the chin was a little stronger than it was in his college yearbook picture, but it was the eyes that told him what he needed to know.

G. D. Woltz.

Gillian Strauss.

Strauss.

Woltz.

Nicky put his hand into his pocket, gripped the pepper spray, put his finger on the trigger, and stepped through the canvas curtains, into Gillian Strauss's world.

59 The man in white at the desk, cooking another run of heroin. The TV blaring an old *Gunsmoke* rerun. The stereo played "Dancing Queen," by ABBA, loud and scratchy.

Maddie. No.

God, no.

Amelia fought the nausea, the heart-shattering grief.

Okay. Maybe . . . maybe she fell on the next building over, Amelia thought. Or a ledge. Maybe she hit an awning . . . or . . . or a Dumpster full of soft garbage bags . . . or . . .

She had to get out of this.

Had to.

Her little girl wasn't dead, see.

Just hurt.

Just . . . *hurt.*

Amelia leaned slightly to the right, then to the left. Right. Left. And began to work on the ropes. But before she could budge them, she looked at the corner of the room, where the two canvas walls met, and thought she might be hallucinating. In fact, she was sure of it. For a moment she thought she saw Nicky standing there, wearing a dark coat, his hands in his pockets, staring into the room with an appropriate amount of disbelief on his face.

"Nick!" the man in white shouted, as if he were expecting a visitor. He stood up. "Come on in!"

Nicky stepped inside, flesh and blood, fully ambulatory. It wasn't a hallucination after all. He stood in the corner, nodded at her. She looked at the man in white and, for the first time, saw his face. His ordinary face. She had seen it before. But where?

"You remember Julia, don't you?" the man in white said, gesturing toward Amelia. "Julia and I are engaged."

Nicky just stared.

"And let me introduce you to the AdVerse Society. This . . . this is my good friend Geoffrey Coldicott." He crossed the room, not missing a beat of the music. He stood behind the soldier-mannequin. "Not much of a kisser, but a blow job to die for. Believe me." He placed his hands on the manne-quin's shoulders. "Between you and me? Not for publication? Off the record and all that? He died screaming *mommymom-mymommymommy*. I swear to God. Like Hayley Mills or something."

"This is so fucked up, man," Nicky said. "You gotta get some help."

"Help? I don't need help." He gestured to another man-nequin. "And this, of course, is Johnny Angel. Johnny is the society's resident thespian. Thespian, not lesbian. *Jenny*'s our resident dyke."

Nicky saw the rotting eyes that were attached to the cowboy mannequin. He had to speak before his mind abandoned him. "You called this Sebastian Keller from my apartment, didn't you?"

"Of course."

"And that was you on-line? You were Prufrock?"

"Call me Al."

"But how did you boot Amelia from the room? You can't just—"

The man in the white suit held up his right hand, made a snipping motion with his fingers. "Wire cutters. I was right outside her house. The phone company fixed it a few hours later. She never knew the phone was out."

"But . . . St. Francis?"

"Long story, Nick. I was going to follow Johnny into the seminary, wait awhile, kill him there. But for some reason I couldn't. It wasn't time, I guess. So I took the job at St. Fran-cis. It was supposed to be temporary, but it turned into a good thing. No one ever looks at the guy who sweeps the church.''

"How did you—''

"Of course, I had to take a lot of side jobs over the years. I had to pay for all this. Landscaping and such. Great work for a college graduate, huh?'' He laughed, humorless, hollow. "I even took a correspondence course in refrigerator repair. Got pretty good, too. Got to repair fridges all over the east side. And do you know what I saw when I stepped into all those kitchens, Nick?''

"What?''

"Drawings,'' he said, as if it made complete sense. "Crayon drawings on the refrigerators. Little drawings of trees and cows and turkeys and boats. Drawings of happy little bungalows with chimneys and curly black smoke. From Vanessa. From Kevin. From Carole and Jessica and Timmy and Gina.''

Amelia closed her eyes. She thought about Maddie's drawings.

Maddie-bear. Gone.

The man in white became more animated. "All those drawings delivered to all those daddies as they sat in their dens with their feet up, smoking their pipes. And I knew, I *knew*, they would never be for me. No report cards, no field-trip notes to sign. That's why this had to happen, Nick. Surely you can see that. These people took my drawings from me. From Julia.'' He sat down, the name somehow taking his thoughts for a moment.

"But why now?'' Nicky asked. "Why *me*?''

"Why now? Because it was time, Nicky. Because it took twenty years for everybody to have enough to lose. When Johnny moved to St. Francis . . . let's just say he would have recognized me eventually. Even with my pop-bottle glasses.'' He reached beneath the desk, took out a carousel of slides, put them in the projector on the shelf, hit the remote. Telephoto shots, night shots. Nicky and Amelia against the schoolhouse wall. Amelia's breasts, Nicky's hands, a freeze-frame of Amelia's hand near Nicky's zipper.

"And you . . . you fell in love, lost your fucking mind. Drugs, sex, murder, suicide. Just the kind of thing a hack free-

lancer would love to write about. Too bad you'll be dead."
He opened the desk drawer, pointed to a pistol. "You're gonna
blow your brains out in just a little while. Catholic guilt and
all."

"Then why did you tell me to walk away?"

"Because you're a fucking journalist. I knew you'd do exactly the opposite."

Nicky ignored the insult. He spread his feet slightly, struck
a pose. "How do you know I don't have a gun in my pocket,
pointed right at you?" he asked. He looked past the man, at
the drawer. Besides the pistol there was also a pair of handcuffs, a set of keys, something red. . . .

"I know," he said.

"You can't be sure."

"Yes I can. The last door you passed through was a metal
detector."

Nicky thought about the can of pepper spray. It was either
plastic, or too small to have been detected. Shit. There goes
the bluff.

"But now that you mention it, I want you to take your
jacket off, lay it on the bed." Reluctantly Nicky complied.

Amelia noticed that when the man in white took his eyes
from Nicky, Nicky took a half step toward the desk.

"But what about all the others?" Nicky asked. "Surely you
fucked up somewhere. Surely there'll be evidence. You can't
tie me to all of this. You can't possibly—"

At that moment Amelia summoned all her strength and
grunted as loud as she could, hoping to draw the man's attention momentarily. She did. Nicky took a full step toward the
desk.

"I'll be with you shortly, Julia, my love. This is business,
I'm afraid. Gil's got to take care of business." He looked back
at Nicky, taking an extra second to focus. He seemed not to
notice the altered proximity. "There's blood from each scene
on the clothes in your closet. A fleck or two of Geoffrey, a
spot of Johnny. I put them there when I picked up the canned
goods. There's no holes, Nicky. Quit looking."

Nicky's mind raced. He remembered Gil staying behind,

drinking his Pepsi. Then it hit him. The semen. The semen in Geoffrey's mouth. A DNA gold mine. "But you did fuck up, Gil. Big time."

Gil looked up, interested, but clearly not concerned. "Did I, now?"

"The semen in Geoffrey's mouth, you sick fuck. They *will* find you."

"You think I put my cock in that man's mouth without a rubber? *Please*. What era are you living in, Nick?"

There was only one other explanation, Nicky thought. And he was right.

"The semen in Geoffrey's mouth was his own," Gil said. "Don't you love it? It'll confuse the hell out of the FBI for years. Don't ask me how I did it, though. Toughest part of this whole thing."

Amelia found another breath somehow, made another noise, low and raspy. The man in white, the man who called himself Gil stood and, instead of looking at her, instead of being drawn by her ruse a second time, spun in place and stabbed Nicky with a syringe.

But Nicky was fast. He shifted his weight—the needle caught him high on his left shoulder—and before Gil could depress the plunger more than halfway, Nicky rolled with it and lashed out with a straight right hand, catching Gil on the point of his chin, driving him into the wall. Gil regained his footing, threw a right hand of his own, stunning Nicky, dropping him to one knee. Then, Gil picked up the desk chair, raised it over his head, and brought it down hard on the back of Nicky's neck. And all that Nicky knew was—

Stars. And pain. Golden Glove tryouts, 1978. Knocked out by a gorilla named Rocco. Never saw it coming, never heard the count.

But he wasn't in the ring now. He was in the—

Gil Strauss. The warehouse. Amelia.

Nicky tried to push himself up with his arms, failed miserably. When he hit the ground his head split with pain. He tried again. And again.

Then, from behind him, he heard Gil open the desk drawer.

The gun, Nicky thought. Jesus Christ, the *gun*. He was going to—

But instead of a loud bang, something warm and fuzzy and soft landed on the side of Nicky's face. Something . . . *familiar*? Calling on every ounce of boxer's discipline against pain he had ever possessed, Nicky found the energy and the courage to roll onto his back, to sit up. The soft thing fell into his lap. He shook his head, tried to loose the cobwebs, the ringing in his ears. He reoriented himself in the room. Gil against the wall, opposite him. Amelia still tied on the bed. How long was he—?

He looked down at his lap and, for a moment, thought he was imagining things. Red. Raspberry red. The flash of familiar red he had seen in the drawer.

It was Meg's beret.

"She's not coming back, Nick," Gil said, removing a loosened, bloody tooth, dropping it into the wastebasket. "They never do. Take it from an expert."

The rage inside Nicky flared, cauterizing his pain.

Gil continued. "She really was beautiful, though. As beautiful as my Julia. It's one of the reasons I figured you would understand all this. You understand loss."

Somehow Nicky was on his feet. He lunged.

Gil dove for the gun in the desk drawer.

But Nicky got there first. He bulled Gil against the wall, stealing the air from his lungs, then set his weight and threw three left hooks in rapid succession, each one landing on Gil's face, stunning him, splitting the flesh over his cheekbone, the final blow shattering two fingers on Nicky's left hand. Nicky finished the flurry with a right cross that exploded Gillian Strauss's nose.

The man in white slumped to the floor: unconscious, still, silent.

Nicky turned to the desk, grabbed the gun out of the drawer, pulled back the hammer, and put it to the back of Gillian Strauss's head. His hand began to shake.

But Strauss didn't move.

And, in an instant, it was over.

*   *   *

The first thing Nicky did was take the gag out of Amelia's mouth. The sudden rush of air into her lungs made her cough, made her retch for a breath. "Thuh-thuh win-win," Amelia tried. "Thuh-thuh win . . . dow . . ." She nodded at the broken window. "Luh-look . . ."

Nicky got the drift, walked over to the broken window, looked out. He looked back at Amelia, shrugged his shoulders.

"Muh-my . . . duh-daughter . . . my . . . Muh-Maddie . . . *Look*!"

Nicky looked again, the hundred feet or so to the ground making things blend together. Willie's car, Dumpsters, lots of garbage bags. "I can't . . ."

Amelia got her wind back. "Go down there and see, Nicky. Please. Now. You have to g-go down there and *see*!"

Nicky crossed the room, stepped onto the bed, looked at the ropes around Amelia's wrists. He would need a knife.

"Go!" Amelia shouted. "Don't worry about us right n-now. Go!"

"Are you—"

"*Yes,*" Amelia said, the emotions closing in on her. "And for God's sake call the police."

Nicky reached into the drawer, took out the handcuffs, and cuffed Strauss's hands behind his back. He held up Strauss's head by the hair. "Amelia, this is Gillian Strauss. Also known as Gillian Daniel Woltz. Also known as Mac." He let Gil's head drop into the small but growing pool of blood coming from his mouth.

Nicky found the hypodermic needle, the one that had been in his shoulder, looked at it, then at Amelia. "Do you know what this is?"

"No."

Nicky thought for a second, then reached over and injected the remainder of the contents into Strauss's leg. "Hack free-lancer? Fuck you."

He then rummaged through Gil's pockets, found a set of keys. He also found some change. "I'll be right back," he said. "But I'll need this." He reached out and pulled hard on

one of the canvas walls. After three attempts it came down,
bringing with it the slide-projected image of a young retarded
girl on a carousel at Cedar Point.

Nicky left the room.

Amelia cried.

And waited.

It took five tries, but the sheet of canvas finally provided him
with enough purchase to get up the oil-slicked ramp. He had
tried every key on Gil's ring before finding the master key to
the doors in the stairwell. Every single move he made seemed
to delay him, seemed to seal the fate of the little girl. Had
Amelia been right about this? he wondered. Had Gil Strauss
gone that far?

He really didn't relish looking into the back alley, but he
had to.

When he got to the top of the ramp, he was just about to
fall backward when his hand closed around the knob. He
closed his eyes, waiting for resistance, and pulled on the huge
steel door.

It opened.

The rush of night air, the streetlamps on East Fifty-first
Street, filled him with a great sense of relief. The sickness at
the top of the warehouse seemed a million miles away now.
But it wasn't. If Amelia was right, it was just around the corner, in the alley.

He looked both ways up the street, found it deserted,
stepped out onto the sidewalk and turned right, toward the
alley behind the building. He stood at the mouth of the alley
and began to visually sort through the debris. Willie's car was
parked halfway to the rear. To the left, a Dumpster, over-
flowing with garbage.

And then he saw it. The burlap bag.

The bag had split open when it hit the ground; the deep red
contents were splayed onto the crumbling asphalt, wet and
warm and steaming in the night air. Nicky steeled himself,
knelt down, peeled back the edge of the bag, saw the orange
hair, the splintered bone, the gobbets of flesh. The bottom of

the bag was soaked with blood, thick with viscera. He turned away, stood up, tried to walk off the overwhelming nausea.

Jesus Christ . . . how . . . how could someone *do* this? He looked skyward, saw the window. It was at least a hundred feet or so. He walked back to the bag, knelt once more, shifted his position to allow for more light, and saw that it wasn't orange hair at all. It was orange . . . fur?

My God, Nicky thought, his heart soaring, his eyes welling with tears.

It wasn't the little girl. It was the dog. The big golden retriever.

Gil had thrown the *dog* out of the window.

And maybe . . . *maybe* that meant that the girl was still alive, still upstairs somewhere.

Nicky couldn't imagine the agony that Amelia was experiencing. He had to get back upstairs and tell her. But first he had to phone the police, before whatever had been in the hypodermic needle kicked in. He sprinted back to Euclid Avenue and the phone booth on the corner. His vision was starting to cloud now, to soften his periphery. It felt like a barbiturate. He fought the drowsiness and dropped the quarter into the phone.

His knees gave a quick trick, buckling momentarily. He held on to the side of the phone booth, dialed 911, waited, his mind misting up by the second. "Come on . . . come *on*. . . ." he said. "Answer the fuggin' . . ."

Nicky glanced at his watch. Hard to focus. Looked like nearly midnight. Midnight on Halloween, he thought. The cops had to be busier than hell. But why doesn't the—

"Nine-one-one emergency, how can I help you?" the voice said.

"Hi . . . uh . . ." Nicky began, but he knew his words were coming out flat and unintelligible. His tongue felt a foot wide. "I'd . . . uh . . . I'd lige do wee-pord a . . . a . . ."

"A *what*, sir? You'll have to speak up."

Nicky's mind was deserting him, as were his limbs. He took a deep breath, tried again. "I . . . would lige . . . to wee-pord . . ."

But that was all that he would say. He slumped to the ground, his mind and body a slave to the drug now. And then his world went dark.

A dark that made the warehouse look like daylight.

60• Amelia stared at the huge expanse of the room, through the space where the canvas wall had hung. Time became an abstract thing. Waiting, waiting. Maddie. Please, God. Nicky, come on. Maddie. No.

Roger still sat in his wheelchair: shackled, naked, unconscious. Amelia looked but could not see if his chest moved, if he was breathing. She wanted to hate him for this, for the horror of this night. But she could not, not now. The sickness of her grief would not allow it.

She looked at the floor. Strauss was still out, too, facedown on the floor, his hands handcuffed behind his back, his white suit slashed with blood.

The music had stopped again, the record player's incessant *brip*ping providing a thought-erasing backdrop to Amelia's dissolving heart. But beneath it, beneath that sound, she heard . . . crying?

Was somebody crying?

Before she could pinpoint the sound, she saw Strauss stirring, coming to. He rolled over onto his back, his face contorting in pain, the blood already drying on his white suit in fat brown streaks along the lapels. He opened his eyes, blinked a few times, tried to focus.

Amelia noticed that he now looked more like the picture in the yearbook. G. D. Woltz. Nicky had broken his jaw and unwittingly undone what must have been a very long and painful operation.

Strauss sat up, his hands still cuffed behind his back. He shook his head side to side, trying to clear his mind. His eyes

were red and damp, glassy. His nose was a flat, purplish mass
of crushed cartilage and mucus. He looked at Amelia. "Wher-
isee?" he asked, slurring his words together.

"Gone," Amelia said. "He went and got the police, you
sick son of a bitch."

Strauss laughed, but it was a mirthless noise. He grimaced
in pain.

Then the sound again. Crying.

Where . . .

Strauss seemed not to hear it. He began to rock side to side,
and eventually got up onto his knees. Even though he was
handcuffed, the fact that he was moving filled Amelia with a
fear she had just begun to relinquish. "Nicky!" she yelled at
the top of her lungs. *"Nicky!"*

Strauss struggled to his feet, backed over to the desk,
reached into the drawer, and removed a set of handcuff keys.
Within moments, he was free.

No, Amelia thought. This can't be happening.

Strauss shook the feeling back into his arms, grabbed the
full hypodermic needle off the desk.

And stumbled toward her.

Music. The Bee Gees now. Loud.

Amelia was sitting on the bed, on top of Nicky's jacket.
Her hands were free, her legs were free. She looked to her
right. Roger's head was now propped up with a cervical collar.
His eyes were slightly opened.

Before Amelia could move, Strauss stepped around the remaining canvas wall. "Walk ober to the winnow," he said to
Amelia, obviously with a great deal of pain. Amelia obeyed,
crossing the room, leaning back against the sill of the window
that overlooked Fifty-first Street.

Strauss had washed the blood from his face, had made an
attempt to wash it out of his jacket. He reached into his pocket
and removed a packet of glossy paper. He opened it, dipped
in with a sharp fingernail, and took a furious snort in his man-
gled nose. Then another. Then another. He crumpled it, tossed
it to the side, and faced Amelia. He turned up the music.

"Now iss *my* durn," he said. "*My* durn to be the pirate."

He walked toward her, unbuckling his belt.

But what Amelia did made him stop in his tracks.

She began to hike up her skirt, slowly, slowly, not taking her eyes from his. She unbuttoned her blouse, let it slide down over her shoulders. She spread her legs slightly.

Confusion in Strauss's eyes. Pained, stoned confusion. Then acceptance. Acceptance of *her* acceptance of the inevitability of the situation. He glanced over at Roger, then reached out to her. She opened her arms to him. He stepped closer, between her legs.

Amelia kissed him, and the revulsion flowed through her like sewage in her veins. She felt his growing erection against her thigh. She reached down, unzipped his zipper. "Gillian," she said directly into his ear.

"Julia," he replied, and closed his eyes.

When he opened them, instead of staring into Amelia's eyes, he found that he was staring at the nozzle of a small can of pepper spray.

Amelia sprayed.

Strauss screamed in agony, tearing at his eyes, flailing his arms like a madman, but Amelia could not hear him over the music. Instead, for a moment, it looked like a silent, tormented ballet as he lurched away from her, trying desperately to find his bearings, spinning, thrashing, his face now a deep blue from the dye in the spray. He stopped, opened his eyes wide with his fingers, found Amelia in the crimson morass of his vision. Then Gillian Strauss dug his feet into the rug and ran at her, propelled by twenty years of hatred, twenty years of sorrow, twenty years of anger.

But, as he had so many years ago, the pirate would best Gillian Strauss one last time.

Amelia dove to the ground as Strauss tripped over the pirate mannequin on the floor, lost his balance, and raged past her. His head burst through the glass, and the sound was a shotgun blast over the music. Amelia scrambled to her feet and turned around to see Strauss stuck halfway through the opening, a thick shard of filthy glass emerging from his back. It had gone clean through him. And for the time being, he could not move.

Or so she thought.

Amelia ran to the desk and grabbed the gun, astounded at how heavy it was. She gathered the last of her strength, pointed it at Strauss's back, pulled back the hammer as she had seen in a million cop shows.

Strauss was still for a moment, then threw back his head and howled in pain as he forced his body straight, snapping the glass off at the frame. He turned, slowly, and faced Amelia, his eyes a red mass of burning flesh now, his small intestine a slithery pink cord on the glass protruding from his abdomen.

"Julia," he managed, wet, feral. He tried to approach her, but he stumbled backwards, leaned against the sill. *"Why, Julia . . . ?"*

But she wasn't Julia. She was Amelia Saintsbury and the monster in front of her had taken her little girl. It was Maddie who steadied her hand.

She pulled the trigger.

The gun roared and tumbled from her grip, but not before slamming a nine-millimeter hollow-point bullet into Gillian Strauss's chest. At this close range, the impact finished the job that inertia had not, carrying him through the window and out into the autumn night, down to the cold pavement a hundred feet below.

Amelia turned, disoriented, revulsed. She located the record player, then struck out at it, plunging the room into a sudden deafening silence. She fell into the desk chair, consumed now by the vast expanse of blackness that was the warehouse, consumed by exhaustion, by the electricity of her sorrow.

Again she heard the crying. Louder now. Amelia tried to calm herself, tried to slow her breathing, tried to pinpoint the sound. . . .

Who was crying? And where was it—

Under the bed.

It was coming from under the bed.

Amelia got down on her knees, and when she felt the coarse texture of the material, when she felt the weight of the second

burlap bag, her heart stammered. She pulled the bag out, re-
joicing in its heft, and untied the top. When she saw the cheap
wig, the suede fringes of the Pocahontas costume, everything
poured forth at once.

"Mob?" Maddie asked, sleepy and obviously disoriented,
thoroughly miserable, but alive, God. *Alive.* "Where's my
candy?"

Amelia pulled her daughter from the bag and held her close,
so close.

A thousand charities owed, now.

A million prayers to be given voice.

Amelia covered Roger with a blanket from the bed, found a
slow, steady pulse. She located Strauss's lair on the other side
of the warehouse, called 911.

Back in the dorm room, Maddie at her side, she stepped
over to the window, just as the wail of the sirens rose in the
distance. She looked down, at the sidewalk on East Fifty-first
Street, at the grim composition she would see every day for
the rest of her life.

White suit. Gray concrete. Red ribbons of blood. A still life
in madness, she thought.

She glanced up at the bruise of sky above the city of Cleveland, at the violet hour of midnight.

Safe now, Maddie-bear.

Safe.

61. The clerk at Cleveland Costume was in her early twenties, pale and brunette, full lips, hips to match. She was the same one who had rented him the costume. He was hoping she would be there. "Hi," she said as he stepped through the door.

"Hi," he replied. He noticed that she fluffed her hair. That was a good sign. "How are you?"

"Just fine, thanks," she said. She took the plastic garment bag from him, along with the bag that held the boots. "And did we have a good time on Halloween?"

"Sort of," he said. "I buckled a few swashes, I guess."

The girl laughed. "You don't sound so sure."

"Well, it was a crazy night round my way. A little more excitement than we're used to."

"Hope nothing bad happened."

"Well, I'm afraid some bad things did. But everyone near and dear to me came out of it just fine. That's the good news."

"Maybe you should go for something a little less provocative next year. Something like a clown or a vampire."

"No. I don't think so. This costume will be fine."

"Okay," she said as she handed his deposit back. "It'll be here waiting for you."

"Terrific," Garth Randolph said with a smile. "Let's just hope I'm the same size."

"Oh, I have a feeling you will be."

"Because I'd really hate to break with tradition," Garth said, walking to the door.

"What do you mean?"

He turned, winked at her. "I've *always* been the pirate."

62 • The healing race came to an end at Christmas. The dose of PCP that Gillian Strauss had given Roger should have been fatal, and Roger had lingered in a coma for three days, but eventually, slowly, he came out of it. He claimed not to remember a thing from that night, only that he had taken a cab to Edgefield Road, paid, and before he had taken three steps, had been chloroformed from behind. He also claimed to have returned to 100 percent of his previous form, but everyone knew it wasn't true. Whenever a word wouldn't come to him, whenever he found that he was repeating himself for the third time in a single conversation, his eyes met Amelia's and her heart broke. There was probably nothing wrong with his mind, but if he thought there was, there might as well have been.

Shelley Roth's name was never mentioned again.

The tragedy, of course, the heartbreak of that terrible night, was Paige. A day didn't go by without her crossing Amelia's mind, her heart. Mutual friends had rallied around Amelia, but they all knew that she and Paige had been close, and that nothing was going to replace her. The police learned that Gillian Strauss owned a few acres out on Sperry Road. It didn't take them long to find the shallow graves. They also found Geoffrey Coldicott's mother.

After Paige's funeral, Roger insisted that they buy the bookstore and try to make a go of it.

The name, of course, stayed.

Dag Randolph stood behind his picture window, the one through which his twelve-year-old son Garth had once chipped

a brand-new Titleist, the one beneath which he had once seduced his young, shy wife, Martha, the only time in their forty-
two-year marriage they had ever made love outside of their
maple four-poster bed, a night now four decades deep in Dag
Randolph's memory, yet still so vivid, so new in his heart.

The snow was relentless, his mood relentlessly grave. As it
had every day for weeks, Dag Randolph's lunch sat untouched
on the TV tray.

His wife and daughter had long since stopped trying to roust
him from his funk. They sat in the kitchen, a cooling pot of
coffee between them.

"And still not a word about that night?" Amelia asked
softly.

"Nothing," Martha whispered. "It's like it never happened." Martha leaned backward, looked into the living room,
then leaned close to her daughter. "He thinks he let everybody
down, you know. Madeleine especially. I can't even mention
Maddie's name without him tearing up and leaving the room.
I don't know what to do. I just don't know. . . ."

Dag Randolph had been taken out of the equation early that
night. The police found him snoozing in the azaleas in the
Cameron backyard, another victim of chloroform. The only
thing broken was the man's pride in his role as grandfather-
protector, as patriarch of a small but needy Randolph clan.

"And what about Garth?" Amelia asked.

Martha just stared, absently. "Gone again, I suppose."

Amelia was worried about her family. What was happening
to them? Would they ever recover from this madness? Would
they ever be the same?

The answer came midmeal on Christmas day when Dag,
without a word, got up from the table, put on his hat and coat,
and left the house, only to return twenty minutes later. He had
a big smile on his face, and in his arms the scruffiest runt of
a golden retriever pup any of them had ever seen.

And it was right around the time Martha Randolph served
her traditional Dutch apple pie and coffee that a beaming,
lovestruck Maddie Saintsbury—with a confused but enthusi-
astic young puppy in tow—lumbered into the dining room and

introduced everyone to the newest member of the Saintsbury family: Molson Lite.

On New Year's Day the pier at Seventy-second Street was deserted, save for the lone figure in black, standing on the rocks. Even the most hard-core fishermen wouldn't come out on a morning like this, Nicky thought. It had to be Joseph. Joseph had called, left a somber message. The two hadn't met on the pier in years.

Nicky parked his car, made his way down the treacherous rocks to where his cousin stood. As always, Father Joseph LaCazio seemed to have a sixth sense about the presence of another human. He didn't turn around, he didn't look.

"Good morning, Nicky."

" 'Morning, Joey. How ya doin'?"

He got his cousin's attention, gave him one of the two cups of McDonald's coffee he carried. In silence they opened their cups, blew on the coffee. When it was cool enough, they sipped, looked out over Lake Erie. Joseph spoke first.

"A murderer, Nicky. A murderer lived at the St. Francis rectory."

"I know, Joey. But you shouldn't—"

"A murderer lived at the rectory and he killed a priest. How does a parish ever get over that?"

Nicky had no idea what to say. How do you begin to revive someone's faith, especially when that person's faith has always dwarfed your own? The police had found a number of bizarre things in Gil Strauss's room. Not the least of which were two dozen scrapbooks containing hundreds, probably thousands, of images cut and pasted from magazines. All the same. Julia's face pasted onto the body of some Playmate or movie star of the day. Farrah. Raquel. Demi. Jodie. Some of the pictures were Gil's face pasted on the body of Christ.

How does a parish get beyond that? Nicky had no idea. But he started moving his lips, and words somehow appeared on his vaporous breath. "Catholics are tough, Joey. You know that. Time will heal all of this. Look at my hand," he said, holding up his bent but healing left hand. "God takes care."

Joseph lit a cigarette, expertly into the wind, the street kid on the pier again. "I knew Gil Strauss a lot of years," he said. "I had no idea. None at all. What the hell kind of priest am I?"

Nicky grabbed Joseph by the shoulders, squared himself in front of him. "The best kind. You hear me? The kind who sees the good in people. Not the evil."

"It's not nearly enough these days, Nicky. Not nearly enough."

"Come on, man. Don't do this to yourself."

"I wish there was a choice," Joseph said.

The two men embraced, a bit awkwardly, trying not to spill their coffees. Nicky wanted to comfort Joseph, to take care of his older cousin who had rescued *him* so many times, but he really had no answers.

So instead, they stood on the rocks, shoulder to shoulder, watching the frigid waves crash into the shore, watching the gulls circle in their odd, seemingly random patterns, patterns that Nicholas Stella used to think were ruled by the moods of the moon, by the whim of the Lake Erie winds.

But he knew better now. He had learned that the fate of people is not random at all, but led instead by history, personal history, the moments of madness we all carry around like deep red scars on our souls.

This Slow-Gathering Storm would be nonfiction, the story of Gillian Strauss and his murderous rampage. About the furthest thing from a romance Amelia could imagine. But that was okay. Amelia decided that she didn't have the words to be a writer, nor the discipline, nor the ability to translate her thoughts onto paper the way some people did.

People like Nicky.

What she *could* do, though, was research. In the weeks that followed that night, in between her victim's therapy sessions at the Justice Center, she became quite proficient with her computer. There was much to learn, much to find out. Strauss was from somewhere. He had a family. Friends.

They would get to the bottom of the Gillian Strauss story.

To that end, Nicky had put together a book proposal that had gotten an immediate response from two publishers. And as they sat in the USAir 727 in late January, waiting for take-off from Hopkins International Airport in Cleveland, heading to New York, it looked to Amelia as if she might have a book in her future after all.

"Ready?" Nicky asked. He wore a navy wool suit, a burgundy tie. He looked like a million bucks.

"Ready," she replied.

She buckled her seat belt, closed her eyes, gripped the armrests, waited for the roar of the engines. And found that she was. Definitely.

Amelia Saintsbury could honestly say that she was ready for anything.

epilogue

Time Present, Time Past

63   Dr. Marsh hung up the phone, made a brief notation on the ledger in front of him. He had spoken to the bank in Cleveland, and was told that their instructions had been to keep mailing the money every month until the account was depleted, an account to which a Mr. Thomas Macavity had suddenly stopped making deposits.

Marsh had never met Mr. Macavity, had never seen him visit the woman. Nor anyone else, for that matter. She had no family, no friends.

Sad, he thought. And now this.

Marsh rose from his desk, filed the report.

Then walked down the hall and stepped into Room 56.

She sat, as always, looking out the window, her shiny gray hair pulled back from her face, lashed into a bow. A girlish thing to do, Marsh had always thought. It made her look younger, even more vulnerable, than her delicate features allowed. Today the bow was lemon yellow. Marsh, who was in his early sixties, still felt a rush of attraction for her. She had just celebrated her fortieth birthday, if *celebrate* was indeed the proper term.

Marsh sat on the edge of the bed, studied her. She did not acknowledge his presence, but that was nothing new. Soon Alice Jilek stepped into the room and placed a hand on his shoulder. Alice was the new head of admissions for the Fostoria Clinic. "Have you told her?" Alice asked softly.

"No," Marsh said. "Not yet."

"Do you think she'll understand?"

"Hard to say. She's been here five years, ever since her mother died. I'm not sure I've reached her once."

"What was her original diagnosis?"

"A heroin overdose, more than twenty years ago now. She jumped from a second-story window, spent a year or so in a body cast. It seems her body recovered, her mind never did. Her mother cared for her for fifteen years. Then she came to Fostoria."

"Shame," Alice said.

"Yes," Marsh replied. He got up, walked over to the window, leaned against the sill.

She looked up at him.

"We're bringing you to a new place, my dear," Marsh said as he took her hand in his. "Soon. A brand-new place. Brand-new people. Do you think you'll like that?"

Julia Raines looked at him, squeezed his hand gently. The doctor was taking her somewhere.

Maybe Gillian will be there, she thought.

Maybe Gillian will finally be there.

And for a long time, as it had been for so many years, it was to that hope she allowed her heart to cling; the notion of some infinitely gentle, infinitely suffering thing.